Accidental Mobster
By: M.M. Cox
ISBN: 978-1-927134-89-4

D0728784

Bluewood Publishing Ltd
Christchurch, 8441, New Zealand
www.bluewoodpublishing.com

Coming Soon by M.M. Cox:

Undercover Wiseguy
Covert Criminal

For news of, or to purchase this or other books please visit.

www.bluewoodpublishing.com

Accidental Mobster

by

M.M. Cox

Jess,
You are going to
do great things. <u>Live</u>
your dreams.
M.M. Cox

Dedication

This book is dedicated to my husband, who inspires me, to my children, who are the best of me, and to my parents, who always believe in me. I thank God every day for the beautiful life he gives me with all of you in it.

And a special thanks to Alyssa, who helped me remember what high school is all about.

Chapter 1

I slam the bathroom door and stare in the mirror as the blood from my head blurs what I see. The sticky fluid irritates my eyes as I struggle to calculate the size of the gash above my right eyebrow. I can feel the blood pumping through my forehead, sending a pulsation of pain with each beat. The person in the mirror looks like a character from a horror movie, and really, I'm not surprised. In fact, my life has been a nightmare tonight, and it wasn't all that great before I dashed in here, blood streaming down my bruised face.

The bathroom I'm standing in as I try to calm my breathing is one of the four rooms in the small house in Ridley, New Jersey, which is the only place that I have ever called home. Tonight, the dark interior of this ratty structure can't be blamed on the night that is creeping slowly in the windows. Instead, I think the gloom is a product of the drama that has just played out in my living room. What I have experienced is a bad dream—but real—and the cut on my forehead proves it.

Because the house is so small, hiding out in the bathroom is pointless. But I'm sure that someone will be coming for me at any moment. Adrenaline is still pushing through me as I jump into the bathtub and hunker down. My body fills the cracked porcelain structure, and I vow I'll make anyone who comes for me drag me away, yelling and kicking. I refuse to leave without a fight. My butt is already feeling tender from my rigid position on the cold ceramic. But I'm not going anywhere—someone is coming for me, and I'm not going to make it easy.

I try not to think about the string of events that brought me to this point, but I can't help myself. The evening ended with everyone leaving the house—and me—behind. Principal Doonesby left the house with a concussion. Del, my dad, left with a pair of handcuffs affixed to his pudgy wrists. My mom left with screams of hysteria, upset over the scuffle that resulted from her own constant selfishness.

She and Mr. Doonesby have been flirting for months. I was well aware of their get-togethers, and I had rolled my eyes at my mom's flirtation and ignored a situation I could do nothing about. I wouldn't be surprised if they were secretly dating. But my dad, an appliance salesman at the local Save-Much, is a jealous guy, and he did not like the idea of battling the middle-school principal for his wife's attention. Dad's uncontrollable temper is often followed by equally uncontrollable fists.

My mother's shampoo bottle sits beside my left shoulder. It's an expensive brand that she swears makes her hair look and feel like a movie star's. I've never seen any difference—her hair is always poofy, dry, and bleached of any natural color. I knock it off the edge of the tub and then hug my shoulders. I'm so angry at her.

My thoughts are racing. I'm fifteen and only a week away from my freshman year of high school. I'm not scared—I've been involved in a few scuffles in school, always ready to give an underdog a little extra help. My best friend Reggie and I are on the wrestling team, and we have a knack for the sport. Because I often find myself standing up for the kids who are bullied, I sometimes get teased for being a "Boy Scout," but overall, the middle school experience hasn't been too painful. I've heard a few girls call me "cute," even though I don't care much for my black hair and green eyes. But none of the girls have much use for a kid as poor as I am. Well, if I was poor then, I'm less than poor now, with neither Dad nor Mom giving me any indication that they will return anytime soon.

What will happen to me? Some stranger will probably be appointed to look after me, unless Mom decides she is still capable of being a parent—a thought that almost makes me laugh. I know I'm more capable of taking care of myself than Mom will ever be. Reggie's family might let me stay for a while, but they are poor too. No, life might be better if I'm on my own. The thought of freedom excites me, but that's when I hear the noise I'm expecting—a knock on the door. I don't answer the knock. I don't even move from my spot in the bathtub. But the intruder comes looking for me anyway. Figures.

"Hellooohh! Danny? Danny Higgins? You here?" The loud, harsh voice is that of a woman; the nasal quality is like ragged fingernails down my back. I shrink down into the tub at the unpleasant sound. My family does not have many friends, but anybody would have been better than a stranger. A stranger means only one thing: Mom has called it quits on being a parent.

Maybe if I keep quiet, this newcomer will give up quickly and go away, but somehow, I know this is too much to ask. I hear high heels clacking on the worn linoleum, a sound that belongs to someone not easily discouraged. The house isn't big; whoever she is, she will eventually find me.

"Danny?" The voice whines like a teenage girl, although the gravel-like quality confirms the woman to be much older. "Danny? I know you're in here. I know you're scared. I'm here to help you."

I don't need your help. I haven't even seen her yet, but the thought of going anywhere with this woman is worse than the prospect of staying with my mom. I scoot down even further in the bathtub. *Please don't find me. I'm better off alone.*

The shower curtain rips open. A tall lady with a stern, straight nose and massive plastic-framed glasses stares down at me. She quickly attempts a sympathetic expression, but I think she looks like a hungry seagull. I have the feeling that I am a fish she is about to snap up for lunch.

"Danny! Oh, my poor boy! You must be so scared." She kneels next to the tub, looking like a creepy clown in her plaid skirt suit.

I jump up, not wanting the harsh voice and smoky breath in my face, and I shrug. "I'm fine."

She stands up, taller than I am. "You're in the bathtub—"

"I was going to take a shower."

The woman is probably pushing six feet tall. I only come to her chin. "Well, I'm Barb Kluwer. I'm from the DA's office," she says smugly, like she deserves an award for it. "I'm here to make sure someone takes care of you." She means to sound nice, maybe even comforting, but I still feel like a hunted animal. She almost sounds like she wants to do away with me.

"I'm fine," I say. "I'll just wait for my mom."

"Oh, honey, your mom isn't coming—" Her voice trails off. She has finally noticed the large gash on my forehead. "Oh, goodness!"

I slap my hand to my head and wince from my touch. "It's nothing," I lie. "Just a scratch. If you'll move out of the way, I'll clean it up." I know I sound rude, but I'm not trying to make friends—not with a

4

six-foot woman who looks like a Scottish bagpiper. She moves to block my path, hands on her hips. Everything about the woman is big. I am not intimidated by her, but I'm not going to push her out of my way. My dad might have trouble controlling his fists, but I would never hit or push a woman—Mom at least taught me that much.

"I said, I'll take care of it! But you need to move." I repeat, feeling my face heating up. I have no patience for this woman. I don't know her, but I hate having her here with her fake sympathy. And all that plaid is hurting my eyes, annoying me. I try to move past her, but she shifts to block me again. I feel my skin prickling with fury and barely keep myself from shoving her.

"Danny, I'm going to take you to the hospital." It is an order.

I stare into her eyes, channeling my stubbornness. "I will take care of it, all right? Just leave me alone! I need some space right now!" The shower walls feel like a cage. My back is to a corner and *she* is closing in on me. My temper is rising too fast—if she doesn't move, I am going to do something we will both regret.

Her face morphs from a look of fake compassion to one that is much less friendly. Her stern features grow angry; she is obviously a woman who expects to win.

"You're going to the hospital," she says coldly, no longer making an attempt to be nice. "I have been appointed by the district attorney to look after your well-being, and we will be giving a statement to the police concerning your father."

I laugh harshly. She doesn't want to help me—she has her own agenda that includes getting me to tattle on my dad. Maybe I should report what my dad did, but this woman is out of her mind if she thinks she can *force* me to do it. "I don't care who you are," I say, unable to control my rage. "I am NOT talking to the police! I wouldn't do anything to get my dad in trouble."

Her face twists, her expression furious. "Your father is already in trouble. He *hit* you. You are obligated to give a statement."

Desperate to gain the upper hand, I give her a nasty smile, hoping to test her patience even more. "I'm not *obligated* to do anything. This cut on my head was my own fault. I don't blame my dad for what happened."

My words are a pin to her balloon. "You don't blame your dad? You don't BLAME your dad?" She is spitting her words, and I wipe some of her saliva from my cheek. "Your father is a violent man. A *bad* man," she hisses. "The principal of your school has been very badly hurt. Even if you don't say anything, your father won't be safe. There will be incriminating evidence and charges against him."

"But it won't be from me. And besides, I'm not sure if Mister Doonesby will be willing to give you a statement. He's got a reputation to protect, you know?" I stand as tall as possible and return Barb's glare with all the confidence I can gather. I know that if she works for the district attorney, she is looking for a slam-dunk case, but I am not going to give her one. Inside I am trying to bury the hurt of what my dad has done to me, but I am not going to show Barb any weakness. I have already been beaten once tonight; it's not going to happen twice.

Her voice is trembling with barely contained fury.

"I think you will change your mind." The statement is definitely a threat. "If you want to end up living with a decent family, you had better do as I say. I can make sure the county social worker finds some foster parents that have some harsh ideas about raising kids." She sneers at me, resembling a gargoyle that I keep on top of my computer.

I feel a quick wave of panic as I realize that this lady holds my future in her gnarled hands. Nothing could be worse than being placed with cruel foster parents. Even being poor with my unhappy parents would be better than living with heartless strangers. I now understand that Barb is going to use her power over my life to blackmail me into ratting on my dad.

She seems to sense my sudden panic, and her gargoyle smile triples in size. "That's right, Danny." Her voice is low and menacing. "I have the authority to make your life completely miserable if you push me. So, if you don't do as I say, you may regret it."

"Or he may not."

A new voice fills the small bathroom. A man I have never seen before stands in the tight hallway right outside the door. In the darkness, I can see the man is not tall, but his body is lean and imposing—he certainly is more than a match for Barb Kluwer. His eyes are the only facial feature visible at the moment, and I can tell he is angry. I stand motionless in the bathtub, unsure if this new stranger is someone I can trust. But I hope he is, because so far, Barb is turning out to be a crappy person, and if it comes to a fight, I'm siding with the new guy, not the woman standing in front of me.

"I'm sorry—who are you?" Although her smile falters, Barb makes an effort to look confident, lifting herself to an imposing height, her high heels making up for any inches she lacks naturally. She is certainly taller than the man, but height alone is not going to give her an advantage.

"I'm here for Danny." The man moves into the light as he speaks, his voice carrying a strong Jersey accent. He appears to be in his mid-forties, with a weathered face that has years of experience etched in tiny wrinkles around his eyes and mouth. He is good-looking and seems genuinely calm and confident, whereas Barb is struggling to appear composed. The man's words give me goose bumps—I can feel them on my arms as I hug them tighter around my body. I do not know whether to be frightened or excited by this stranger's claim on me.

"Well, sir, I am also here for Danny and I believe I have the law behind me." Barb smirks at the man, obviously gaining more confidence in her court-appointed role. "And you still haven't told me who you are," she accuses, as if the man has committed a crime for which she would be more than happy to arrest him.

But Barb's confidence can't change the cool self-assurance of the man. "Well, that's all great," he says. "But I believe my authority will surpass yours. Danny is coming with me."

Whoever this man is, he seems to know exactly who I am, even though he has yet to say anything to me. But at the moment, with Barb ready to whisk me off to some crazy foster family unless I give a statement against my dad, I am willing to take a chance on this stranger.

However, Barb is not ready to wave the white flag of surrender just yet. "No. I don't care who you are. I'm Barb Kluwer, the DA's assistant, and Danny is my property."

The man's coolness finally melts. He starts laughing, and it is so catching, I find myself chuckling, despite the fact that I really feel like shoving Barb toward the gaping toilet for calling me her property. I have no idea why the man is so amused or why I feel like laughing right along with him. But it feels good to laugh, whatever the reason.

The man's laughter fades, and he instantly becomes cool once more. "Well, Ms Kluwer, I'm not sure you would want your superiors to know that you promote foster homes that are less than kind to troubled kids, or that you are talking to Danny without proper authorization. Or you may not want your boss to know that you are *blackmailing* a child into testifying against his own father."

I flinch at being called a child, yet I am thrilled the man heard all of Barb's threats.

Barb cringes; she knows she is caught. She glares at the man, perhaps hoping that her hatred will be enough to destroy his confidence.

"That's a ridiculous accusation you've made," she snaps. The man does not respond. All three of us know Barb has lost. "What would it take to make you walk away?" she asks in final desperation.

The man shakes his head. "I won't," he answers. "When you go back to your office, you may want to have a chat with your boss about me. He may refresh your memory concerning who I am."

Her eyes narrow. "Who are you?"

The man smiles as if he were having the most pleasant conversation of his life. "Why, Ms Kluwer, have I not told you?" He is grinning now, showing a full set of white, perfect teeth. "I'm Gino Vigliotti— Danny's godfather."

* * * *

I sit quietly in the passenger seat of a pristine Lexus SUV as Gino climbs into the driver's seat. I still haven't said a word to him.

After hearing Gino's name, Barb left the house with threats of revenge and legal consequences (and much to my amusement, she tripped over the toilet as she hurried out of the bathroom).

Gino grabbed a washcloth from the sink and cleaned the cut on my head with warm water. I stood completely still, unsure of what to say or do. I felt that I should say thanks or ask a few questions, but instead, I kept silent while the warm cloth cleaned the blood from my head. Then Gino grabbed another washcloth and pressed it to my cut.

"Here," he said gruffly, moving my own hand to the cloth. "Hold this until we get to the hospital."

At first I was alarmed. Was Gino also planning to make me give a statement concerning my dad? Had I been saved from one fire only to jump into another?

Gino must have known what I was thinking. "We'll just tell them you took a spill down the stairs," he said. "I'd like to skip the hospital completely, but you need stitches." He then took me gently by the arm and guided me to the vehicle in which I now sit, holding the cloth carefully to the cut on my head.

I struggle to find words to say, but my mind is blank. I finally realize just how awful the events of the last several hours have been. And I have no idea what is going to happen next.

The charcoal gray exterior of Gino's Lexus is simple, but the inside is complete luxury. As I settle into the soft leather seat, I realize that I have never seen, much less ridden in, anything like this. I spend a few moments staring at the sleek GPS system mounted in the dashboard, which is only outdone by the DVD player situated a little further down the console. Everything is automatic—mirrors, seat belts, locks, windows, and seats—and the rear view mirror is outfitted with a compass and an outside temperature gauge. The most fascinating item to me, however, is the stereo system, which has an MP3 player plugged into an elaborate satellite radio. I have never known an adult who owned an MP3 player.

The SUV drives smoothly, and I lean back against the seat.

"Be careful, Danny," Gino warns. "Don't get blood on the seats." I quickly sit up. Gino's tone of voice is not irritated, just frank. I can appreciate frank. My dad has never said anything to me that did not carry a threat of violence.

The hospital is about as much fun as five stitches can be. The doctor and nurses study Gino suspiciously when he tells them the tale about me taking a tumble down the recently mopped stairs. But Gino seems unconcerned by their scowls, and I have to bite my lip to keep from smiling. The only stairs in my shabby little house are the two crumbling concrete steps that lead up to the front door.

The doctor is gentle as he examines my head, as if sorry for not confronting Gino about the real cause of my injury. I appreciate the kindness, but I also feel a little guilty about Gino taking the blame for my dad's actions. I try not to think about my dad—I don't want to lose my resolve to protect him. But the events of the evening have certainly shown me that, of the few people in my life, Del Higgins is not someone I will ever be able to trust again. I have always felt, deep down, that my dad would be there for me when it truly counted—that years of verbal abuse and a bad temper would be put aside if I was in a true crisis. Those feelings are gone. I wince at a sharp stab of pain in my forehead. Yes, definitely gone.

The doctor pulls out a needle of alarming size. "I'm going to inject this into your head so you won't feel any pain from the stitches. It'll just sting for a moment."

I grit my teeth, thinking it strange that pain is necessary to avoid more pain. But I can't let Gino know that the needle scares me. I hardly know this man—my godfather?—but I don't want to show him any weakness. I feel that being brave is a quick way to earn Gino's respect. And that, more than anything else, is what I want most at this moment.

The stitches take only minutes. As the doctor finishes, Gino briefly inspects my head and gives a small nod of approval. The doctor eyes him warily. "We'll need you to sign some paperwork, Mister Higgins."

Gino shakes his head. "It's Mister Vigliotti. Gino Vigliotti."

The doctor glances down at my chart. "You're not the father?"

Gino shakes his head. "No, I'm his godfather."

The doctor drops the chart to his side. He is now openly glaring at Gino. "I'm sorry, Mister Vigliotti. We're going to need to speak to one of the parents."

"That won't be necessary," Gino says casually. I am impressed that Gino is unfazed by the doctor's hostility. "I gave the nurse the necessary paperwork.

His mother, Penny Higgins, made sure everything is in order."

The doctor is surprised, but he doesn't push the issue. He has too many patients to spend any more time worrying about me. I'm shocked by what Gino has just said. First, I have never heard Mom go by the name "Penny." She has firmly told my dad many times that her parents named her Penelope, and by God, who was she to shorten what must have been important to them. I always thought that my mom just enjoyed the uniqueness of Penelope, whereas Penny sounded ordinary—like the coin.

But I am most surprised by Gino's claim that Mom herself gathered the necessary paperwork to give him temporary care of me. I do not think my mother ever had a responsible moment in her life. And how had she been able to pull herself together so quickly? Only a few hours have passed since she was led from the house screaming like an angry toddler. Yet, I am also hopeful. My mom would not leave me with someone she didn't trust, would she? Well, I guess it depends on how desperate she is.

Gino heads for the door. "Let's go."

I jump down from the examining table and quickly follow him. He fills out a zillion forms before we can leave, but we are soon out of the hospital and back in the Lexus. I'm already becoming attached to the vehicle. As someone who has never had nice things, especially not new things, the SUV is a window into a lifestyle that I have only ever heard about and never dreamed I would experience.

The drive starts out much like the first one did. Neither Gino nor I speak a word. However, my curiosity eventually wins out, and I nervously clear my throat. "Mister Vigliotti, I—I guess you know my mom?"

Gino stares straight ahead. "Call me Gino, Danny. And of course I know your mom—I'm your godfather. I don't think someone would choose a stranger for that, do you?"

Gino's gruff answer does nothing to ease my nerves, but I find that this man I barely know impresses me. "No, I guess not," I say quietly. "It's just—I've never heard of you. I'm not even sure I know what a godfather is."

I am not prepared for Gino's abrupt laugh. He shakes his head as he chuckles. "Well, that's not really your fault," he says, a grin spanning his tanned features. "If I were a good godfather, I guess you'd know what role I'm supposed to fill. But I'm making up for lost time now. Your mom ignored me for years, probably to save up for a really big favor like she's asking now."

I don't like being a *favor*. "I'm sorry to be any trouble," I say. "I probably could have been left on my own and been just fine. I've practically been taking care of myself my whole life anyway."

Gino's face immediately turns serious. "Danny, I didn't mean it to sound like you're any burden at all. It's just that I haven't heard from your mom in ages, so I was a little surprised by her call." He pauses and then glances at me. "I'm glad I'll get a chance to know you, Danny, while you stay with us in Newcastle."

I turn to Gino in surprise because I had assumed he was taking me home. "I'll be staying with you?"

"Yes—for a little while. Your mom needs to get some affairs in order before she's able to be a parent again. Or maybe a parent for the first time." He smiles quickly at me. "You seem like a tough guy. You'll be a good influence on my kids—they're spoiled rotten, and I doubt they would be able to survive very long without my wife and me to pamper them."

Kids? This is all becoming very complicated. Here is a perfect stranger taking me in for a few days, with children of his own. How will Gino's kids feel about me invading their space? Because I've never had a sibling, I have no idea how it will feel to live with other kids.

"How old are they?" I ask.

Gino rolls his eyes. "Not old enough. Or maybe too old. I don't know. Julia is sixteen, and Vince is seventeen. Vince is old enough to drive, of course, which makes me really nervous, and Julia's got a boyfriend who's a freshman in college. That's my next project—to put an end to that!" He laughs again, as though scaring off a college student will be fun.

So both of Gino's kids are around my age. I wonder what that will be like. And will Gino's wife be okay with me staying in their home? I can't imagine how angry my own mom would be if she had to take in another teenager. Some days, she barely tolerates *me* in the house.

"Um, look," I say, hesitating, "I don't want to intrude on your family. We could just stay at my house, you know, until my mom comes back."

Gino smirks. "I don't know about you, Danny, but I think I'd prefer to stay at my house. You might prefer it too, once you get there."

"I just meant, you know, I don't want to put anyone out. I definitely don't mind sleeping on the sofa. I hate to be in the way."

"Don't worry about it, Danny. No one's sleeping on a sofa. Even the dog's got a bed—that spoiled ankle-biter. Don't worry about the family. They'll all be glad to have you. And if not, they can go stay in your house for a few days, and they'll come crawling back!"

I'm a little insulted. "Hey, my house isn't that bad. My parents did the best they could." I notice Gino's look of doubt. "Okay, okay. Maybe not 'the best they could,' but I'm not complaining."

Gino smiles. "We'll see what you think a couple days from now."

With that, Gino pulls the Lexus into the driveway of a beautiful, ivory-colored stucco house. Not a house, a mansion. I lean back, trying to take in the enormous structure with one glance, and I can't.

Gino opens the door and steps out of the SUV. "Come on. I'll introduce you to the family."

Suddenly, I panic. "Uh, Gino, I completely forgot! I need to get some stuff. I don't even have a toothbrush! Maybe we should go back to my house and I can pack a bag. I'll be really quick. But I'll need some stuff." I am rambling, desperate to be somewhere familiar again. This is all overwhelming.

"Don't worry. I'll send someone to your place to get your stuff."

"They won't know what I need!" I say quickly.

"How about everything?"

"Everything?" I have still not moved from my seat. "Just how long am I staying here?"

Gino shrugs. "Don't know. Might be a while." He closes the door and motions for me to follow him. I can feel my chest tighten. How can I be intimidated by a mansion? Certainly most teenagers would be thrilled with the idea of moving from a tiny house to an enormous one in a matter of a day. The problem is, this isn't really my house and this isn't really my family, and no matter how amazing this place may be, this isn't my home.

"Danny, come on!" Gino's voice is muffled outside the SUV. I take a deep breath, open the door, and step out onto a cobblestone driveway. Gino is staring up at the house, shaking his head. "The fact that this house looks more like it should be in Arizona than in Jersey always annoys me when I bring someone new over. But Ronnie loves the architecture, so we've got stucco walls and a tile roof. Ridiculous!" Gino turns to me. "Just remember, a happy wife makes a happy life!" He laughs and starts walking toward the front door.

"Great," I say, a little sarcastically. "But I don't even have a girlfriend. Although driving a Lexus might help." I point my thumb over my shoulder at the SUV.

Gino chuckles. "Hah! Don't even think about it! But we'll work on the girlfriend thing." He grins. "I think this is going to be fun."

I give him a weak smile. "Maybe. I'm still not sure I haven't been kidnapped."

Gino shakes his head. "Kid, if you've been kidnapped, this is the best day of your life." And with that, he continues up the driveway and through the front door, leaving me standing alone, with a bloody washcloth in my hand and a sense that my life may have changed forever.

Chapter 2

Veronica "Ronnie" Vigliotti could pass for a TV mom. First of all, she's petite, but slender in a gorgeous and curvy way, not an "I eat only celery and carrots" way. She has dark, reddish-brown hair and dark blue eyes that are strangely warm. Whereas my mom has tanned every drop of moisture out of her skin and looks like a dried apricot, Ronnie's skin is smooth and fair, with a hint of color from taking in just the right amount of sun. I do not even have a chance to examine the oversized hallway (or, as I would later be informed, the *foyer*) before I am wrapped in her small, strong arms.

After hugging me fiercely (I wonder where such a tiny woman gets so much strength), Ronnie takes my shoulders and holds me at arm's length, looking me up and down. "Look at you. *Look* at you." She gasps, smiling. Her voice carries the same Jersey accent as Gino's, just lighter and prettier. "You are adorable," she breathes, "I mean—*handsome.* Who would have thought such a darling boy would have come from Penny and—"

"Ronnie!" Gino coughs, interrupting her. I see him shoot her a warning look. "Take it easy. You'll scare him away. Look at him, like a deer in headlights." Gino's eyes seem to communicate something to her he isn't going to say out loud, because she puts her hand to her mouth right away. Gino turns to me. "She has that effect on a lot of the kids' friends." He lowers his voice to a spooky whisper. "One encounter with Ronnie and they never come back."

Ronnie grins and slaps him playfully. I have never seen two married people behave like that, and I immediately feel uncomfortable.

"The kids! We must introduce them!" Ronnie moves to the foot of the staircase, an elegant curving structure that is a perfect match for the white marble that decorates the large hall. In fact, I'm pretty sure my house might fit in this house's hallway. *Just* the hallway.

"Jules! Vince!"

Ronnie's one flaw, I think, is that the volume of her voice might be able to bring down a smaller, less sturdy house.

"Jules, Vince, now!"

I have to keep myself from covering my ears. Suddenly, I hear a shriek of frustration coming from the top of the stairs.

"Mom, seriously! *Seriously!*" A teenage girl is at the top of the steps, blue eyes blazing, her brown curly hair brushing against flushed cheeks. "I. Am. On. The. Phone!" The girl pronounces each word as a single sentence. "And it's *Julia*. You didn't name me *Jules*. It's Julia!"

A tiny, furry, black and tan terrier sits yapping at her feet. She glares at it, raising one finger in the air. "Shut up, Baxter!" Baxter pays her no attention.

Julia is pretty. No, she is *beautiful*. She looks much like her mother, with the same wavy reddish-brown hair and blue eyes, but Julia has the height that Ronnie lacks. I try not to stare, and I can feel my jaw dropping lower than what would certainly be considered "cool," but this girl is hot. Very, very hot. And I immediately know that she is *way* out of my league and that, for some reason, she already dislikes me. In fact, at the moment, she seems to hate everyone.

Julia lifts her cell phone to her ear and turns away from her parents. "I'm sorry, honey. Gino and Ronnie can be *so* frustrating! Yes, I know you have a big test...I can't help you study tomorrow, I'm getting my hair cut..."

"Julia." Gino says the name in a low voice, but it is enough to make Julia jump and turn around.

Gino glares up at his daughter. "If you don't come down now, the only person cutting your hair will be me. Can you say, buzz cut?"

Julia's eyes widen. "I'll call you back," she tells her caller, then she snaps the phone shut and stiffly walks down the stairs, as a queen would come down to meet her subjects. Baxter follows, yapping excitedly until he sees Gino—then he quickly struggles back up the staircase.

Gino continues to glare at his daughter. "It's *Dad*, Julia, not *Gino*. It will always be *Dad*. As long as I'm paying the bills, that's the way it will *always* be."

Julia rolls her eyes. Twice. "*Fine*," she says. But obviously, she makes clear with her face, it isn't fine.

Ronnie motions toward me. "Julia, this is Danny. He'll be staying with us for a while."

Julia finally notices me. She studies me intently for a few moments, her eyes quickly jumping from one feature to the next, finally settling on the stitches on my forehead. I stare back at her, knowing that my face is turning red. Then she quickly dismisses me, her beautiful eyes flicking back to her parents. "Why?" she asks, not too kindly.

"Because he needs a place to stay," Gino says firmly. "And I'm his godfather."

Julia takes this information in with no expression. "Will he be going to school with us?"

"Perhaps."

I am more surprised than Julia by this piece of news. She simply turns on her heel and arrogantly lifts her head. "Just don't expect me to be a tour guide," she sniffs before heading back up the stairs. A burly teenage boy passes her at the top and descends the steps in a few huge leaps.

"Hey, Dad, Joe said he just got a Camaro on the lot that's in perfect condition! He said he'd give us a great deal!"

Gino appears unmoved by his son's enthusiasm. "He said he'd give *us* a deal?"

"Oh, come on! You said you'd help me get a car!" wails the teenager, whom I know must be Gino's son, Vince. He is tall, like his sister, but where she is graceful and slim, Vince is bulky, with dark eyes and scruffy black hair. Vince glances at me, his eyes quickly finding the stitches on my head, before directing his attention back to his father.

"I told you I'd help you with half," Gino is saying. "Now, if you think you can come up with the other half needed for a Camaro—"

Vince's face turns red. "Oh yeah, right, like you don't have the money to help me get this car!"

Gino's voice is almost as cool as it had been with the loud, obnoxious Barb Kluwer. "I'm not your bank, Vince. It's my money, and I decide when and where it gets spent, not you."

I am a little unsettled by Gino's tone. With the exception of a few bursts of laughter, he seems to be an extremely calm guy with a tough guy exterior. But something about the edge in Gino's voice makes me uneasy.

Vince throws his hands in the air dramatically. "Fine! I'll go find a crappy car, and you can come pick me up when it breaks down at school and everyone makes fun of me!" Vince runs back up the stairs, taking the steps three at a time. His hammering footsteps cause the whole structure to tremble.

Gino and Ronnie ignore him, turning their attention once more to me. "Well, we already ate dinner," Ronnie says casually, as though her almost two hundred pound son were not about to take down the entire house. "But, Danny, we've got leftovers. How does macaroni and cheese sound? Mine is strictly homemade!" She looks at me expectantly, but she doesn't need to worry. I am so hungry, I would eat just about anything; macaroni and cheese sounds, well, unbelievably great.

Ronnie directs me through the enormous living room to the equally enormous kitchen and nudges me into a seat at the large oak table. I sit silently once more, racking my brain for something to say, but I am too exhausted to make conversation. Gino has disappeared for the moment.

"Here you go!" says Ronnie, placing an oversized bowl of steaming macaroni and cheese in front of me. "Now, if you need anything else, you just let me know. Or help yourself—this is your home." She pauses, uncertainly. "At least, it's your home as long as you want to stay here." She turns back to the kitchen and begins unloading the dishwasher. After a few moments of nothing but the sound of clattering dishes (and several delicious mouthfuls of mac and cheese for me), Ronnie again makes an attempt at conversation.

"So, Danny," she says casually, her Jersey accent shaping the sound of her words. "What grade are you going into this year?"

I swallow quickly. Too quickly. The hot macaroni burns my throat on its way to my stomach. "Uh, ninth grade. I'll be a freshman—unfortunately."

"Unfortunately? No, that's fantastic!" Ronnie says it like she truly means it. "High school is wonderful!"

I feel sure that high school was probably a good experience for Ronnie. If her daughter Julia is any indication, Ronnie has never struggled in the looks department. And let's face it, in high school, few kids see past a person's appearance. I look okay, but being poor has a limiting effect on my wardrobe, and therefore, my overall reputation. My ratty jeans may have been cool had they come from a socially approved, expensive mall store, but jeans from the local Save-Much are less than acceptable to my peers.

Ronnie ignores the fact that I have not responded. "Danny, you'll just love high school. The dances, the dating—it's all so much fun! And now you'll get to go to Vince and Julia's school. It's just a fantastic place!"

I stare at her, but she is too busy jamming silverware into their slots in a drawer to notice.

I might not be going back to Ridley, I realize and feel as though Gino has not been completely honest with me. Have they removed me from my home for good? Is my mother abandoning me, giving me to strangers?

I guess circumstances could be worse. The Vigliottis are obviously wealthy—Mom may be thinking that she is doing this for my own good. And maybe this is for my own good, and I am being ungrateful for being taken in by such a family. But even with the kindness shown to me by Gino and Ronnie, I can't help but feel lonely at this particular moment. And now that my stomach is full, I feel like the only thing that might bring me any comfort is sleep.

Thankfully, Ronnie seems to notice my exhaustion. "Hey, let's get you set up in one of the spare bedrooms," she says gently, taking my empty bowl from me and placing it in the sink. "I've got one that will be perfect—toward the back of the house on the ground floor. No one will bother you there."

It is just the thing I need to hear.

* * * *

The morning sun hits me full in the face. I open my eyes wearily, expecting to see my bedroom in my house in Ridley. Several moments pass before I realize that I am in a sunny guest room towards the back of the Vigliotti's small mansion, that I am in a bed that would fit at least two more people my size, and that there is a furry little creature who is curled up and snoring, his head resting on my foot.

"Baxter?" I call quietly, trying to remember how the dog had come to be in my room. And, for that matter, how did its dwarfish little body make it up onto this big bed? The dog lifts his head lazily at the sound of his name. "Who are these people you live with?" I ask, gazing into the little black eyes that stare back at me intently. Dad once told me that someone could determine a dog's intelligence by whether it was able to make eye contact. Whether this is true or not, Dad also believes that pets are dirty and too expensive and that they should be avoided at all costs. Except, I think, that with the occasional rat in our house, a small terrier or a cat would have been useful in my home.

Baxter, however, is not a dog that appears to have spent much time running after rats—or, for that matter, running at all. For being as small as he is, Baxter has a rather round belly that hints of too much food and an absence of any meaningful exercise. But I have to admit, he is a cute little guy, even if he is definitely not the most macho pet a person could own.

I stay in bed several minutes, letting myself enjoy the softness of the mattress and the silky sheets. I have never, ever slept in a bed like this. Once, at my grandmother's house, I was able to sleep in a queen size bed; however, it was not nearly as nice as this bed, and the springs creaked whenever I rolled over. My bed at home is far worse—in fact, it is not even a bed, but a futon Dad bought at a yard sale. But this bed is not the only item that makes staying at the Vigliotti house so amazing—the room is quiet, protecting me from any noise coming from other parts of the house. This is also a stark contrast to my house, because I can't remember a morning that I did not wake up to slamming doors and shouting between my parents.

I can't get used to this. I will eventually be forced to return to my life in Ridley, so I cannot get accustomed to this lifestyle. I am poor, and this type of living, if I ever experience it again, is far in my future, when I make my own way in the world. Gino is my godfather, not my dad. And sooner or later, I will be headed back to live with my real family.

I suddenly feel an overwhelming urge to call my friend Reggie and tell him everything that has happened to me. I'll have to ask Ronnie if I can make a quick call. With that thought fixed in my mind, I climb out of the bed and take a shower in the adjoining bathroom. Having my own bathroom is another luxury because I don't worry about taking too long or someone barging in the door. Complete privacy is something I have always wanted but have never experienced. I *can't* get used to this life. I can't live with more disappointment.

Baxter is still on the bed when I exit the bathroom, and he is staring at the floor and whining as though the carpet were a bottomless pit, unreachable for his scrawny legs.

"Here," I say, picking him up and setting him on the floor. Baxter immediately starts to wag his tail and bounces around the room, yipping excitedly.

"Easy there, little guy," I say, trying not to laugh. "Just give me a minute to put on some clothes. I think if I walk out of here naked, my temporary parents will kick me out immediately!" I throw on an extra large T-shirt I find draped over the back of the chair (taken without Vince's knowledge, I'm guessing, by Ronnie, who took my own bloody shirt from me the night before). Then I put on my own pair of jeans, which are definitely in need of either a wash or the garbage can.

I hope that I have a chance to pick up my things today. I don't have much, but I could at least use some of my own clothes. Maybe I'll try to catch a bus back to my house—in the past that's been the only way I've been able to participate in any activities at school, as my parents have more important things to do with their time, including drinking beer, watching television, and arguing endlessly over where last week's paycheck disappeared.

I follow the yipping Baxter down the hall and through the living room toward the kitchen. The house is quiet, and I wonder whether anyone is home. My question is answered when I reach the immaculate, oversized kitchen; Vince is slouched in a kitchen chair, slurping a bowl of cereal and intently reading the back of the box.

He turns from the box of Cocoa Nuggets as Baxter puts a paw on his pant leg, eagerly waiting for some food. Vince shakes his leg. "Get off me, *Bastard*. You can't have chocolate, dumb dog. It will kill you. So don't tempt me…"

I stand silently at the counter, debating what to say, when Vince notices Baxter is not the only newcomer in the kitchen. He nods his head at the cereal box. "You want some of this cocoa crap? Bowls are in the cabinet to the left of the sink. Spoons are in the drawer on the right."

I find a bowl and spoon and sit down at the kitchen table across from Vince. I shake the box of Cocoa Nuggets at my bowl and pour just a spoonful of milk over the dark brown puffed cereal. Vince is watching me with interest, so I try to make conversation.

"Where is everyone?"

Vince shrugs. "Dad's not home yet. Mom's at a tennis lesson, and Julia's sleeping. And she won't be getting out of bed anytime soon, because she's *lazy*."

I am most interested in what Vince said first. "Gino's not home yet? Where did he go?"

"Out." Vince replies cryptically, and then his gaze trails to the back of the cereal box. "Hey, this says the longest one syllable word in the English language is 'screeched'."

I try to sound interested. "Oh?" I pause. "Your dad wasn't taking care of anything to do with me, was he?"

Vince's eyes remain on the box. "I doubt it. That's just his normal hours." He looks at me meaningfully.

I have no idea what Vince is trying to say. "Okay. Well, I've got to go back to Ridley then, because I need some clothes and stuff."

Vince reaches in his pocket and pulls out a credit card, tossing it on the table. "No, don't worry about it. Mom gave me this and told me to take you shopping for school clothes and other junk. She wouldn't give me cash because she thinks I'll take it for myself." He grins. "Smart lady."

I stare at the credit card. "I don't need your parents to buy me stuff. I just need to get to Ridley. All I need is a few bucks for a bus fare."

Vince is staring at me as though I'm crazy, or maybe from another planet. "You're not going back to your place. Mom said so. She said she wanted me to make sure you spent at least seven hundred dollars on stuff you need, but you could spend up to a thousand. That's the limit she set."

I know my jaw is hanging open unattractively. A thousand dollars? That is more than twice what my parents scrounge up each month to pay the rent. I don't think all the clothes I have ever owned would add up to a thousand dollars. How could I ever spend that much money just to buy clothes?

Vince is amused by my shock. "Hey, if you don't want it, I could easily spend it on myself. Besides, I'm not thrilled that I have to chauffeur a *freshman* around. Then again, if you don't come home with some crap, I'm going to get in trouble. And I need to play things right. I've got to convince them to help me buy the Camaro. Besides, if I take you shopping, I get to drive the Lexus. And let me tell you—me driving the Lexus is a totally worth-it experience. When you're in that thing, the girls can't keep their hands off you." He grins again and takes another slurping bite of cereal.

I grin too, but it's because I am trying to imagine girls unable to keep their hands off of the slurping Vince. I think of the comfortable life Vince has, and suddenly, I have to fight down the urge to use every single penny Ronnie has given me. "I won't spend the money. I'm not even related to you guys. I don't need your money."

Vince rolls his eyes. "Face it. You definitely need it. Just take it. A thousand bucks in this house is a night on the town for my dad, a few haircuts for my mom, or a designer bag for my sister. It's nothing. So get off your underprivileged high horse and be grateful."

I glance at the side of the refrigerator, having noticed earlier a smattering of coupons held in place with colorful magnets from different states. "You're saying your family always spends money like this?" I ask doubtfully.

Vince follows my eyes to the magnets. "Oh, believe me, my mom likes to act like she's saving money—clipping coupons, buying items on sale, driving a practical minivan to her social things—but she's as big a spender as the rest of us. She just needs to find ways to justify it, which is *not* like the rest of us." He glares at me. "So enjoy the money and quit whining."

I am not trying to be ungrateful, but surely the Vigliottis will want something from me in return. My dad has told me over and over that every gift comes with some sort of price attached. "Look, I'll pay them back," I offer lamely.

Vince laughs, milk and cereal exploding from his mouth back into his bowl. I wipe away a droplet of milk that has landed on my nose. "Pay them back?" Vince is having difficulty pulling himself together. "That would be a first! Good luck with that! My dad would probably beat you senseless for trying!"

I flinch at Vince's words and am abruptly reminded that I am here because my dad, Del, struck me. I recall hitting my head on the battered coffee table on my way to the floor. The memory is painful, and I subconsciously reach up to touch the stitches near my temple.

Vince's eyes widen. "Hey, look, I'm sorry. I didn't mean it. That was a stupid thing to joke about. My dad said, well, he said that your dad—"

"Don't worry about it," I cut in. I can't talk about last night's events, and I'm desperate to change the subject, so I pick up the credit card on the table. I've made up my mind—I deserve this, right? "Should we go spend some money?" I ask.

Vince smiles. "I'll get the Lexus."

Chapter 3

For a Saturday morning, the mall is quiet. I expect that most people are doing some last-minute outside activities before the start of a new school year. The Newcastle mall is far nicer than the one in Ridley. My dad has always thought the mall is absolutely unnecessary (what could someone buy there that couldn't be bought for half the price at Save-Much?), and Mom has spent so much money on department store makeup that there is little cash left to buy much else. For that reason, I have no idea where to start.

Luckily, Vince seems to have no trouble putting the little plastic credit card to work almost immediately. He leads me into an expensive sunglasses store and begins to flirt with the leggy, tanned teenage girl standing behind the cash register. In less than five minutes, I have a pair of sunglasses sitting on my nose.

"What do you think?" Vince asks casually, but he isn't looking at me. He is staring at the girl's long legs.

I shrug. "They're fine. But I'm not sure sunglasses count as a school item. And if I spend a hundred and fifty bucks on these, I'm definitely not going to be able to buy much of anything else."

Vince rolls his eyes and shoots the girl a charming smile. Despite his husky body, he certainly seems to be attracting positive attention from her. "This kid is unbelievable," Vince says to her. "It's like he's never spent money before in his life." He turns to me. "This doesn't count against your tab at all. You were being such a pain at the breakfast table, I forgot to tell you my dad left us some money to spend too." He pulls out two hundred dollars in cash and hands it to the girl. "Keep the change," he says, smiling.

She shakes her head. "We're not allowed!" she squeaks.

Vince looks around the empty store. "Hey, who's going to know?"

She giggles nervously and takes the cash. All of it.

In less than two hours, I have four pairs of jeans, at least ten new shirts, an expensive backpack, three pairs of brand-name sneakers, khaki and athletic shorts, and some bath items from a drugstore. But my items are nothing compared with what Vince has purchased. Despite his mom's warning to only use the card for me, Vince has used the plastic to buy several expensive clothing items and some cologne for himself, saving most of the cash from Gino for his "car fund".

"Let's get out of here," Vince says, glancing at our numerous shopping bags. "We're beginning to look like chicks."

Several minutes and a few potential speeding tickets later, we are racing down the interstate, and I can tell we're not headed back to the house. "I gotta stop to make," Vince says casually, as though the SUV were not flying down the road at ninety miles an hour. I feel exhilarated by the speed, and I'm positive that the Higgins family has never owned any vehicle that could even come close to going seventy miles an hour, much less ninety.

I'm suddenly struck by a thought. "Is this your dad's car?" I ask.

"Yup."

"Then why isn't he using it right now?"

Vince grins. "He doesn't use the Lexus for work much. I think it would cramp his style."

I'm confused, but I don't push the issue. Vince is difficult to read, and I want to make a good impression on him. We quickly leave the nicer part of Newcastle and enter the older section of town. Exiting the highway, Vince drives the Lexus down a narrow street that winds through weathered, grubby buildings. The area isn't shabby or dirty, just somewhat neglected. The buildings may have been the center of Newcastle a few decades ago. Vince pulls the Lexus in front of an aged brick two-story building featuring a weathered sign reading, "Jimmy's Diner."

I give Vince a questioning look and receive a grin in return. "This is the office!" he says cheerfully. Vince turns off the ignition and hops out, but as I begin to open my door, he holds up his hand. "Stay here. I'll be right back—don't move." And with that, he slams the door and disappears into the building.

I'm not in the SUV for three minutes before the sweat begins to drip down my face. Vince didn't even leave the keys in the ignition, so I can't turn on the air conditioner. The middle of August is not a good time to be sitting in a dark, sealed vehicle during the hottest part of the day. I wait three more minutes before calling it quits and stepping out of the SUV. The ninety degree weather feels cool and refreshing compared with the stagnant air in the vehicle. I quietly shut the door and try to lean against the SUV's exterior, but I quickly jump away from the scorching metal. So I'm standing next to the Lexus, feeling awkward, annoyed, and curious all at once.

Three more minutes, and I am seriously considering whether I might follow Vince inside the restaurant. Did he actually think I would wait in the car in such steamy weather? And I'm wondering what

Vince is doing at a place like this. Maybe this guy has activities going on that his parents don't know about. If that is the case, I don't want to know about them either.

A second later, my theory is blown to pieces, because through the tinted glass of the driver's side window, I'm surprised to see Gino exit the restaurant, roughly dragging Vince by the arm. Vince is talking very fast, his usually husky voice sounding strangely high-pitched.

"Dad! I'm sorry. But I had to ask you, and I can never get you on the phone!"

Gino spins Vince around to face him directly. Gino's face is hard, his body tense. "There's a reason for that, and you know it!" His voice is seething with anger.

My body becomes rigid, and I pull myself out of Gino's line of sight. Being so new to the family, I do not want any of Gino's fury directed at me. The Gino from last night was tough, yet kind. There's no kindness in that voice now.

"I'm sorry! I'm sorry!" Vince stammers. "I just wanted to talk—"

"You can wait 'til I get home!" Gino says fiercely. "You should never, ever come here!" He pauses, and a moment of uncomfortable silence hangs in the muggy air. "You didn't bring anyone with you, did you?"

I can't hear Vince respond, but I figure that Vince must have said no, because Gino says nothing more than "Get outta here!" before tramping angrily back into the restaurant.

I remain motionless next to the SUV until Vince comes around the side. He seems relieved to see me. "Good move," Vince says. "If he had known you were here with me, he would have killed me!"

Vince lumbers back to the other side of the Lexus and climbs into the driver's seat. I get in on my side and wait silently as long as I can help it. Then, when I realize that we aren't going anywhere, I ask, "What is this place?"

Vince turns his head toward me, but his eyes are looking through me, glazed. Vince seems stunned, as though he hadn't expected his dad to react as he did.

"Has your dad ever been like that? You know, before?"

Vince finally seems to come out of his trance, his eyes narrowing as they focus on my face. "Look, Danny. I should never have come here. Let's go."

He puts the Lexus in reverse and backs out quickly, the dirt of the parking lot swirling up and covering the hood of the SUV. The vehicle jerks back and then forward as Vince switches gears and roars away from the restaurant. However, if I thought we were headed back to the house, I was wrong. A few blocks down, Vince pulls up in front of another shabby building with the words "Mike's Movies" on the sign. He says nothing to me this time; he just exits the vehicle and hustles into the store. I stay put for a moment, but I already know I won't last long in this heat. I can only imagine what kind of movie Vince has gone into the store to get, but I think it's probably not something Ronnie would approve of.

Two minutes later, just as I am about to get out of the SUV again, Vince exits the store, a DVD case in his left hand and a Snickers bar in his right. He climbs back into the SUV without a word and tosses the movie to me.

"*Goodfellas*?" I ask.

"It's the best movie ever made."

I shake my head doubtfully. "Yeah—I don't agree. In fact, I actually think it's kind of dumb."

Vince glares at me. "Are you kidding me?" He shakes his head in disbelief. "Then you're stupid. This movie is an absolute classic. As far as Mafia movies go, there's nothing like it."

"Okay, if you're into the *Mafia*," I agree. "Is that why you like it? Organized crime and all that nonsense?"

"Nonsense!" Vince yells, speeding up and allowing the SUV to swerve a little out of control. I grip the leather of my seat, my palms layered in sweat.

"No, not nonsense! I just meant, you know, some people are really into mob stuff!" I say quickly, keeping my voice calm.

Vince slows the SUV, but I can see that he is steamed.

"Look, I'm sorry. I didn't mean to disrespect your movie," I say.

"It's just that it, well—it always motivates me," he answers, his body language telling me I have quickly made his bad mood worse.

I lean back in the seat, not sure what to say after Vince's blowup. I am ready to get back to the house and shower away all this sweat. I search for a new topic. "Hey, Vince, you play sports?"

Vince shakes his head, and his eyes take on that strange vacancy I saw at the diner. "No. I'm just not very good at anything. My dad hates that I don't."

I definitely don't know what to say now, so I say nothing. I'm sure we are headed back to the house, but a few minutes later, my hopes are crushed again. Vince is pulling into a used-car lot that sits at the entrance to the highway. At least, I assume it is a used-car lot, because bright green price stickers have been placed on the windshields of the army of shiny cars covering the large dirt lot. However, no sign indicates any dealership name.

Perhaps the classic Corvettes or the sleek silver Porsche should have caught my eyes first, but it is actually a girl that grabs my attention as Vince parks the SUV. She looks to be in her mid-teens, and she is stretched out on her stomach on a blanket she has placed on the hood of a gleaming Cadillac. She is wearing a red and white striped bikini and has large bulky sunglasses sitting atop her head of straight blond hair. As she concentrates on a glossy magazine, her legs swing back and forth casually behind her.

I am still staring at her as Vince puts the SUV in park and hops out, slamming the door without a single word to me. Curious about the sunbathing girl, I clamber after Vince. Vince goes right up to her, and she lazily lifts her eyes when he gives an abrupt cough. Her eyes are brown, big, and expressive, and at the moment, those eyes are expressing that she is not happy to see Vince.

Vince glares back at her. "Where's your dad?"

She rolls her eyes. "Oh, I don't know. Earning a living. Selling cars, maybe?" she answers sarcastically. She glances at me, her expression annoyed. She appraises me quickly, and her eyes narrow on my stitches. "Who's this? One of your bullies-in-training? Does he help you beat up the other little kids on the playground? Or do you send him off to buy your Snickers for you?"

Vince grunts in irritation and stuffs his half-empty candy wrapper in his pocket. "You're such a snot, Portia. I'm not a bully. And I barely know this kid. My dad took him in for a few days. Family crap or something."

I'm surprised by the way Vince has quickly shrugged off any connection with me after being somewhat friendly through the morning. I don't care to be called a "kid," and more importantly, I don't want to discuss my family problems with a beautiful girl I've just met.

"Hi," I say, stepping forward and extending my hand. "I'm Danny. I'm just staying with the Vigliottis for a few days." I'm pleasantly surprised to see Portia's scowl quickly turn to a smile.

"Hi, Danny. It's nice to meet you. I'm sorry you have to stay with Vince. I try to have as little contact with him as possible." She shoots another annoyed look at Vince, whose face flushes in irritation.

"You only wish you could have *contact* with me, Portia," Vince snaps. "Too bad you're a dorky freshman. As a junior, I shouldn't even be seen talking to you!" And with that, Vince stalks away.

Portia smiles as he marches toward the little brick building sitting in the middle of the lot, and then she turns her attention back to me. "He is such a jerk. I've got no time for his sulkiness. And the insults—he is *such* a charmer."

I can't help but smile. Portia is being nice to me *and* she is pretty. This is going down as a very good day for me. "I don't know him very well, but I'd say he *is* a little moody," I add helpfully.

She laughs—not a high-pitched teenage girl giggle, but a full, hearty laugh. "Moody?" she gasps. "Oh, that's an understatement! You definitely haven't spent much time with him. Lucky *you*! My family has known his family my whole life. And it has been such

38

torture to put up with him." She finally settles down, and her face turns serious. Her large brown eyes search my face. "What happened to your head?"

I instinctively cover my stitches with my hand. "Nothing. Just an accident."

She nods, almost as though she has connected the pieces in her head. "I'm sorry about your family stuff."

I shake my head quickly. "It's not a big deal. Vince shouldn't have said anything."

Portia doesn't look away, and I feel she is reading me. I'm suddenly uncomfortable, as though she were invading my privacy. "I can tell you're hurting, Danny," she says softly. "You don't have to act tough. I'm *surrounded* by tough."

I stare back at her, wanting to say more, but knowing I cannot confide in someone who is still a stranger, striped bikini or not. "Thanks, but it's okay. I'm fine."

She nods again, slipping off the Cadillac and stepping into rhinestone-covered flip-flops. She is standing extremely close to me, and I inhale deeply to keep my breathing steady. My mind is screaming at me—*don't say or do anything stupid!*

Portia steps in front of me, her eyes a few inches below mine. She grins. "You're cute, Danny. Don't hang out with Vince too much. You seem nice, and he might be a bad influence."

I have the urge to hug her. Her no-nonsense personality is so attractive. Most of the girls I know have only about half the confidence of the blonde standing in front of me. I want to say something smooth, something that will match her confidence. I clear my throat, then say, "Portia? What a great name. It's like the car?"

I immediately turn red, knowing how completely stupid that comment sounded.

Portia begins to laugh so hard she has to hug her arms to her stomach. "Oh, Danny, you *are* cute. Like the car? I must be making you nervous! I'm sorry!"

She can't stop laughing, and I rake my mind for a quick response, something to save my shredded dignity. But the moment is lost to the sound of yelling coming from the far corner of the lot.

Vince obviously has not found what or whom he was looking for inside the brick building, because he is now facing off with two teenage boys. Portia sucks in a deep breath and takes off running toward the group, and I run after her, the words "It's like the car" still ringing shamefully in my ears.

One of the boys pushes Vince as Portia and I run within earshot. Vince rushes the other teenager, but he stops when Portia screams "No!" Everyone turns to look at her. She stops running, plants her hands on her hips, and glares at the group of boys before her. "That's enough! You can't fight on my dad's lot!"

"Oh, really?" The boy who pushed Vince is sneering at Portia, looking at her in a way that makes me angry. The boy isn't quite as burly as Vince, but he definitely outsizes me by an inch or two in height and at least ten pounds. He is dark, like Vince, but where Vince has a round face, this boy's face is narrow, his eyes large and his nose sharp. His buddy is similar in looks, if not in body build; he is small, but almost as wide as he is tall, built like a torpedo. The first teenager glances at me and then quickly smirks. "Who's the Frankenstein, Portia?"

I again put my hand to my stitched forehead, and I feel my heart begin to beat with anticipation, just as it always does before a wrestling match. I can sense the conflict, and I know a fight is likely, if not unavoidable. Even the size of this other teenager and his bulky friend are not enough to make me stand down. If only Reggie were here to help me, because I have no idea how strong a fighter Vince is or whether I can trust him to back me up.

"No! All of you, stop it! I know what you're going to do! Don't make me get my dad!" Portia's strong voice holds a note of panic. If I could stop the fight, I would be her hero (or at least she might still pay attention to me), but I am struggling with my urge to demonstrate my skills to this arrogant kid, to Vince, and, most importantly, to the pretty blonde standing next to me.

I feel my inner conscience take over (or is it the striped bikini—I don't know for sure). "All right, let's all calm down. Nobody wants any trouble here," I say heroically.

Vince and the other teenage boys are all staring at me in disgust. Of course, they all want trouble. Heck, I want trouble too. Portia is the only one looking for a peaceful end to this face off. My arms tingle with the thought of rushing the smirking teenager.

I never have a chance to make a decision. The other teenager rushes me first, closing the distance between us in seconds. I react instinctively, but late. Crouching, I duck and grab at the other teen's knees, attempting a double-leg takedown. The teen's surprise attack and momentum allows him to escape my grab. He stumbles several steps past me, but he quickly regains his balance. The fight is on.

Vince immediately begins swinging at the smaller boy, and I feel a tinge of resentment that burly Vince is taking on the smaller of our two opponents. But I don't have time to think about whether the fight is fair. The other teen is coming at me once more; I jump back from his swinging fists, ducking one punch before sending a blow to his stomach.

"Stop it!" Portia screams. But no one pays her any attention, and I am certain that I am the only one who feels even the slightest hint of guilt.

The other teen comes forward again and flings his fist with his whole body at my jaw, but this kid's haymaker gives me the advantage. As he goes off balance from the momentum of his missed swing, I dip to the side and throw my arms around his stomach, pick him up off his feet, and use my leg to sweep his legs out from underneath him. The move is perfect except for his last desperate attempt to go down fighting. He headbutts me, slamming the back of his skull into my forehead, and unfortunately, the gash on my head. I drop my opponent from high in the air and grab my forehead. My head is throbbing wildly, but until I see the blood on the back of the other kid's head, I don't realize that my stitches have been ripped open. The other teenager is sputtering, having lost his breath in the fall. I wait, debating whether I should end the fight now with a couple more punches.

"Break it up! Now!" A hand grabs my shirt collar, almost lifting me completely off my feet. I catch my balance and my breath as I am released, and I spin to look at the man who grabbed me. Large, fleshy arms extend from an equally fleshy body. But the man isn't exactly fat—he is more like a contestant in the World's Strongest Man competition. I brush myself off as Vince and the teenager he has been pummeling rise to their feet—Vince with a bloody lip and the other teenager with a much bloodier nose. Vince and I have been moderately successful, but the outcome is now a draw.

The man turns to face my opponent, who is struggling to his feet, his eyes full of rage. "Tommy!" the man booms, his voice rough and deep, "I told you to stay away from here unless you are handing me money for a car."

Tommy glares at the man, his nose wrinkling. "Hey, Joe. What is that I smell? Grease? Must be a car salesman nearby."

I gape at Tommy in shock. How can he be so disrespectful to an adult, and such a large one at that? Portia is also shocked by Tommy's comment, and, having obviously forgotten her previous anti-fighting stance, she takes a few steps toward Tommy, grabs him by the shoulders, and knees him in the crotch. Tommy doubles over with a howl of pain, brings his arm up, and swings it at Portia, smacking her across the face.

I reactively move toward Tommy, but Joe has Tommy by the neck of his shirt before I can take two steps. Joe shoves him roughly up against a nearby car and holds Tommy inches from his face.

"How dare you!" Joe roars, enraged. "How dare you touch her! The only reason you're still alive is because of your father!"

Tommy glares fiercely at Joe, although he looks a little less confident than he did a few minutes before. "Sorry," he mutters, although he doesn't sound even close to meaning it.

Although Vince has backed away from the action, as has the other teenager, I am amazed at my own confidence as I walk over to Portia and put my hand on her shoulder, and I feel a small surge of excitement when she doesn't move away. I stand with her, glaring at the battered Tommy. What is this kid thinking? Joe is three times his size and obviously protective of his daughter.

But Joe does nothing more. He holds Tommy up against the car for a few seconds longer, his face impassive as he stares down at Tommy. Then he lets the teen go, turns around, and walks away. Joe nudges Portia away from me and guides her gently by her elbow from all of us. Joe doesn't even turn his head when he says, "Don't any of you come back here unless you've got enough cash in your dirty little hands to buy a car."

Tommy motions to his friend. "Come on, we'll be back soon. I've got a Camaro waiting for me." He makes a face at Vince, who, to my surprise, merely watches the other teenagers as they walk in the opposite direction.

"What was that?" I ask, shocked by the bizarre events.

Vince curses and kicks at the dirt with a dusty sneaker. His clothes, which were spotless and ironed this morning, are now grimy and wrinkled. I know I don't look much better. Between Vince's bloody lip and my reopened gash, I expect that the trouble is far from over. "Well, you definitely hold your own in a fight," I say, unable to hide my exhilaration.

"Let's go," Vince says crossly. "What a total waste of time."

Chapter 4

All hell breaks loose at the Vigliotti house. Ronnie is already fuming about Vince's generous use of her credit card for his own purposes (she apparently has a very close relationship with one of the credit card customer service representatives), and our battered appearance only stokes her temper further. I experience the full volume of her irritation and am again amazed at the strength of the voice coming from this tiny woman. She is displeased with Vince's rumpled clothing and split lip, but when she sees my bleeding forehead, she goes ballistic.

"Vince!" she howls. "I can't trust you with anything! Anything at all! First the credit card, and now you're getting Danny involved in your fights!"

Vince slumps into a chair at the kitchen table. He seems tired and angry, but he shows little concern for his mother's rage. He shoots me an evil smile. "Actually, Danny started fighting before I did."

"What? That's ridiculous!" Ronnie spins to face me. "Tell me he's lying!"

I glare at Vince, who shrugs, as though this is a game. I feel like punching Vince in his split lip. Getting in trouble like this is a quick way to earn a ticket right back to Ridley, or worse, into the hands of Barb Kluwer.

"I'm sorry, Missus Vigliotti. I don't know if it makes any difference, but the other kid made the first move," I offer weakly. "I was just defending myself."

Ronnie turns to Vince, who has taken the box of Cocoa Nuggets from the table and is using his grimy hand to scoop dry cereal into his mouth. I make a mental note to bypass the Cocoa Nuggets tomorrow morning. That is, if there is a tomorrow morning at the Vigliotti house for me.

"Yeah, the other kid moved first," Vince answers, grinning at me. "Danny actually made a weak attempt to stop the fight before it started, but I'm pretty sure his only motivation for that was the hottie standing next to him."

Ronnie shakes her head in frustration, but I keep my eyes on Vince, trying to gauge his motivation. Vince's tendency to joke is obvious. The problem is, I don't know whether Vince is teasing his mother or trying to get me to take the blame. Vince and I certainly aren't friends, but we fought on the same team today, and I guess I expect a degree of loyalty for facing off with strangers.

"Well, that's great—that's just great!" Ronnie is still furious. "And the other kids, they look like you two?"

"Worse." Vince smirks. "Danny's a champ. Although the beating he gave Tommy didn't seem to keep that butt-head from being a snot-nosed brat to Joe Saviano."

Ronnie puts her hand immediately to her chest. "Tommy? Tommy Gallo?"

Vince glares at her defiantly. "Yeah, Tommy was the one who started everything."

Ronnie is staring at him, but she no longer seems angry. She looks frightened.

"Vince, I told you not to provoke that boy. I told you to leave him alone! You know why!"

I can't help but feel I am missing information that would make Ronnie's behavior make sense. Vince is no longer smirking; he angrily slams the Cocoa Nuggets on the table, causing crispy chocolate pieces to come flying out of the box.

"I don't care who he is—or who his father is!" Vince says loudly. "If he's going to rush at me, fists flying, then I'm going to reply with some fist flying of my own. And Danny's no different. He's not going to sit there and allow Tommy to give him a bloody head for no reason. And I'm glad to have him on my side. It's about time Tommy had some competition. The whole school is tired of his bullying."

Vince meets my eyes with a look of respect, and I can't help but feel a little proud.

Ronnie, however, is not as touched by Vince's words. She steps forward and puts her hands on his shoulders, her eyes pleading as they look into his. "It's not about being brave or even about self-defense, Vince. It's about keeping you safe—keeping this family safe. Making sure your father doesn't suffer for what happens among boys on the playground."

Vince shakes her off. "Playground? Seriously, Mom! Don't say crap like that. And I don't care! You hear me, I don't care!"

He flies from the room, and several seconds later the stairs are again treated to his pounding feet.

Ronnie turns to me, her face pale. "Well," she says, "I guess it's back to the hospital for you."

* * * *

I gingerly touch the new set of stitches in my forehead and realize that my gash will probably take longer to heal now that I have hit my head twice. But at the moment, I don't care. I am on the phone at the

Vigliotti house and am sitting in the office chatting with Reggie, trying to update my friend on the strange turn of events without being too specific concerning what happened to me in Ridley. No one needs to know that my dad crossed the line; I feel that any information might make its way back to Barb Kluwer, who is certainly still working on getting hold of me, if I have judged her correctly.

"Okay, so your parents got in a fight, decided to split for a while, and now you're staying with your godfather in New Jersey? Man, I don't know, Danny, that sounds a little crazy!"

I can understand Reggie's disbelief. The whole thing is somewhat absurd. "I know it's weird. But it gets better—I'm staying in one of the most fantastic houses I've ever seen, and today they bought me all these nice new clothes. *And* I've got a great big bedroom and bathroom!"

"Wow, with all that, you'll never come back to Ridley!" Reggie is joking, but I can hear the slight strain in his voice.

"Oh, I'll be coming back. Ronnie hinted that I might go to school here for a while, though."

"Really? That's no good! We were going to be starters on the wrestling team this year!"

I can sense Reggie's disappointment. How would I feel if my best friend abandoned me? Yet, I am having a difficult time feeling the same disappointment. Reggie and I have a great friendship, but today has been an eye-opening experience in what living in a wealthy, happy home might be like. Well, perhaps they are not one hundred percent happy, but every family has their problems, right? I keep having this nagging feeling that I should not get too attached to these people or this lifestyle. But for the moment, I am going to let myself enjoy the feeling of being a teenager who, for once, is not forced to worry about buying groceries, paying bills, or playing peacemaker to fighting parents.

"So, who are these people?" Reggie asks. "What's a godfather?"

"Ronnie said a godfather is supposed to look out for his godchild's spiritual upbringing. I think it's a Catholic thing, which I don't quite understand because I don't remember my parents going to a Catholic church. Or any church for that matter."

"Yeah, that's kind of strange. We don't have that in my church. You said the last name was Vigliotti? That sounds Italian."

"I guess," I answer.

Reggie sucks in a deep breath of air. "Hey! You don't think they're in the mob or something, do you?" He sounds excited.

"Oh, come on, Reggie! Seriously? You need to cut down on watching so much TV."

"I don't watch much. But just think about it—they're Italian, they live in New Jersey, and he's your godfather!"

I roll my eyes, knowing Reggie cannot see my frustration, but I can hear the edge in my voice as I reply. "Knock it off. I told you godfathers were a Catholic thing. And not every Italian is a mobster!"

"Yeah, but some of them are!"

Gino steps into the office doorway, an odd expression on his face, and I smile in silent greeting. "Reggie, I've got to go now. I'll call you again soon."

Reggie sighs. "Fine. I'll talk to you later."

"Talk to ya later." I hang up the phone and swivel my chair to face Gino.

"So," Gino begins, his voice gruff, "I heard that you made another trip to the hospital today. And that you met some new friends at Joe Saviano's lot."

My body goes rigid. I have no idea how to answer Gino. Does he know I was at the diner? Should I apologize? Is Gino thinking twice about bringing me to stay at the Vigliotti house? "Uh, Vince and I, we had, um, what you might call a disagreement with some other teenagers." Geez! Is that the best I can come up with? Now *I* sound like a mobster!

"Just be careful, okay." Gino's tone is strict, but surprisingly, not angry. "Ronnie and I don't always agree about fighting—I don't think you should always back down—but just be smart about it. Tommy Gallo is not a kid you want to tangle with unless it's absolutely unavoidable. You may be able to kick his butt—good for you. But that kid has a very powerful father, and it's not smart to provoke him."

"I didn't provoke—"

"I know." Gino cuts in. "Vince told me. But nevertheless, you are grounded for one week. We've got to make Ronnie happy. Vince is grounded for three—he lied about bringing you to the diner."

I feel my face flush. One day at the Vigliotti's and I'm already causing trouble. At home, I'm usually so responsible, and now I feel like I'm behaving like a poster boy for troubled teens. I want to make a good impression on the Vigliottis, but now they might send me away. "I'm very sorry, Gino. I'll understand if you want to send me back to Ridley. Just don't send me to Barb Kluwer." I hate the pleading tone in my voice.

Gino smiles and shakes his head. "Danny, you are not going back to Ridley until Penny is ready for you to come home. You've got a really screwed up idea about family. Just because you make a mistake doesn't mean we give up on you. Heck, if that were true, Julia and Vince would have been given away a long time ago! You're a good kid—I know that. So don't worry about it."

A brief silence follows. If Gino considers me part of the family, I know I could never come up with the right words to thank him for that kind of acceptance.

Gino motions to me. "Let's go grab some dinner. And your stuff from home has arrived."

* * * *

Being grounded at the Vigliotti house is like a fun-packed snow day. The first day of our punishment, Vince and I play video games all morning in the game room (I catch on quickly, even though I can count on one hand the number of times I've played a video game). The game room is equipped with an enormous TV and a state-of-the-art stereo system, which means that every game is an audiovisual thrill. Then we order pizza (on Ronnie's credit card, of course), watch *Goodfellas* (which isn't quite as dumb as I remembered), and go online to debate which Hollywood actress is most "talented."

Despite Vince's sketchy loyalty during the fight yesterday, I feel we are forming some sort of friendship. I have started to realize that Vince is a bit of a loner, but that he is enjoying my company, despite my freshman status. I wonder if this is what having a sibling is like.

In addition to watching *Goodfellas*, Vince and I consume an assortment of mob movies, every one of which Vince seems to have seen before. I have to sit through several seasons of *Sopranos* (the "good ones," as Vince observes), and by the end of my exposure to various Mafia stories, I know that a *wiseguy*, a *made man*, or a *button man* is a guy who dedicates his life to the Mafia, that a *gumata* is a mobster's girlfriend, and that getting whacked or "hit" means you're not long for the earth.

After overdosing on video games the first day, on day two Vince introduces me to FaceSpace, a website where Vince chats with other kids his age. Well, "kids" means mostly girls; despite Vince's loner personality, he obviously has plenty of time to flirt. And he appears to have quite a few fans. Between texting on his cell phone (I'm envious because I've never had a phone) and e-mailing, he has a large network of friends.

The rest of the week rushes by in what seems like minutes, and I find myself easily becoming accustomed to the Vigliotti lifestyle. Ronnie cooks amazing meals every night, and I am already packing on a few pounds—I'll have to be a little more careful if I am going to try out for wrestling. Going to Mass on Sunday is quite a new experience for me, and not completely unpleasant. My only church experience so far has been at Reggie's Baptist church in Ridley, which is extremely different from this one.

Someone is letting Baxter into my room at night (although I always forget to ask who), and I hate to admit that I enjoy walking the little dog around the fancy neighborhood. Vince often joins me on these walks, even though he spends most of the time teasing me about getting attached to a dog that is really more like a rat. I don't mind the teasing or the dog, and I decide that if and when I go back to Ridley, I will force my parents to get me a dog to make up for traumatizing me. But maybe I'll ask for something a little less girly than Baxter.

Julia ignores me as easily as she ignores everyone else at the Vigliotti house. Whenever I see her, she makes an effort to show me just how little I matter in her life. I could care less—she is certainly gorgeous, but after meeting Portia, Julia's snooty attitude makes her slightly less attractive. In fact, I'm glad that my lack of interest seems to irritate her.

"She's usually worshipped by boys, so she's offended by any male interest that is less than extreme," Vince tells me. "I'd show her some attention if you want her to be friendly."

I just shrug, but am thrilled with the little power I hold.

The day before school begins, I am finally becoming comfortable with the idea of attending Newcastle High. High school would be a challenge regardless of whether I went to Ridley or Newcastle, and Newcastle may actually be a better experience because I have the connections and the clothes that I never had in Ridley. However, I know my reputation as a good wrestler at Ridley won't matter at Newcastle unless I prove myself. What if I'm not as good or can't make the team? This motivates me to go jogging and work out in the Vigliotti's home gym, especially with all the pizza Vince and I have been consuming. Vince mocks me when I work out and has no intention of joining me.

That same day, my mom shows up on the Vigliotti doorstep. I am still damp from my after-jogging shower as I answer the doorbell and am ashamed of the panic I feel when I see her. Mom looks terrible. Her bleached hair is pulled back from her face in a limp ponytail, and her face is clear of the usual five pounds of makeup she applies daily. The bruise on her left cheek is conspicuous in the glaring sunlight. Her green eyes are bloodshot, and the wrinkles around them seem to have been etched overnight. I would never have considered my mother beautiful, but now she appears weary and miserable. A battered Volkswagen sits in the driveway; I remember it belongs to the lady who owns the salon where Mom works.

"Hi," I say quietly. "Are you okay?"

She nods, her eyes brimming with tears as she notices the stitches in my head. "I'm so sorry. I'm so, so sorry."

"Have you come to get me?" I ask abruptly, even though I wish I didn't have to hear the answer.

But to my surprise, she shakes her head, a tear trailing down her tanned, crinkled face.

I feel relief, but I don't want Mom to cry, especially not out on the Vigliotti doorstep. I pull her inside the house. She immediately appears out of place in the luxurious environment. Is that how I looked when I arrived here? I wait as she takes in the impressive foyer and elegant staircase; she seems to be lost in thought, so I finally clear my throat.

Mom turns to face me. "It's been so long. I had forgotten how wonderful everything was."

"Yeah—it's pretty amazing. How do you know these people?"

She ignores my question, and I wonder whether I will ever find out how a woman like my mom knows people like the Vigliottis. Instead, she looks me over, her eyes skimming my new clothes. "Are you okay, Danny? Do you like it here?" she asks.

I shrug; I don't know how much to tell her, thinking I will hurt her feelings if she knew *how* much I like it at the Vigliotti's. "It's fine. It's easy to get used to the nice stuff, I guess. What happened to Dad?" I ask, changing the subject.

"I'm not sure. I've been staying with Sue. I guess he's back at the house. No one's pressing charges, so the city's not going to waste their time with it," she says, her face expressionless.

So, Mr. Doonesby didn't press charges, I realize. Maybe my principal feels guilty about the whole mess.

He should.

Mom continues to study me, staring at my head for a long moment, and I shift from one leg to another, feeling uncomfortable under her scrutiny. "But are *you* okay? After everything—you know—how are you handling it?" she asks breathlessly, as though she almost can't ask the question, just as the look on her face says she doesn't really want an answer.

I stare at her. I can think of many things to say— many things I want to shout at her. The pain and loneliness take hold of me, threatening to become angry words. So I say nothing. Isn't that what she wants anyway? What good would anger be for either of us now? Neither of us can handle it, neither of us wants it. She should leave, just as she did a few weeks ago. Leave and let me live this new life that is the only item of worth she has ever given me.

I can feel myself trying to tell her these things with my expression, and fortunately, whether Mom understands the exact message or just my emotions, my meaning seems to push its way through.

"I've gotta go, Danny. I still have so much that needs to be done before we can be a family again." Her eyes look at me hopefully.

I feel heartless as I gaze back at her without giving any sign that there is still hope for our relationship. I can't forgive her, at least, not at this moment—and not for some time to come. Even though I am feeling selfish now, she is the one who was selfish. That selfishness took me from her, and perhaps, that is exactly what self-centered people deserve.

She puts a hand on my shoulder, and I stand motionless. I can't hug her—not yet. A few more tears stream from her eyes, and she turns and leaves the house. I have given her no indication that I miss her, and now she is leaving again. And I am ashamed that I am glad.

* * * *

Later that night, I lay my clothes out and gather my school supplies into my expensive new backpack. I am so excited and nervous about the next day that I wonder if I will get any sleep. I want to make a good impression and blend into the background all at the same time. And I find myself wondering if I will see Portia, and if so, will she be friendly like she was before? And will Vince pretend that he barely knows me, ignoring the last week of fun we've had together in order to not appear to be "friends" with a freshman? I decide that's probably a good possibility based on Vince's past behavior.

I choose a pair of jeans and a green polo shirt and wipe a scuff mark from my shoe. I try to think of what else I might need. My sunglasses! I skim the room and rack my brain for where I might have left them. Then I remember the argument Vince and I had on the way to pick up milk for Ronnie. Vince, who had once again been driving the Lexus, had grabbed my expensive shades from my face and had thrown them in the backseat after an argument over the score on a recent video game. I had grabbed for Vince's sunglasses in retaliation, but I quickly gave up when Vince's attempt to fight me off resulted in the Lexus swerving toward the guardrail of the highway. I now realize I never retrieved my glasses from the backseat.

The house is quiet as I leave my room and make my way toward the garage. Ronnie is having a girls night out, and Vince and Julia are probably in their rooms, although almost certainly not in bed yet—it's only nine p.m. Gino is nowhere to be found, and I guess that he is out, possibly working. Ronnie explained that Gino is a computer networking specialist who works mostly during the night on company computers so as not to disrupt the company's normal daily business. I do not think Gino fits the stereotype of a computer technician, but then, I don't know many computer technicians. At any rate, he must be very good, judging by the way this family spends money.

I switch on the light in the garage and open the back door of the Lexus. I start searching the seat and floor for my sunglasses and eventually shut the door when the vehicle starts beeping. Thankfully, the interior lights remain on as I continue my search.

Several minutes later, I am sweaty and frustrated. I climb over the backseat and into the large rear area of the SUV. Some junk is back here (Ronnie has a complete winter roadside emergency kit—even in the middle of August), and the interior lights click off as I strike my knee on a snow shovel and grit my teeth in pain. I decide to stop searching just as my hand feels the smooth lens of my sunglasses. I rub them on my T-shirt and lay on my side for a moment, enjoying the pitch-black quiet inside the vehicle. However, the heat is too much for me, and I am just about to climb back over the seat when the front doors of the Lexus suddenly open.

"Let's go, Frank," I hear Gino say. "We've gotta get to Iggy before he kills Capriotti."

Chapter 5

I frantically squeeze myself up against the back of the rear seat, barely daring to breathe. I wish I had sat up the minute the Lexus doors opened and warned the men that I was in here, but as soon as Gino spoke those chilling words, I had followed my instinct to crouch down and hide. Now I can't show myself; I only hope that I have misunderstood what Gino said about killing and that I can get out of this car undiscovered.

Can Gino and this Frank guy see me from their seats in the front of the Lexus? The vehicle is large; if they aren't looking for me, they might not notice me. But maybe they will need something from the back seat. What will they do if they find me? Did Gino actually say someone was going to get killed?

I know so little about Gino, even though I have spent over a week at the Vigliotti house. I had guessed that Gino was gone much of the time because he is busy with work; the Vigliotti lifestyle is certainly an expensive one, and Gino probably works long hours to make the big bucks. But what is Gino planning now? Is this part of his work? Maybe I misunderstood Gino— maybe he was speaking in computer terms that I don't understand.

"Are you sure the Lexus is clean?" Frank asks Gino.

I strain to hear Gino's answer. "Yeah, I have my guy sweep it for bugs every week. But I'll tell you more later. We'll switch vehicles at the diner."

I feel a brief moment of relief. Gino and Frank are not planning to stay in the Lexus. Once they leave, maybe I can make a run for it and take a taxi home. After a week at the Vigliotti's, I always have some cash in my pocket and hopefully it will be enough to get me back to the house.

"Just one thing," I hear Frank say. "What did Capriotti do to get Iggy so upset? Iggy's a captain. Doesn't make sense for him to go off on his own and take Capriotti out. What could have made him so angry that he would kill a district attorney?"

Gino swears. "I don't know. But Iggy knows better. We all take orders from Ray, and Ray can't afford to lose Capriotti. The man is a parasite for sure, but he's in a position of power, and if something happens to him, who knows if his replacement would cooperate with us. Iggy knows that, so Capriotti must have done something really stupid this time. But nobody's allowed to kill him, so I guess we gotta get to Iggy first."

My body is so rigid with anxiety, I feel my back and shoulders start to ache. I somehow know that something terrible is about to happen, and I only hope I can get out in time to get away. And yet, I hate to admit that I am beginning to feel just a little curious about the whole thing. What is Gino involved in?

Reggie's words come flooding back to me; I remember the excitement in his voice when he suggested that Gino was in the mob. Is that possible? What does computer technology have to do with Mafia activity? In every movie or show I have seen about the mob (and I have seen a lot of those in the last week with Vince), mobsters have been involved with loan sharking, the garbage industry, gambling, and money laundering—but computers? Maybe Gino has nothing to do with computers at all. Maybe it's all a cover. I suddenly feel I must find out.

The vehicle slows and pulls onto a dirt surface. We must be at the diner, but I don't dare lift my head. I have to control my curiosity and focus on freeing myself from the SUV and getting safely away from whatever is going to happen. I want to know, and yet, I don't. I like my new life in Newcastle. Finding out that Gino is some sort of criminal will ruin everything.

"Hey, look!" Frank says excitedly. "There's Iggy now! We won't have to chase him down after all. Maybe he's changed his mind."

"Not likely," Gino grumbles, and he abruptly puts the SUV in park and jumps out. Frank follows, and I find that although I am finally alone in the vehicle, I must still wait to escape. I hear angry voices outside and, as soon as the interior lights dim, I lift my head just enough to peer out of the tinted rear window. My eyes search the darkness outside, barely able to make out figures in the street a few buildings down from the diner.

Once my eyes adjust better to the night, I am able to identify Gino, and I suppose the younger, tall man standing next to Gino is Frank. The two men face off with a small, chubby older guy. This must be Iggy. I see Gino reach out and push Iggy roughly up against the side of a building. I raise myself up a little on my arm, knowing I shouldn't watch, and yet unable to take my eyes from the scene.

What I see next almost makes me sick. Gino stands back from Iggy and points at Frank. Frank starts punching Iggy. The older man is no match for the athletic Frank, and Gino stands back and watches Iggy get pummeled. Gino then pulls out a gun from under his jacket, and I find that I want to beat on the glass of the car window, just to keep the inevitable from happening. I'm stunned and frightened at the same time. Is that really my godfather, the guy who rescued me, threatening someone's life? What will I do if I see Gino commit murder?

But luckily, I'm not forced to make that decision. Frank stops beating Iggy and pulls Gino aside, pushing the barrel of the handgun toward the ground and talking quickly. Iggy leans back against the building, too dazed to move, blood streaming from his nose. Gino tucks the gun back under his jacket, and he and Frank leave Iggy slumped against the building, but alive. They are coming back toward the Lexus, and I duck back down and fold myself up even tighter against the back seat, realizing that I missed my opportunity to escape.

But Gino and Frank do not come back to the SUV. I hear another car pull out of the lot and lift my head to see the two leaving in an old battered pickup truck. The truck pulls away from the diner and quickly disappears down the road.

With Gino and Frank gone, I now only need to worry about Iggy, who can't be too much of a threat in his present condition. The older man takes a long time to move away from the building, and I begin to feel reckless in my impatience. Maybe I should just make a run for it? Would the older man notice me? I check myself as I remember that Gino said Iggy had planned to do some killing of his own tonight.

After an agonizing half hour, Iggy finally clears out, and I cautiously climb over the backseat of the Lexus and open the back door. When I'm sure no one is around, I sprint down the empty street toward the highway. Three blocks later, I finally find a pay phone, and as I wait for the taxi (talking the driver into coming to Old Newcastle late at night is not an easy task), I realize that my sunglasses are still sitting somewhere in the back of the Lexus.

* * * *

I barely sleep at all. The little bit that I do manage is filled with hazy dreams that include Tommy Gallo and Frank beating the living daylights out of me, and Gino pointing a gun in my face. I wake up drenched in sweat, trying desperately to make sense of what I witnessed at the diner. Gino is not the hero I made him out to be, but am I sure this all really happened? I placed the taxi fare receipt in my pocket just for that purpose—so I wouldn't be able to convince myself I didn't see anything wrong.

Why can't I just let this go? Why am I preventing myself from forgetting what I saw? For some odd, frustrating reason, and despite the fact that my parents have taken no trouble to teach me good values, I have an overwhelming dislike of foul play.

I don't know whether Iggy deserved his beating or not. Gino had mentioned that Iggy planned to kill someone, so maybe Iggy is a person who got what was coming to him. But I'm finding any reason to excuse Gino, because this situation involves not only him, but also the whole Vigliotti family. Somehow, I can't imagine that good-natured Ronnie has any idea that Gino is involved in something so violent. And yet, she was concerned about the Gallo kid. Vince may know something about this. Is that why he is so obsessed with mob movies? How long has Gino been doing this type of thing? Is there a mob in Newcastle?

I have so many questions—none of which can be answered at this moment. I need to get more rest so I can take on the first day of school and be ready for Tommy Gallo and Portia Saviano, both of whom make me nervous for very different reasons. I finally fall into a more peaceful sleep, but not before realizing that Baxter isn't sleeping on my bed.

* * * *

By the time I am dressed for school the next morning, I have a plan. Things are always clearer to me in the morning. Instead of judging Gino on what I observed last night from the back of the SUV, I decide to launch a full-scale investigation of my own before I make any hasty decisions.

But before I get started, I have to get through my first day of school. When I stride into the kitchen, Vince is slurping a bowl of Cocoa Nuggets and Julia is sipping orange juice and reading the latest issue of *Vogue*. Both of them ignore me, which I had expected. For Julia, giving me the cold shoulder is nothing new; Vince on the other hand, is establishing the distance he expects me to keep on the first day of school. Vince can't be seen as friends with a freshman, and I know Vince well enough by now to understand the snub isn't personal. At least, Vince doesn't necessarily mean he doesn't want my friendship—but the fact that we are buddies can't be obvious at Newcastle High without hurting his reputation.

Ronnie is bustling around the kitchen with her usual energy. She fixes me an English muffin and poached egg when I decline a bowl of Cocoa Nuggets. I'm thrilled to have someone make me breakfast—just another experience to add to my ever-growing list of why I love it here. Vince leaves the table quickly (and angrily) when Julia suggests he needs more deodorant, and I eat my breakfast in silence. Ronnie leaves the kitchen to get ready for a tennis lesson, and I am about to head back to the bedroom to grab my backpack when Julia puts her hand on my arm.

I look at her curiously. "What's up?"

She glances at the door through which Ronnie and Vince just exited the kitchen and then says, in a quiet voice, "Where were you last night?"

I try to hide my surprise. My arm stiffens under her hand, and I hope she doesn't feel it. "What do you mean?" I ask innocently.

"Baxter doesn't want to sleep with me anymore. In case you haven't noticed, Baxter has been sleeping on your bed the past week."

I forget for a moment that Julia knows I was absent last night. I am suddenly more interested in the fact that Julia has been putting the dog in my room. "But Baxter can't get on the bed," I say. "So you've been sneaking into my room and putting him there? That's a little creepy."

She abruptly withdraws her hand as though burned. "Oh, please. He's been scratching at your door every night. I have no choice. You haven't heard me because you sleep like a hibernating bear—you have a horrible snoring problem. It's *quite* attractive," she finishes sarcastically.

I grin. "You're like a stalker."

Her face flushes. "What matters is that you were gone for a good part of the night," she accuses.

I attempt to make my face unreadable, as I have seen Gino accomplish many times before. Julia is glaring at me, and I know she isn't going to let the issue go. I must appease her in case she decides to tell Ronnie, or worse—Gino.

"Look," I say casually, "I had to take a walk. Starting high school, being in a new place—it's just a lot of pressure. Okay?"

She continues to study me, but after a few seconds, she takes a sip of orange juice and abruptly leaves the table. I wonder whether she could tell I was lying.

* * * *

As we pull up in front of the school, I am thrilled that the first person I see at Newcastle High is Portia Saviano. I am not as thrilled, however, to see that she has her arm around the shoulders of another boy. I hope it is a sign of Portia's friendliness and not an indication that she has a boyfriend. The other boy is barely as tall as Portia and slender. But no matter what the kid looks like, Portia is draped all over him, and that is not helping to ease my first-day nerves.

Vince has driven us to school in the Vigliotti's "practical" car—the minivan. I was surprised by this because it's not exactly legal. At seventeen, Vince isn't allowed to drive more than one passenger if a parent isn't in the car. But if Ronnie doesn't have any objections, then I'm certainly not going to say anything.

I am up front with Vince, and Julia, in constant text-messaging mode, is in the far back. Vince drops us off impatiently (he obviously does not want to be seen with his sister and a freshman, or he may be worried about someone seeing him driving a minivan) and drives off to find parking in the student lot. Julia immediately turns her back on me and strides toward a group of girls that appear equally as snooty, if not quite as beautiful, as Julia. I cautiously approach Portia and her male accessory from behind, wondering how she will react to me. Last time I saw her, I had just beat the snot out of Tommy Gallo. I don't know whether this has earned me points with her or not.

"Portia?" I call out a little too quickly and loudly, wanting to take her attention not only from the other boy but also from the several girls who are surrounding her and talking way too fast about summer break. One girl is blabbing about a guy at the GAP, spitting through her braces and brushing frizzy brown hair away from her chubby face. No one seems to be paying her much attention, and I appear to be a welcome distraction for the group.

"Danny!" Portia says happily, unwrapping herself from the other boy and making my confidence spike. I return her smile.

"Hey."

She puts her arm around my shoulders and propels me toward the group of teenagers. Frizzy-haired girl has finally quit talking; actually, no one is speaking at all. Everyone is staring at me (and my stitches) with curiosity. That is, everyone except the boy over whom Portia was previously draped. He is glaring at me and making no effort to hide his dislike. I can't blame him.

"Danny, I'd like you to meet Tony Chen," Portia says, removing her arm from me and standing between me and the other kid. "I've known him for years. My dad sold his dad his first car after they moved from China."

I immediately hate Tony simply because he has known Portia for years, and I have only known her for about five minutes. How can I compete with someone who has a lifetime of knowledge about what Portia likes and what she doesn't? I know I have some serious ground to make up.

"Hi, Tony," I say, keeping my tone as relaxed as possible. I need to learn more about my competition before I can gain the upper hand.

"Hi," Tony replies, equally casual. He is studying me with suspicion.

"Tony and I double-team at school," Portia says. "I'm the artsy one. I like to write, give speeches, and create presentations. Tony's the practical one. He helps me with math and science homework."

I realize that Tony is much further ahead than I thought. *Double-team*? Portia is practically telling me that she and Tony are girlfriend and boyfriend. I feel my confidence drop.

"Is it true you're staying at the Vigliotti house?" Frizzy-haired girl cuts in, moving closer to me. "What happened to your head? I heard you were in a fight with Tommy and that you beat him up!"

I quickly shift away from her; she makes me uneasy with her rapid-fire questions. I choose only one of her questions to answer. "Yeah, I'm staying at the Vigliotti's," I reply, but I'm not looking at her. I'm watching Tony's face, because at the name Vigliotti, Tony's jaw tightens. If Tony disliked me before, I think he might hate me now, and I wonder why the name makes Tony angry. Portia does not seem to notice Tony's reaction.

"Do you want to hang around with us today?" she asks me quietly, so that the giggling, chattering girls won't hear her.

I stare at her, surprised. Of course I do. Well, I don't really want to hang out with Tony—but I definitely want to hang out with her—all day, every day. "Sure," I say, trying not to sound too eager.

"Great! Because if our experience in middle school is any indication, we need one more member on our team. Now we'll have personality, brains—" She smiles at me "—and muscle."

Chapter 6

So I'm the bodyguard. Portia seems to like me because she feels safe with me. That's okay—I would rather be the bodyguard than the nerd. I could never be the nerdy guy, even though I have always managed to get decent grades at school. A kid can get good grades *and* pull off being cool as long as the good grades don't define who you are. I'm glad that the girls I've met know I beat Tommy in a fight—if everyone thinks the stitches are from fighting Tommy, I can hide the fact that I'm from a poor town and belong to hopeless parents.

I know it's only a matter of time before I will confront Tommy Gallo again. Tommy is a sophomore at Newcastle High, like Julia, so his reputation is already established. And I also know from Vince that Tommy's reputation is one of a tough guy—a tough guy who is hated and feared by *everyone*.

I asked Vince why Tommy was so intimidating, especially when I personally know that Tommy is beatable—any decent wrestler or boxer could take him down. Vince chose to ignore the question, which has only increased my curiosity. I now know that the Gallo family is not only connected to Gino in some way, but that they hold a certain degree of power that can force Joe Saviano to back away from a kid who just hit his daughter.

But I, unlike the others, am not going to worry about Tommy's connections. I'm an outsider, and even if I'm living at the Vigliotti's house, I'm disconnected from them. I don't know who Tommy's dad is, and I don't care.

As though my thoughts cause him to materialize, Tommy suddenly appears in the school hall. He is flanked by his torpedo-like friend who fought Vince as well as an extremely tall kid with white blond hair. I know I can't just start fighting, at least, not here in the school hallway. But the look on Tommy's face hints that he obviously feels we have some unfinished business. I remember Tommy striking Portia and feel angry all over again. Portia is stiff beside me; she must be thinking about what Tommy did to her too. However, I decide, with some difficulty, to let Tommy make the first move.

Tommy studies me, but he doesn't appear angry—he appears smug. That worries me more than anything else. What does Tommy know that I don't? I pretty much beat Tommy in our fight; shouldn't he be angry? He takes a step toward me, and I feel Portia surge forward. She also has some unfinished business, but I instinctively hold her back by the arm, not wanting her to get hurt by Tommy again. Tommy laughs at my protective action, and Portia stomps on my foot, forcing me to let go. She steps away from me and scowls.

"So, the gutter-rat is making a play for the used-car hottie. Isn't that really pathetic?"

Tommy's buddies laugh at his lame joke, but the rest of us remain motionless. I am uneasy about Tommy's new nickname for me. What does this kid know? Tommy reaches his hand toward me; he holds a piece of folded paper in it. I lean forward cautiously and take it, expecting to be rushed at any moment. I keep the note in my hand but don't unfold it, and Tommy smirks. "See you after school!" he says, turning away from us and walking down the hall, the other bullies trailing behind him.

Portia makes a short, irritated noise and turns to me. "Why did you stop me, Danny?" she asks heatedly.

"I thought you wanted me to protect you guys," I reply.

"I do. It's just—well—he deserves to be smacked in the face!"

I try not to smile but can't help myself. That is the first unkind comment I have heard from Portia. And I agree wholeheartedly with her; Tommy deserves to be smacked.

"What's on the paper?" Tony asks.

I glance down at the paper and slowly unfold it, wondering what Tommy would write to me.

"I'm surprised he can write at all," Tony says, half jokingly.

I lift my head and grin, surprised by Tony's attempt at humor. Tony gives me a weak smile back. We may be able to get along, I think, but of course, that depends on where Portia decides to direct her affection. I could never be friends with Tony if Tony were Portia's boyfriend. Then I read the note, and suddenly, my competition with Tony seems like the least of my worries.

"What does it say?" Portia asks.

I hand her the note. "He wants me to meet him."

Portia reads the note slowly. "Meet me in the gym after school, or prepare to have everyone know who you really are." She purses her lips together. "What's that supposed to mean?"

I shake my head. "I have no idea," I answer, but in my mind I think I *may* have an idea. It couldn't be the fight we had last week—Tommy would have nothing to gain by revealing *that* to the people at the school. What else does Tommy know about me? He had called me a gutter-rat. That's not exactly true, but it's getting close. Tommy can't know anything about me that's personal—can he?

"So, what are you hiding?" Tony asks, attempting to sound curious, but I can sense the edge of suspicion in his voice. I look at Portia. She is studying me intently, yet she doesn't ask any questions. I feel frustrated, even though I don't know for sure what Tommy knows. I must be patient to find out what is going on—and patience, unfortunately, is not something that comes easy for me.

* * * *

By the end of the first day of school, I realize that high school is going to be completely different from middle school. Of course, the change in school districts only makes that difference bigger. The classes are going to be much more challenging—no longer can I do the bare minimum and still manage to make an A. I already have a ton of homework and am worried about being able to finish it in one evening. Of course, completing my homework would probably not be a problem if I wasn't so concerned with planning my personal investigation of Gino, which I hope to begin tonight.

The teachers are more energetic and less stressed than those in Ridley. My schedule will alternate every other day, and I am glad that I won't have to worry about algebra until tomorrow. So far, I think I will get along with my teachers. I especially like the homeroom and history teacher, Miss Lowe—not only because she is nice but also because she is hot, for a teacher anyway. By the interest from the other guys in the class, I know I'm not the only student impressed with her appearance. The English teacher, Mr. Capriotti, seems like a good guy also, but I am distracted by the fact that he shares a last name with the man Gino mentioned last night.

Portia, Tony and I all have biology as our final class of the day, so after the bell, we stroll down the hallway toward our lockers. Portia seems to have a friend tucked into every corner of the school, but she obviously spends the most time with Tony, much to my dismay. At the moment, the three of us are joined by one of those friends, a small, curvy girl with long, straight dark hair and brown eyes. Portia introduces her as Evie Alvarez, and she's pretty but talks too much about her dad, a Newcastle detective.

I'm hoping Evie won't always be hanging around us because she seems endlessly interested in the Vigliottis. And I'm also a little ticked at Portia because she told Evie about Tommy wanting to meet me after school. Evie is very curious about that too, but I have given her nothing but a grunt or head movement in answer to her volley of questions. I'm actually a little afraid she might follow me there.

That thought leads me to wonder if Portia will want to come with me when I face off with Tommy. I can't let her because I just don't know what Tommy is going to say, and I don't want to lose Portia as a friend if the truth comes out about my past. I think of how uninterested in me the girls in Ridley were when they found out which neighborhood I lived in or where my dad worked. And those were Ridley girls—hardly much better off than I! I don't believe Portia is that shallow, but I'm not going to take the chance. Especially when I'm competing with boy genius, Tony.

We stop at our lockers, and I pull out the books I need for my homework. Portia asks Tony if we can all get together to tackle biology homework tonight. He nods, and she turns to me. "You want to study with us tonight?"

I shake my head. I know it's strange to turn down a girl that I'm really into, especially when that means she'll be spending that time with Tony. But I must figure out what to do about Gino before I concentrate on anything else. Biology homework comes in a distant second. I notice the exultant look on Tony's face, and I momentarily have second thoughts.

Portia frowns at me. "You're not going to see Tommy, are you?"

"I've got to. I need to know what he wants."

"You can't go by yourself," she states, although she doesn't volunteer to go with me.

"Maybe I'll make Vince come. He owes me for helping him kick Tommy's butt." I try to smile as I say this, but the fact is that Vince is the only person I can take who already knows about my past *and* can help me out if the situation calls for it.

"So, you're worried about something that Tommy knows about you," Tony states, not too nicely. "What are you hiding from us?"

Evie's eyes grow wide with interest as Portia turns to glare at Tony.

Tony shrugs. "Well, if he doesn't have a *dirty* past, then he wouldn't have anything to be worried about, would he?"

Tony's smug tone irritates me. "Well, Tony. I'm sure you're quite perfect. If only we could all be so squeaky clean," I say sarcastically, furiously slamming my locker. I then turn my back on them and stride down the hall, half hoping Portia will chase me down. She doesn't.

As I walk away, I attempt to let go of my rage so that I can talk to Tommy with a level head. In the mood I'm in right now, I feel like beating the crap out of that bully. I need to find Vince and ask whether he will go with me to meet Tommy and company.

I find Vince sitting alone on a bench outside the school and am somewhat surprised that he is not socializing with anyone else, although less surprised to find him munching on a Snickers.

Vince rolls his eyes when he sees me. "Well, it's about freakin' time! Now, we've just got to go surgically remove Julia from her bratty clones."

I can't help but laugh, but then I quickly tell Vince I need his help to confront Tommy. Vince seems flattered by the invitation. "Of course, let's go beat the snot out of that little snot."

"What about Julia?" I ask.

"She has more rides home than she could use in a school year. She can take care of herself—or she can wait," Vince replies, obviously concerned very little with any inconvenience his sister may be forced to experience by his sudden disappearance.

We make our way to the gym, which is actually crowded with girls at cheerleading tryouts. I see Tommy and his two friends standing in the corner, ogling the girls in their tight athletic clothing. I'm glad that Tommy has not added anyone else to his entourage, because it means that Vince and I are only outnumbered three to two. Unfortunately, that could be just enough to tip the scales in Tommy's favor if the meeting ends in a fight.

Tommy jerks his thumb toward the doors at the side of the gym, and Vince and I shuffle past the crowd of girls to follow them outside. Before opening the doors to walk out, I turn to Vince. "Back me up, man. No matter what happens, don't run out on me."

Vince seems genuinely offended. "Hey, I'm here now, right? I kinda think I know how this meeting might go, and I'm ready for a fight if you are."

"Let's just see what they want first," I reply, pushing open the heavy metal door.

In the bright August sun, Tommy and his buddies face us, as if ready to pounce. Maybe a rematch is all Tommy wants. Better yet, maybe he doesn't have any information about me after all. Vince and I walk within a few yards of Tommy and wait for someone from the other side to make the first move.

But Tommy doesn't rush me like he did at the car lot. Instead, his mouth curves into a sneer, a look that makes me more uneasy than if Tommy ran up to me and threw a punch. "What do you want, Tommy?" I finally ask, deciding that the sooner things get started, the sooner this will all be over with, for better or for worse.

Tommy's grin widens. "So tough, aren't you, gutter-rat? I should have known you weren't a Newcastle kid. You're a filthy kid from a filthy town. Ridley, is it? I think that's where Newcastle dumps its garbage. That's the only thing Ridley has—a big pile of garbage."

Tommy's rant is ridiculous, and yet, he is saying the very thing that I am afraid the other kids will think if they find out I'm from Ridley. My heart starts pumping furiously, and my hands tingle with anticipation. I want to fight Tommy and make him promise to keep his mouth shut. Vince is restless beside me, but we wait. Tommy has not yet played his hand.

"And then," Tommy continues, "I found out that you're not only from that rat-hole, but you're on the bottom of the food-chain there, which really makes you scum. Apparently, you're so scummy your crappy parents didn't even want you."

I can barely hold myself back now. "What's your point, Tommy?" I ask angrily.

Tommy is thrilled with my hostility. "Kids here *hate* Ridley. It's the butt of everyone's joke. Even Portia hates it." He pauses for a moment to let that statement sink in. "I suppose you probably don't want people around here to know you come from that garbage dump. But more than that, you probably don't want everyone to know your mom's a slut."

That's it. I've been set in motion. I spring toward Tommy, Vince on my heels.

"Doonesby's here, you know."

Tommy's words bring me to a halt just as I'm lifting my fist to drive it into his nose. Vince skids to a stop behind me. I want to punch the smirk off Tommy's face, but at the name of my old middle school principal, I hold back. "Who's Doonesby?" I ask, hoping Tommy won't sense my strong interest in the name.

"Well, apparently, after dating a *student's* married mother, he was fired from his old job in Ridley," Tommy explains. "However, he had won a ton of awards or something during his career, so I guess the county decided to downgrade him to a teaching position in a place where no one would recognize him. And Newcastle is about as different from Ridley as it gets.

People from Newcastle don't visit Ridley, and people from Ridley are so flat broke they can't even afford the bus ride here."

I quickly realize that Tommy knows my mother is the one who had been spending time with Mr. Doonesby. How Tommy had been able to get that information, I don't know. As angry as Tommy is making me by ridiculing me and my family, I also feel that some of those remarks are true. Ridley is a trashy town, and many of the people who live there act like trash too. I can't let Tommy reveal all this stuff about me to the students at Newcastle or I'll be an outcast. I enjoyed the flirty looks I got from the girls this morning; they can't know I come from the nastiest town in New Jersey. Tommy definitely has the upper hand.

Vince, however, is not quite defeated, probably because it's not his reputation that's in danger. "Tommy, Danny's already way more popular than you. Everyone hates you. You're the scum around here, not Danny."

I stare at Vince. That was quite the statement from a kid who has proven himself to be extremely shallow up until this moment.

Tommy starts laughing. "Oh, right. Well, at least I'm not a dumb Vigliotti. Your dad's just as stupid as you are. He's going to end up dead in a ditch somewhere—maybe Ridley," Tommy taunts.

Vince rushes him immediately, but Tommy's two friends step in and hold him back. Vince is like an angry bear, struggling violently and cursing like a drunken sailor, but he can't shake them both. I close the last foot of space between myself and Tommy, push him to the ground, and pin him.

"Leave Vince alone," I say.

Tommy is not concerned. "In a minute. As soon as you agree to do what I say."

"Or?" I prompt, holding my arm against his chest, close to his neck.

"Or else."

I frown at him but then rise to my feet and step back, letting Tommy raise himself up on his elbows. "What could you possibly want from me?" I demand. "You said it yourself—I'm nobody."

"You're right. You're nothing, gutter-rat," Tommy replies, casually getting to his knees and brushing himself off, his expression smug. "However, you've got some information about Doonesby that I don't think he'd be too thrilled to have spread around the school."

I look at Tommy in surprise. "Why in the world would I blackmail Mister Doonesby? He could easily call my bluff. I don't want people to know that stuff anymore than he does."

"Then you'll have to convince him you don't care about your reputation. Even though we both know you do." Tommy grins as he stands, obviously pleased that he has me cornered. "You see, I'm not a real whiz at math. It's just not something I'm really concerned about, you know? But apparently, I'm not getting a car until I get an 'A' in that stupid class. So I may need a little help from our dirt-bag of a math teacher, and my buddies might too. Isn't that right, guys?"

But Tommy's buddies can't answer him. One against two, Vince has somehow managed to gain the advantage. He has thrown the shorter kid to the ground and is now facing off with the freakishly tall, white-blond teenager.

Tommy swears. "You two are worthless. Get off the ground, Paul! Kurt, just leave Vigliotti alone!"

Paul scrambles up, and Kurt backs away from Vince.

"Don't agree to do anything he asks you, Danny!" Vince orders.

I turn to Tommy. "Why not blackmail Doonesby yourself?"

"Oh, I don't really like to get my hands dirty," Tommy replies.

My eyes narrow. *Liar,* I think. *You're setting me up.* But really, what can I do at this moment? I must keep Tommy from revealing my past to the entire school until I can come up with another plan.

I turn to Vince. "What choice do I have?"

Chapter 7

The ride home is quiet. Vince is still seething from the afternoon's non-fight, and I can tell he is angry at me for accepting Tommy's terms. I want to explain to Vince that I'm not going along with Tommy's plan, but I'm forced to agree to it until I can figure out a way to keep Tommy quiet.

With the exception of the Tommy incident, the first day of school was better than I had expected; so far, the other kids (and most importantly, the girls) are friendly. Will that change if they find out where I'm from—or worse, my connection to Mr. Doonesby? I can feel anger at my mom building inside of me again. Even now, when I have the chance to make a fresh start, her actions are haunting me. The kids at Newcastle are from wealthy families with good names. Or are they? I glance at the sullen Vince and think about Gino and Tommy's dad. I remind myself that, beneath the surface, things might not be as they seem. There is only one way to find out.

I think about Mr. Capriotti and again wonder whether the name has any connection to the one I heard last night. The English teacher seems nice, and I have difficulty believing he could be connected to the violent activity I witnessed yesterday. I have so much digging to do and, somehow, I must find time for a couple hours of homework.

As Vince pulls up to the house, I notice a souped-up Honda in the driveway. When we walk inside the house, I see Julia and a tanned, blonde teen with huge muscles snuggling on the couch. They are kissing in between chatting on their cell phones, and I find myself feeling alternately grossed out by the blatant display of affection and amused by the fact that the two are talking more to outside callers than to each other.

As I set my backpack down on the hall floor with a loud *thunk*, I see Julia shoot me a superior look, which does nothing more than remind me that most pretty girls are like Julia, and fewer are like Portia. I experience a momentary pang of regret that Portia is spending time with Tony this evening, not with me, and that this was of my own doing.

I know I should tackle my homework first, but I am impatient to start working on my plan to investigate Gino's activities. Gino is probably upstairs asleep at the moment, so I go first to his office, knowing I won't be noticed by Vince, who has probably retreated to his video games, or by Julia, who has a college student attached to her face. I take a brief look around the office, but nothing seems unusual. There are no papers saying, "More mob activity planned tonight," and I feel foolish for hoping to find something so obvious.

I start searching the office thoroughly, knowing that at any time Gino might come down the stairs and catch me. Surely I could come up with some story since he doesn't know that I have anything to suspect. I spot a box underneath the computer desk, but when I try to unlatch it, I realize it is locked. Not to be discouraged easily, I check the top drawer of the desk, the one in which people always keep pens and junk, and jackpot: I find a little key.

I'm always puzzled by people who leave keys so close to the items they open. But even as my pulse pounds with excitement when the key turns the lock on the box, I am disappointed to find nothing inside except a baggie with yet another key and a scrap of paper that reads, "Gallo" followed by a number code. Well, the last thing I need is any more trouble with the Gallos, so I replace the baggie, lock the box, and put the key back. But I jump in the air when I hear footsteps in the hallway and leap behind the desk just as Julia glides by on her way out the door.

I roll my eyes. Not too much to worry about there.

I have almost given up on finding anything worthwhile when I notice that Gino's jacket is draped over the chair. Telling myself not to get too excited, I pick it up and check both pockets. Nothing. As I lay it over the chair once more, I feel defeated. I'm standing in the middle of the room, out of ideas, when I hear another set of footsteps. I know it's Gino because I can hear him on the phone. Quickly, I start to pick up the house phone so that I appear to be making a call, but Gino doesn't make it to the office. I can't see him, but I know he must be only a few feet from the door.

"Tomorrow? He knows it's dangerous for him to go there, right?" Gino says to the person on the other end. "There's a chance someone in law enforcement could see him. They know where we meet."

I stand motionless, my hand on the phone, ready to lift it if Gino comes into view. "Fine. Nine-thirty. Tell him to meet us in the parking lot." Gino slams his cell phone shut, and I instinctively pick up the phone and start laughing into it.

"Reggie, that's hilarious! I can't believe that happened on the first day of school!" I laugh hysterically as Gino comes to stand in the office door, and I think his eyes are judging whether I heard any of his conversation. I'm desperately trying to appear that I haven't.

"No way! That's awesome. Wish I could have seen that!" I continue.

Gino smiles and heads for the front door. I collapse in the office chair just as the busy signal begins to blare from the phone. As Gino shuts the front door, I replace the phone and immediately pick it up again. I now have all the information I need. The specifics are not clear, but I think I can fill in the blanks. It's time to call for some help.

Reggie answers after two rings. "Hello?"

"Hey, Reggie, it's Danny."

"Hey, Danny," Reggie responds, without much enthusiasm. "I guess you're going to Newcastle this year then, huh?"

"Just for a while," I answer.

A long pause follows. I know Reggie is hurt by my leaving him alone at Ridley High our freshman year. "Look, Reggie, I wish I were there," I lie. I do miss Reggie, but not Ridley. "It's just not the same here." *At least that's the truth.*

"Yeah, I'm sure it's real tough," Reggie shoots back sarcastically.

"I can't help it! My parents can't have me right now, and this is the best option, all right?"

"All right." Reggie says, but he sounds irritated.

I choose to ignore Reggie's hurt feelings for the moment. Instead, I start laying the groundwork for my plan. "Just because I live all the way over here doesn't mean we can't still hang out. In fact, I think I may have a little project we could do together."

Reggie doesn't say anything, but I may at least have my friend's attention.

"Let's just say some of your suspicions about my new family might not have been so off base," I hint.

Fortunately, Reggie catches on immediately. "Really?" he replies, his voice excited.

"Yeah, really. And it looks like I might need your help to find out for sure."

"Okay. What do you want me to do?" Reggie asks, his voice eager, but now a little uncertain.

"You still have that crappy excuse for a car?" I joke, but I can't hide my jealousy. Reggie not only has a car, but because he spends part of his time in Pennsylvania with his dad, he has his driver's license in that state, which is less restrictive than New Jersey.

"Oh, real nice, Danny," Reggie growls. "Of course I do. But you better show my car some respect if you want a ride."

"Yeah, somehow it's hard to respect a beetle, even if it's an old one," I shoot back. "But it will work fine for what we need to do."

"Which is what?"

I pause, not sure how much information to divulge while any Vigliottis could be in the house. "Meet me at the bus stop for Old Newcastle at nine-fifteen tomorrow night and I promise I'll answer all your questions."

* * * *

My accomplishments during the rest of the evening are small, at least as far as my schoolwork is concerned. I shouldn't ignore biology, history, and English homework, but my excitement for tomorrow night's task consumes most of my thoughts and energy.

Dinner takes thirty minutes and involves probing questions from Ronnie about the first day of school.

She receives answers from all three of us teenagers that I know do nothing to satisfy her avid curiosity.

Gino has dinner with the family, but he doesn't seem overly interested in his children's activities, although he does order all of us to get our homework done. He eats silently, with Ronnie shooting him concerned glances, which tells me that Gino is not always so silent and cranky at dinner. Gino's face brightens when the doorbell rings. He tells Vince to answer the door, and the man who is led into the kitchen by the grouchy teenager is someone I already know.

Gino introduces Frank Moretti to the family, and I take a moment to analyze him because I saw so little of him during my accidental spying the night before. Frank is quite a bit younger than Gino, with short brown hair and light skin. He doesn't have a strong Italian face, but his nose has the slight crookedness of one that has been broken. He is taller than Gino, probably at least six feet. Ronnie is her typical friendly self and invites Frank to sit down for some dinner, and although he seems willing, Gino quickly tells her they have somewhere to go. He strides out of the kitchen with Frank following closely behind, leaving Ronnie standing with a half-empty serving bowl in her hands and a hurt expression on her face. The rest of dinner is very, very quiet.

Later in the evening, Julia annoys me for about ten minutes when I am actually trying to do some homework in my room. She wants to interview me for an article for her journalism class, and she sits in the middle of my bed as I work at the little desk that is more ornate than functional. At this point, I decide to clarify to Julia that no one at Newcastle is to know where I grew up.

"You haven't told anyone where I'm from, have you?" I ask her sharply.

She sniffs. "Of course not. I would never tell my friends someone from *Ridley* was staying at my house. I told them you were from Boston."

"Why? I don't know anything about Boston!"

"Then I suppose you had better learn something about it. I'm sure people will be *really* curious," she comments, stretching her bare feet out on my bed and wriggling her bright pink toes.

"Couldn't you have just made a town up?" I say, poking a hole with my pen through the paper that holds the three sentences representing what needs to be a three page history essay in less than two days.

"You can't just make up towns! People will know they're not real. Besides, Boston is exciting!" She is sprawled across my bed, now on her back, staring at the ceiling.

"Thanks, just what I need. More problems." I rip up my paper and vow to use Vince's computer to write the essay instead.

"More problems?" Julia asks expectantly, raising herself up on one slender arm, her wavy hair going in every direction. I think she looks much prettier without her usual layer of makeup, but I quickly remind myself that she is a selfish girl who unquestionably has infinite ulterior motives.

"I meant 'problems' as in all this homework I have to do this week," I answer and start digging through my backpack, trying to appear busy. "Anything else I can help you with?" I ask in an irritated tone.

She scowls and scoots to the edge of the bed. "No. I'll just make up other stuff about you. At least my story will make you sound more interesting than you really are."

Julia hops off the bed and walks to the door, before turning to me once more. "You should be nice to me, Danny. I influence a lot of people—especially girls—at Newcastle."

She walks out the door, and I roll my eyes. I decide against doing any more homework in favor of working a little more on tomorrow night's plan. I want to think through every detail because I hate to drag Reggie into something dangerous without being prepared.

At nine-thirty, just as I am contemplating putting a little more effort into outlining my history essay, Vince stops by and asks if I want to play a few video games.

"You finished your homework?" I ask.

"No. What do you care?" Vince replies, sounding more like an aggravated three-year-old than an eleventh grader.

I shrug. I have to admit that playing a video game sounds like more fun than writing about the Louisiana Purchase, so I scramble off the bed and up to the game room with Vince. We race cars through the hilly streets of San Francisco, trying to set course records or run the other cars off the road. Usually Vince wants to play something violent, which means a lot of gore and death, but I like car racing more. If I had lots of money, one of the first things I would buy is a classic car with so much power under the hood that not even Vince's future Camaro could keep up.

After an hour of speeding through the city, Ronnie shows up to put an end to our game. Vince fights with her, which gives me the opportunity to sneak downstairs and into my bedroom. I catch Julia opening the door to put Baxter inside.

"See, I'm here," I say, making a mental note to figure out a way to keep Julia away from my room tomorrow night.

She says nothing and hands me the squirming dog before heading back up the stairs. I take Baxter in and set him on the bed. The dog quickly curls into a ball on the comforter and stares at me.

"I should finish my homework, shouldn't I?" I ask. Baxter merely gazes up at me with a blank expression. "No, I can see it in your eyes, Baxter. You're ready to go to sleep, and so am I." With that, I change into a clean T-shirt and boxers, get under the covers, and fall asleep, wondering how I can convince Portia that I'd make a great boyfriend.

* * * *

The next day at school, I am so excited and anxious about my plan to follow Gino that I barely tune into the conversation going on between Portia and Tony. This is not a problem until Portia asks me a direct question.

"Do you think she's pretty?" We are standing in the busy hallway next to our lockers before last period, and Portia is looking straight at me.

"Uh, I don't know," I answer, unsure whom Portia means. I never like this type of question because it usually means someone is trying to set me up with a girl. I especially don't like this question coming from Portia. She is the girl I am interested in, not one of her giggling, gossipy friends.

"What do you mean, you don't know?" She asks disbelievingly. "She either is or she isn't, right?"

I'm immediately frustrated. Portia has so far acted differently from the other girls, which I like. Now she sounds just like them. "Why?" I ask, my guard up.

She rolls her eyes. "Well, usually I wouldn't care, but Evie thinks Julia will get the role of Juliet in the school play only because she's pretty."

Oh, we're talking about Julia, I realize. I answer Portia with a shrug. "What does it matter?"

"Well, for one thing, I really love Shakespeare. And seriously, it's like every girl's dream to play Juliet, one of the most infamous heroines of all time!"

I put several overly large books in my locker. "Having never been a girl, I wouldn't know. If it's such a great role, do you think I should try out for it?" I try not to smile, but can't resist.

Portia pushes me playfully. "You dork! They want someone *pretty!*"

"Well, then, you've definitely got the role," I say sincerely—maybe a little too sincerely, because Portia blushes as she smiles. *But,* I think, *she did smile.*

Tony, however, is not smiling. He coughs, interrupting our playful back-and-forth. "So, Danny, you never told us—where are you from?"

I stop rearranging my locker; Tony's question catches me completely off-guard. I turn and glare at Tony, but I know the question is a fair one. Because I am new to Newcastle, the question was sure to be asked eventually. In fact, Julia has already fielded questions about where I'm from. But somehow, coming from Tony, the question sounds like an accusation.

I start rearranging my locker again, hoping that Tony and Portia won't hear the dishonesty in my voice.

"Boston," I reply, hating myself for saying it, but knowing that I must stay consistent with whatever Julia is spreading around the school.

"Boston?" Tony repeats, sounding completely unconvinced.

"*Really?*" Portia asks eagerly. She grips her books to her chest, her eyes shining with excitement. "That's cool!"

Great, I think, feeling awful. This was going to be a difficult story to maintain. I've never been dishonest like this before.

"You don't sound like you're from Boston." Tony remarks.

"Parents are from Jersey," I say, thinking fast.

"I have relatives in Boston—they live in Cambridge. You go there much?" Tony challenges.

"No, I don't know that area well," I answer, thinking at least that statement is true. The bell rings at that moment, saving me from Tony's interrogation. "I've got algebra, guys. I gotta go." I walk in the other direction, wondering if I am headed the right way. Fortunately, the classroom I am looking for is just around the corner. I walk in the door and almost run into a person with an extremely familiar face.

"Hello, Mister Doonesby," I say quietly.

Chapter 8

Mr. Doonesby obviously had no idea that I would be attending Newcastle High. He twitches as we make eye contact, then he tries to speak, chokes on his words, and quickly excuses himself from the room, his awkwardly tall, lanky body clumsily knocking over a can of pencils as he backs out the door. I knew our first meeting would be rough, but I hadn't expected him to run away like a scared animal.

I find a desk and wait, but Mr. Doonesby does not come back immediately. Evie files into the room with several other students and quickly takes a seat next to me. She isn't easy to ignore, but her chattiness is somewhat forgivable because she is pretty. Evie is tiny and dynamic, annoying and appealing all at the same time. I realize that personality flaws can be overpowered by good looks and charm—at least, that's how it works in high school.

"Hi, Danny! You should have seen our teacher, Mister Doonesby. He was walking down the hall when I came in, and he looked like he had seen a ghost!"

"Really?" I reply, flipping open my book and trying to appear interested in exponents.

"Yes, really. Maybe if he's ill, we'll get out of class," she says hopefully.

But Evie is not destined to get her wish. Mr. Doonesby comes back to class five minutes later, his face still pale. He doesn't make eye contact with me, but introduces himself to the rest of the class as a middle-aged mathaholic who enjoys running, grilling, and reading science fiction. *And hanging out with a student's married mother,* I think sourly.

Mr. Doonesby teaches the entire algebra class without once looking at me, which is impressive because I'm sitting in the middle of the classroom, burning holes into his forehead with an angry scowl. I'm somewhat surprised by my anger, because without Mr. Doonesby's shenanigans, I wouldn't be living the life of luxury at the Vigliotti's place. But I'm so angry at my former principal that I almost think for a moment that Tommy's plan to blackmail Doonesby will be fun. Then I remember that Tommy is my enemy and that Mom was the one who started the flirtation with my principal. But even these thoughts don't help me feel much better about sitting in class with a man who separated my parents, unhappy as they were together.

At the end of class, Evie and I make our way to the door, but before I'm through it, Mr. Doonesby calls me over. "Can I see you for a minute?" he asks.

I nod and wave to Evie, who glances curiously at me and reluctantly exits the room, leaving me alone with the demoted principal.

"Danny," Mr. Doonesby starts, but then coughs to clear his throat. He pauses and stares at me, his eyes almost as bloodshot as Mom's had been when she visited me at the Vigliotti's. "Danny, I'm—I'm sorry."

I shrug. "Whatever. You don't have to apologize to me." I start to turn away, but Mr. Doonesby catches my arm. I barely hold back the urge to wrench it away.

"Yes, yes, I do," Mr. Doonesby says, his voice growing a little stronger. "What I did was terrible. I shouldn't have—I shouldn't have interfered in your life."

I am steaming. "Interfered? With *my* life? How about my mom's life? She's miserable right now! And it's all because of you!"

"Really? You mean, she's miserable without me?" Doonesby asks expectantly.

Now I do jerk my arm away. "Leave me alone! Don't talk to me, and don't you dare talk to my mom!" I stalk out of the classroom, not turning around once. I can't take another word from him, or I might just finish what Dad started.

* * * *

The night is extremely hot and sticky as I wait at the bus stop, drenched in sweat, my palms soaked. I am dressed in dark jeans and a black hoodie, both throwbacks to my Ridley days, which means neither item of clothing could have cost more than ten dollars. But I am now wishing I had chosen something less cozy. The hoodie is suffocating me.

Ten minutes pass, and I begin to feel a little nervous. Did Reggie forget, or worse, has he blown me off? I have already put so much work into tonight's plan—I put Baxter in my room early (to ward off any suspicion from Julia), and I told Ronnie that I was going to bed early because of a stomachache. That should keep everyone away for a while. After stashing some money in my pocket, I jogged down to the corner gas station, where I used the pay phone to call a taxi to take me to the nearest bus station, which was over by the high school. The taxi driver was not thrilled with the short ride and cheap fare, but I tipped him enough to lessen his disappointment. From there, I rode the bus to Old Newcastle, along with a strange assortment of people typical of the late hour. After so much effort to get here, I can't walk away from my plan now. But without a car, I can't do anything. Where is Reggie?

The beetle finally pulls to the curb at nine-thirty, fifteen minutes late. But my "where were you?" is cut off by the look on Reggie's face.

"Hey, man, sorry I'm late. One of the Newcastle cops thought I was up to no good. Took me a little while to get him off my back."

I nod, briefly imagining how a Newcastle cop might see Reggie. My friend's dark complexion sometimes makes people respond unfairly to him. "Don't worry about it," I offer as I climb into the passenger seat. "But we've got to get rolling. The meeting I heard about is supposed to be taking place now."

I can sense that Reggie wants to ask questions, but instead he listens quietly as I give him directions to the diner. I bring us around the back of the building and have Reggie kill his headlights. I hope we can arrive undiscovered, but I'm not yet familiar with the area, so we are taking a chance no matter how careful we are. Despite the danger, I can't help but be excited.

As we pull next to a dumpster sitting up against the building that's adjacent to the diner, I try not to feel disappointed by the lack of activity in the parking lot. The buildings appear deserted, and not a single vehicle sits in the lot. I hate to have my plans come to nothing, especially because I brought Reggie all the way out here to help me.

Reggie is scanning the area. "What are we looking for?" he asks, sounding puzzled.

I shake my head, feeling frustration build inside me. "I'm not sure exactly."

"You're not sure?" Reggie asks with an edge of irritation in his voice.

"No, not positive. But something should be going on in that parking lot," I say and point at the diner, as though Reggie has not already figured out that this is the object of our surveillance.

"Great!" Reggie's sarcasm is unmistakable. "I drive all the way out here for you, and all you can do is—"

"Shut up, Reggie," I interrupt. "There's someone there."

Sure enough, two men have come around the side of the diner. Reggie and I fall silent and shrink down into our seats. The beetle is well hidden by the dumpster, and I know the men probably won't see it— but I'm nervous anyway. I have no idea how these guys will react if they realize they are being watched, but I have a suspicion that they will not be happy. Reggie and I must be invisible for our own safety.

The two men seem to be arguing, and I wonder whether this might end in violence, just like my unplanned ride in the Lexus two nights before. The argument carries on for several minutes before both men disappear once more around the side of the building. I put my hand on the car door handle and start to open the door as quietly as possible.

"What's going on, Danny?" Reggie demands in a harsh whisper.

I pause. I know that Reggie has a right to know what he is getting into. He has followed me blindly until now, and that shows a great deal of trust.

"I think my godfather, Gino, is in the Mafia," I reply.

Reggie rolls his eyes. "Duh! I think I figured that one out by now. How do you know? What's happened?"

"Well, I don't know anything for sure. But I did hear Gino talking about someone trying to kill somebody, and then I saw him and another man beat up the would-be killer and put a gun in his face. And Gino talked about using some person in power—someone named Capriotti."

Reggie's eyes narrow. "Capriotti? I wonder if he meant the district attorney."

I am surprised by Reggie's knowledge. "How do you know who the district attorney is?"

"'Cause I had a run-in with him just last year."

My eyes widen. "You were in trouble?" I ask, but then I smile. "You're messing with me."

Reggie grins. "Yeah. Actually, I met him when I was on the debate team." He pauses thoughtfully. "I don't know quite how to describe him, but he's not the kind of guy you feel like trusting. He's very slick."

"Well, that would make sense, especially if he's working with the Mafia."

Reggie grabs his own car door handle. "So, what's the plan?"

I feel embarrassed. "I really thought any action would take place in the parking lot. But maybe everyone's inside. I'm going to get out and try to look through a window or sneak in the door."

"Let's go," Reggie says, and before I can consider the consequences of walking toward a building that might be full of violent, angry men, we are creeping across the dusty lot toward what might become an extremely dangerous situation.

Within minutes, I realize that the building doesn't have windows. The only way we are going to be able to find out what is going on is to go inside the diner itself. I know I can't take a chance of going in the front door, and I am at a disadvantage because I have no idea what the layout is inside the building. But the only other option is to turn around and go home, and I just can't do that, not when I am already here. Reggie points to a door on the far right side of the diner, and I nod. It is the only other door we have seen other than the front door. But when I try the handle, it's locked.

"Do you have anything we can use to pick it?" I ask.

"Hey, it's not like I carry a lock picking kit around with me. Isn't that racial profiling?" Reggie jokes, but I'm not in the mood for humor. I roll my eyes, frustrated. I may have been able to pick the lock—Mom habitually locked us out of the house, and I was good at tricking the lock with her bobby pin, which usually made me feel sure that our house was vulnerable to the most inexperienced of burglars.

But without any tool to pick the lock, our investigation is at a standstill. After a few more minutes of trying to come up with a solution, we decide to walk back to the car to wait a little longer. Just as we start back, however, the door opens. I grab Reggie's shirt and we smash ourselves up against the wall. A man emerges from the diner, props the door open with a nearby rock, and walks a small distance from the diner while unzipping his pants to take a pee in the lot next door.

I cannot believe how lucky this is. I know my idea is foolish, but this is our one chance to get inside the diner. I pick up a small stone next to my foot and toss it as far as I can in the opposite direction of the diner. The man flinches when he hears it land, and not knowing what it is, zips up his pants and starts toward the noise, away from the diner. Reggie and I take a few quick steps around the side of the diner and through the propped door.

If it is dark outside, the blackness that greets us inside the door is worse. Reggie bumps into me as I stop, unsure of where to go or even what is on the floor in front of me. I know we must move quickly—the man outside will not be distracted for long.

I put my hand out in front of me. Nothing is there. I shuffle a few steps forward, and my hand finally reaches the wall, but I don't know which direction to turn. We hear footsteps on the gravel outside—the man is returning. I take a few steps backward and bump into Reggie. "We've got to get out!" I whisper, panicked by the crunching steps behind us. I can barely see the way out.

"No, it's too late," Reggie answers. He grabs my arm and pushes me to the left. I muffle my own cry of pain as a wooden crate smashes into my shin, and Reggie almost topples over another crate as we hurry to get out of the man's path. I think we will run into a wall very quickly, but instead, we manage to stumble through a narrow doorway and into a very small bathroom, as I find out when my hip bumps a sink. Reggie starts to close the door, but stops when it lets out a high-pitched squeak. We stand motionless in the bathroom, waiting for the man to enter and hoping that, somehow, he will not see us standing here.

Chapter 9

My eyes adjust to the darkness just as the man reenters the building. He flips the light switch and closes the door, and I know that Reggie and I are completely visible now, even though the bathroom is to the side of what I can see is a half-empty storage room. But the man must have had a little too much to drink, because he stumbles over the same crate that I struck with my shin only a few seconds before. The man swears and continues to the next door, which creaks with age as he opens it and exits the storage room, killing the lights behind him.

I stand still while my eyes readjust to the darkness. Reggie is moving around beside me. "What are you doing?" I whisper, trying to decide whether we should attempt to follow the man through the next door.

"Look!" Reggie whispers, while climbing onto the toilet lid. I follow his pointing finger upward, where a small grated window is letting in a few pinpricks of light. I return to the storage room and feel around for the crate that injured me a few minutes before. I drag it to the toilet and stand next to Reggie, our heads practically touching as we peer through the tiny slits into the lighted room beyond.

I know immediately that I am lucky not to have followed the man through the other door, because it leads directly into a large room filled with men. Reggie takes a sharp breath, even as my own body tenses with fear at having only a wall between us and what probably is a room packed with Mafia wiseguys. They are counting money and are arranged in a loose circle around a large, imposing man with a bald head and horn-rimmed glasses, seated at the center of the activity. The room is smoky, and I'm having trouble getting a good view from between the slats.

I scan the room for Gino, hoping that maybe I'm wrong and Gino isn't associated with these men.

Reggie elbows me. "Which one is Gino?" he asks so softly that I can barely hear him.

I shake my head. "I can't find him."

"So should we stay put or get out of here?"

I can hear the anxiousness in Reggie's voice, but I'm reluctant to leave. I've been lucky to get this far without being discovered and am curious about what is going on in this diner. I have a pretty good idea that these men are not doing good things, but I don't know that for sure. The only act of violence I've witnessed so far was from Frank the other night. I stay rooted to my crate, and Reggie waits silently beside me.

I struggle to pick out any specific words from the various conversations flowing around the room. Reggie shifts uneasily, so I am just about to step off the crate and tell him we can go when the front door of the diner opens. Standing in the door frame are Frank and Gino, and between them they hold a thin, older Asian man, who appears terrified, yet defiant, as he is held captive.

The hefty bald man turns in his seat as Gino and Frank enter. The frown spanning his thick facial features deepens as he sees their hostage. The room falls silent; Reggie and I barely breathe.

"Ray, this is Chen," Gino tells the bald man as he pulls the older man toward him. Ray sits quietly for several long moments staring at Chen, who glares boldly back.

"I am tired of your threats," Chen says, a slight tremor in his voice. "I don't want you involved in my business! I won't pay your outrageous extortion, Mister Gallo!"

Gino shoves Chen down into a chair. "Shut up!"

I'm surprised by the name Chen just said. That name is all too familiar to me now. I study Ray Gallo closely, looking for any resemblance to Tommy Gallo. With Ray Gallo's heavy features, I have trouble seeing much similarity, and yet, Ray and Tommy definitely possess the same cruel twist to their mouths.

"Who is this again?" Ray asks Gino in a deep, gravelly voice, motioning to Frank.

"Frank Moretti, *a friend of mine,*" Gino says meaningfully. "He's been working in the area for a while now. He's got some connections that have been really helpful."

Ray nods and turns his attention back to Chen. Chen continues to sit still, but as I watch him more closely, I notice a trickle of blood coming from Chen's upper lip. I don't want to think that Gino may have beaten this man or even allowed Frank to do it.

I still can't believe that Gino, the man who has been so kind to me in my hour of need, the man who rescued me from the clutches of Barb Kluwer, could treat others so brutally. Surely this man Chen must have done something awful, right? Hadn't Iggy been about to kill someone else? Perhaps Gino simply keeps bad men from doing bad things. If so, Gino's rough treatment of Iggy, and now Chen, would be justified.

Reggie tugs on my sleeve and points at Gino. I nod, knowing my friend is trying to identify my godfather.

Ray turns slowly to Gino, ignoring the rebellious glare of his captive. "Where's Capriotti?" Ray asks. He points at a large man standing nearby. "Donny there said you told him nine-thirty."

Yes, you did say nine-thirty, I think, giving myself credit for being right about that. I want to see if this Capriotti guy is actually the district attorney that Reggie had mentioned.

Gino shakes his head. "Frank said Capriotti won't be coming. Apparently Capriotti thinks it is too 'compromising.' His words, not mine. I think he's just a chicken."

Ray nods and again eyes Chen like cornered prey. "So you bring me this bony, washed-up businessman instead? Why the hell would you expose me to this riffraff? You need the underboss to help you do your job or something?"

Gino scowls. "He hasn't paid in three weeks. But he said he might bargain with you."

Ray glares at Chen. "The bargain is this – if you don't pay, we'll let our virus wreak havoc on your computers."

Chen smirks. "That's the point. I'm not afraid of your weak, ineffective viruses. I only said I would bargain so I could tell this to your face!"

Ray's eyes narrow, and he turns to Gino. "This fool is playing you. Is he really immune to the virus?"

"Yes, last week we breached his firewall but were unable to release the virus onto his system. He's got someone at his company who knows this thing better than our guys. I don't know how, but his system is stronger than our virus."

"That so?" Ray asks, not particularly interested in a reply. He strokes his wide chin with thick fingers. "So Mister Chen believes he is invincible."

Chen lifts his head proudly. "My system is very strong, perhaps indestructible! I do not need to pay your outrageous price to maintain my network. You cannot touch it!"

Ray doesn't reply, but he nods to two men beside him. Gino and Frank take a step back as Donny and another man pick Chen up out of his chair and throw him to the floor. They proceed to kick him, then they lift him from the floor, and Donny holds Chen as the other man punches him twice. Chen is on the verge of passing out, his face bloody. He is still gasping from the violent kicks that were delivered to his stomach.

Reggie glances at me helplessly, but we can't do anything to stop the violence. Or can we? I can't think of anything that would not put our lives in danger. I glance at Gino, willing my godfather to put an end to the undeserved beating. I think Gino looks uncomfortable, but he does nothing. However, Gino's associate Frank seems even more upset, and he finally says, "Look, if you guys beat him to death, we'll never get our money!"

Ray glares at Frank for questioning his authority, but he finally motions for his men to stop beating Chen. "See, Mister Chen," Ray says, chuckling at the man's misfortune. "We may not be able to touch your network, but we can touch you. And we can get to your family too. You have kids, yes?"

Chen is conscious, but barely. Yet, his eyes widen at the mention of his family.

"Well," Ray continues, "I would recommend that you pay your fees, or your children may get a taste of the fun you're having this evening."

Donny starts to again pummel Chen, and I don't think the older man can stay conscious much longer. Why won't they stop? How can they continue to beat this frail man without killing him? Frank moves forward as if to say something, but another guy holds him back.

I look at Reggie again. We must do something. "Go to the car and get out of here," I whisper.

"You want to leave now? While they're distracted? What about that man?"

"No, I want you to go get in your car and get out of here now. Make as much noise as you can. Just don't let them see you or your license plate."

Reggie doesn't budge. "By myself? No! What are you going to do?"

"I'm going to stop that beating and then hide. So I need them to think that anyone who was here is getting away in your car. You'll keep them from looking for me."

"No way. It's too dangerous for you to stay!"

"I have to, Reggie. The best way to protect both of us is for you to go and for me to hide. I can get home once they all leave." I glance through the slats at the beating still taking place—was Chen even conscious now? "Otherwise, they may kill him."

Reggie nods. "Okay."

"Now."

"Now?"

"Now!" I say, almost too loudly.

Reggie scrambles off the crate, trying to make as little noise as possible. I know the men in the diner are distracted and have little chance of hearing Reggie's movement. Reggie pauses before he leaves the bathroom. "Do you want me to call the police?"

I glance back through the grate at Gino, disbelieving my desire to protect him. "No. No, I don't."

Reggie pauses, as if wanting to argue with me, but then he turns and hurries toward the door.

I wait several seconds after Reggie leaves; I want to ensure that he gets safely to his car. I want Reggie to escape, but I also need him to distract these men if I'm going to be able to hide safely. When I feel I can wait no longer, I grab a half empty metal paint can and throw it as hard as I can against the door leading to the diner.

I know I have only a few seconds to get into the bathroom and behind the door before a dozen or so mobsters are headed into the storage room, ready to beat—or maybe even kill—anyone who has been spying on their activities. If I timed things correctly, Reggie will be rolling out of the parking lot momentarily, making the men think that whoever made the commotion is getting away. Reggie is in as much danger as I am, but separating was the only way we could stop the beating and have the best chance of escape.

I slam the back door to the diner for effect and then speed into the bathroom, but I forget about the crate that I moved. As I trip over it again, I feel the hard wooden edge slice across my shin. I let out a silent howl, feeling sure that the splintered wood has drawn blood this time, and clamber behind the flimsy wooden door. I'm desperately hoping that somehow, my foolish scheme will work.

I flatten myself against the wall as the door leading into the diner bursts open, big, angry men streaming through it, their faces alarmed. One stops to pick up the paint can sitting on the floor, but the rest race toward the back door. I'm sure someone will see me—my heavy breathing thunders in my ears as sweat trickles down my legs, which are shaking from the pain and adrenalin coursing through my body.

Reggie's timing couldn't have been more perfect. Just as the men begin stumbling through the back door, I hear the unmistakable rumble from the beetle's old muffler as Reggie speeds over the gravel out of the parking lot. The men are frantic in their haste to get outside, knowing their spy might be escaping. I hear car doors slamming and motors revving as the men take off after Reggie, and I hope that for just this once, the beetle won't break down. Suddenly, I wonder whether Reggie's job is more dangerous than mine.

I know I must get out of the diner as quickly as possible, but I can't be sure that everyone has left. I'm glad for my hesitation when three more men walk through the interior door into the back room: Frank, Gino, and Ray.

"What was that?" Ray asks, cursing under his breath.

Gino shrugs and shakes his head, his face worried.

"How could this person get in?" Ray snaps, infuriated. "This door locks from the inside!"

"I don't know," Gino answers unhelpfully. "But a lot of guys go out to grab a cigarette or take a pee, since the toilet doesn't work."

I freeze as Gino mentions the bathroom, knowing that any of the three might glance involuntarily at the room.

"Well, they had better catch him," Ray replies, his tone threatening. "I'm not coming down here anymore if my identity can't be protected. In fact, I shouldn't be seen with half the people who were in that room!"

Gino nods. "I know. I feel the same way." He motions to the door leading into the diner. "I'm going to take Chen home. You coming, Frank?"

Frank is staring at the back door. "In a minute. I'll meet you outside."

Gino and Ray retreat into the diner, Ray mumbling about the danger they are all in. I watch Frank through the small slit between the door and the wall that I'm pressed up against, wondering why the younger man doesn't follow the others back into the diner. I need Frank to leave so I can escape.

As soon as the door closes, Frank turns toward the bathroom, his eyes on the crate that I tripped over in my hurry to get behind the door. I look at the crate, which is to my left, and my heart almost stops at the sight of it. In the spot where I hit my shin, blood is streaked across the wood. Will Frank realize that it's blood? I stand motionless, too afraid to breathe.

Frank moves toward the bathroom, switches on the light, and crouches down to examine the crate. He is only a foot away from me now, and he would only need to turn slightly to his left to see me. After a moment, Frank stands up, his eyes leaving the crate and shifting to the dirt from Reggie's shoe that litters the toilet lid. Then he turns to his left and swings back the squeaking door behind which I'm hiding. And in that moment, I am face to face with one of Ray Gallo's mobsters, staring into the eyes of a man who is sure to beat the living daylights out of me, if he doesn't kill me first.

Chapter 10

I finally know what it feels like to have seconds seem like days. I am flattened against the bathroom door, my escape now blocked by the imposing body of Frank Moretti, whose expression is hard as he stares down at me. I don't know what to do, although I'm sure Frank will probably rat me out immediately. Will Gino keep me from being harmed, or will he let these mobsters do with me whatever they like? Should I try to push past Frank and make a run for it? Frank took Iggy down with several punches, so I know my chances of escaping this man are slim to none.

The door leading into the main room opens again, and as it does, Frank immediately switches off the light so I can't be seen. Gino's head pokes through the door, "What's taking so long? You coming or what?"

"Yeah, I'm coming," Frank answers, shoving the bathroom door against me as though no one were behind it. I also notice that Frank's leg is blocking the bloody streak on the crate. "Just looking around a bit."

Gino seems curious. "Find anything useful?"

"No, not a thing," Frank answers quickly, leaving the bathroom. "Nothing at all." He follows Gino back into the diner, switching off the light in the storage room.

Stunned, I want to sink to the floor in relief, but I'm too scared to move. I wait and hear car doors slam and engines rev, then I stand on the toilet lid and see that the diner is empty and dark. I stumble toward the back door, open it a crack, and search the parking lot.

Everyone is gone—not a single man remains. I check around the front of the building, but find that it is deserted as well. And so I leave, limping to the pay phone to call a taxi and go home, more confused than ever and wondering why Frank, a mobster who I saw beat a man bloody, would protect a spying teenager who saw incriminating evidence.

I ask the taxi to stop at a gas station three blocks away from the Vigliotti home. The gas station has a pay phone, and I quickly insert coins and wait uneasily for Reggie to pick up the phone.

"Hello?" It's Reggie's mom.

"Oh, hi, Missus Allen. I was trying to get in touch with Reggie."

"At this hour of the night?" she asks suspiciously.

"I was up late doing homework," I lie. "And I need help with something."

"Well, I'm sorry, Danny. But Reggie just went to bed. He's in big trouble for staying out way, way past his curfew. I don't know what's gotten into him!"

Relief rushes through me. Reggie made it home safely. "That's okay, I'll figure it out. Thanks!"

"Okay, but don't study so hard, Danny. You need to get some sleep," Mrs. Allen admonishes.

Sleep? I think. *How am I ever going to sleep?* I hang up the phone and limp home, hoping to do just that.

* * * *

I actually have no difficulty sleeping—the waking up in the morning part is the problem. My alarm faithfully beeps at six-thirty, and after one unsatisfying round with the snooze button, I wake up wondering whether I should have called the police. Is Chen okay? Had Ray and Gino returned him to his house like they said they would? Am I a terrible person for condemning and protecting Gino at the same time? Would Frank beat me up like he had beaten Iggy?

I drag myself out from under the sheets and take a stab at trying to look as though I had not been up until one a.m., had not seen a helpless man beaten into a bloody mess, and had not been caught in the act by a brutal mobster. My bloodshot eyes give me away; beneath each of them, the flesh is purple and puffy, a telltale sign of a late, rough night. But the condition of my face would be manageable if my leg was not throbbing so sharply. I wonder how I will ever get around school without limping and enduring the questions that are sure to follow.

Even if Gino doesn't guess that I was the spy last night, I know my godfather will be curious about the injury, and I'm not certain I will be able to lie to Gino convincingly. But maybe I won't be able to cover up where I was last night anyway—Frank works for Gino, right? And he met me the other night at dinner, so he may have already alerted Gino to the fact that I was the one spying. Or maybe worse, Frank is planning to blackmail me, which would be stupid because I don't have a penny of my own.

I leave my room warily, wondering what danger lies in store for me. The kitchen is quiet. Breakfast dishes have already been stacked in the sink, and I realize that I'm moving much slower than usual, trying to account for my hurt leg. I hear the roar of the minivan's engine from the garage and rush toward the noise, afraid that Vince and Julia will take off for school without me. But just as I reach for the handle of the door leading into the garage, Julia catches my arm.

"What's up?" I ask, attempting to keep the guilt and exhaustion out of my voice. At the same time, I'm relieved to know she isn't in the car yet either.

She doesn't say anything for a long moment, placing her hands on her hips and staring me directly in the eyes. I'm extremely uncomfortable, but I hold her gaze.

"Where were you last night?" she asks, her tone already accusing.

"What are you talking about?" I snap, trying to sound as though she's being unfair.

"I came down to check on Baxter. You weren't in bed," she replies, her face triumphant.

I inwardly groaned. What's the deal? Julia could barely stand to look at me when I first arrived at the Vigliotti house. Now she can't seem to stay away. I'm tired of her games, but I must come up with something she will find believable. "I went to Ridley to see some of my friends, okay?" I say. "It's hard, you know, starting over."

"What were you doing with them?" she asks, as though she expects that anyone from Ridley would obviously be up to no good.

"Geez, you're nosy. We were just hanging out. Shooting basketball, playing video games—that kind of thing."

She eyes me suspiciously. "Who has parents who would let them stay up that late on a school night?"

"Kids from Ridley," I shoot back. "Just lay off, okay?"

"*Okay,*" she agrees, rolling her eyes. "You're so rude, sometimes."

"I'm rude? Why don't you stop breaking into my bedroom at night?"

She scowls at me. "I'm not breaking in! This is my house, not yours! If anyone's an intruder, it's—" Julia stops. "Whatever," she says quickly, turning toward the garage. She opens the door to the blaring of the horn. Vince is not a patient person, and he glares at us coldly as we climb into the van.

Vince guns the vehicle out of the garage and almost hits a small car coming down the road behind us. Julia screams at him, and he bellows back at her, while I lay my aching head in my hands and close my eyes. I desperately want to call Reggie and discuss what happened the night before. I want to tell him that I might disappear forever. But first, I must endure an entire day of school with an aching head and an injured leg. This is going to be an extremely long day.

* * * *

"Danny, you look so tired!" Portia puts her hand on my neck and gives a few quick squeezes. Her touch feels amazing, and for a moment, I forget about everything but her hands touching my neck.

"He looks like crap," Tony offers, eyeing me with his usual suspicion.

"Oh, come on, Tony! Can't you be nice for once?" Portia snaps.

Tony scowls at me with no intention of being nice, but to Portia he merely mumbles, "Fine."

"Good!" She starts down the hallway toward our first period class, which still won't begin for another ten minutes. Before entering the room, she sets her backpack on the floor and pulls out a videocassette.

"Tony, I need you to do me a favor." He nods eagerly, shooting me a superior look. "This is my mom's favorite video in the world—it's of my first Christmas," Portia continues, showing him the weathered box. "But it's getting worn out! Doesn't your dad's company transfer video to DVD? Do you think I might be able to get this copied for her birthday? I'll pay him for it."

"His company does all kinds of electronic media management for businesses," Tony brags, "but they do have video transfer equipment. I'll get it done—no cost to you."

"Thank you so much," she exclaims. She gives him a quick hug, as she is often inclined to do, and I feel jealousy course through me once again. Does she have any idea what she is doing to us? Tony beams at her sudden show of affection, but I am watching her face. No, Portia appears completely innocent of the torture and competition she is inflicting on her friends. "Tell your dad 'thank you' for me," she adds.

Tony nods. "I will—if I ever see him again!"

Portia and I both look at him questioningly. He shrugs. "I'm just kidding, really, but my mom's pretty mad. He went out to dinner with some colleagues last night, and he probably had too much to drink and stayed over. But Mom is furious!"

Portia turns to me. "Missus Chen is pretty strict," she explains.

I can't reply. I just stand there, staring back at her, trying to keep my features from showing my panic. Tony's last name seems to float before my eyes, and I have a sudden, horrible suspicion that I have already seen Mr. Chen and that Tony's father is suffering from something far worse than a hangover. I have a terrible realization that if Mr. Chen has not come home yet, he may not have made it through the night.

My abrupt change is quickly noticed. "What's wrong, Danny?" Portia asks, concern filling her voice. "Are you all right?"

"So, your dad does a lot of computer stuff?" I ask Tony awkwardly, my tongue feeling too large for my mouth.

Tony studies me, his eyes narrowing. "Yeah, I'd say so. He taught me everything I know—except that now I do all of his network security." Tony is obviously proud of his dad's trust. "My dad is always saying that if kids can break into a system, then it will take a kid to keep them out! I get paid and everything." He shoots Portia a confident smile.

"I think I'm going to throw up," I reply, not untruthfully, as I stagger toward the men's bathroom. Tony steps back from me, but Portia leans up against me, supporting me and helping me to the door, her face almost as white as mine.

"Come on, Tony!" she says, drawing the curious stares of other students lingering in the hall.

Tony grudgingly offers his shoulder to me, but I shake my head and reluctantly struggle away from Portia's grasp. "I'm fine, I'm fine," I reassure them. "I'll just walk down to the nurse's office and see if she can give me some Pepto. Let Ms Lowe know where I've gone."

Portia is worried, but she nods and lets me go. I start down the hall as she and Tony enter the classroom, but as soon as I'm sure that they can no longer see me, I switch directions and head for the library. By this time, my leg is starting to throb painfully again, so I walk a little slower than I would have liked. My guilt deepens as I think about everything I should have done the night before. I had seen something terrible take place, but I didn't call the police; I didn't tell anyone that a helpless man had been beaten, perhaps to death. Maybe I'm an accessory to murder, just by keeping my mouth closed.

The librarian is not around, so I'm able to silently make my way to a computer and quickly get online. I immediately pull up a local news website, searching for any report of a dead or badly injured man. No news referencing Tony's dad is to be found, but I know that this doesn't mean Mr. Chen is safe.

I am just about to check out the local police report when I'm discovered by my English teacher, Mr. Capriotti. "Hey, Danny, you need to be in class," he says earnestly, and I'm momentarily impressed with the teacher's ability to recall my name after just one class.

"Yeah, I know," I say, getting up and heading for the door. "Sorry!"

I hurry out of the library and almost plow into Mr. Doonesby as I rush out the door. We're both startled, but Mr. Doonesby recovers more quickly than I and puts his hand once more on my arm. "Danny! Are you okay?"

I lean out of Mr. Doonesby's grasp, trying to keep my chaotic emotions in check. "Yes, I'm just late for class." I start to make my way past my old principal and head down the hall.

"Danny, I wanted to talk to you about that article by Julia Vigliotti."

I stop immediately. I have no idea what Julia wrote, with the exception of my being from Boston. But Mr. Doonesby's remark makes me think I may regret having let her use me as a subject for her article.

"Yeah? What about it?" I ask, attempting to sound casual.

Mr. Doonesby holds up a slim newspaper that I recognize as the school's weekly publication. He points to an article that spans the column on the far right side of the front page. "This is quite a story."

I can't see much from where I'm standing—all the black print blurs into unreadable text. But I can make out the headline, which reads, "New kid on Newcastle block has hobnobbed with stars." I groan. Julia's creativity may have gotten a little out of control, and I never realized her article would actually be published.

"You have a very exciting past," Mr. Doonesby comments dryly.

I glare at my old principal. "Well, I haven't read it. But I guarantee I'll prefer that story to the real one. And really, you should too. You wouldn't want people here to know our little 'connection,' right?" I don't like the way my voice sounds, but I'm still too angry to be polite to Mr. Doonesby.

Mr. Doonesby's face turns white. "That wouldn't be good for either of us," he agrees.

I briefly think of Tommy's threat to expose me unless I blackmail Mr. Doonesby. With Julia's article, I now have more to lose than when I was just worried about Tommy telling everyone I'm from Ridley. At this moment, I have Mr. Doonesby exactly where I need him, but somehow, I can't follow through with blackmailing him to give Tommy good math grades. Instead, I turn away without another word and walk down the hall toward my homeroom, trying to hide my limp and wishing I had told Julia to be honest—wishing I myself had been honest.

However, I never make it to class. Just as I turn the corner, Portia rushes out of the classroom and starts down the hall in the opposite direction.

"Portia!" I call.

She stops and turns. "I thought you were going to the nurse's office."

"I was, but I got lost," I reply, thinking I have lied so much at this point, what is one more?

Portia doesn't acknowledge my excuse. "It's Tony, Danny. Something terrible happened. The principal came to get him. I don't know what's wrong!"

I stay silent, not able to tell her that something has probably happened to Tony's dad.

Portia waits for me to catch up to her. "I told Ms Lowe I needed to go to the bathroom. I can't sit there and not know!" she says.

I nod. "I understand. Let's go the principal's office and see if we can find anything out."

We start down the hall in silence. Portia is chewing on her lip, and I can't think of anything to say that will make her less anxious. She stops suddenly and turns to me. "Do you think something happened to his dad?"

I try not to let my face tell her what I really think. I put my hand on her shoulder and look into her eyes. "Maybe," I say. "But don't get too upset until you know exactly what's going on."

She nods, and we continue down the hall. I try not to be overwhelmed by my exhaustion. Between my late night activities and my fear about Tony's dad, I feel terrible.

When we reach the principal's office, we peer through the blinds covering the window. The secretary is sitting at the front desk, and no one else is in sight. I motion to Portia, and we go into the office.

"May I help you?" the secretary asks coolly. "Why aren't you two in class?"

Portia steps up to her desk anxiously. "We're looking for Tony Chen. I'm his best friend, and I want to know what happened to him!"

The secretary regards her suspiciously. "I'm not feeding school gossip. If he's your friend, he'll eventually tell you himself."

Portia bursts into tears. "Please just tell me if everything's okay!"

The secretary is moved by Portia's sobbing. She heaves her heavy body out of her chair and around the desk, putting her arm around Portia's shoulders and guiding her to a chair. "Hey, it's okay." She glances at me. "She's really his friend?"

I nod. "They've been friends since they were little."

"Everything's going to be okay," she promises Portia, patting her back. "Tony's father was injured and hospitalized, but he's going to be okay."

Portia pulls back from her, searching the secretary's face with wide eyes. "His dad?"

"Yes," the secretary confirms. "But he'll be okay."

Portia turns to me. "I've got to talk to him!"

"Tony needs to concentrate on his dad right now," I say, relieved that Mr. Chen is alive. "We'll talk to him as soon as we can."

Portia stands up. "You're right. But I need to call my parents to tell them."

The secretary points to her desk. "You can use my phone. What's your name?"

"Portia. Portia Saviano." She walks to the desk and picks up the phone, turning her back to me and the secretary, whose attention turns quickly to me.

"And you are?"

"Danny Higgins."

Her face lights up with recognition. "Danny Higgins? I just got a phone call about you!"

I freeze, wondering what part of my recent activities has finally caught up with me.

"Your brother called. He said that he has your lunch, and that he would meet you in front of the school. But I thought you were staying with the Vigliottis?"

I'm glad Portia is still on the phone with her parents. "I *am* staying with the Vigliottis," I reply, not sure what else to say. News certainly travels fast around the school.

"Do you have a brother?"

I think quickly about whether I should answer yes or no. I find that I'm curious, but also a little hesitant of claiming a brother. "Yes," I answer finally. "Sometimes he brings me lunch. He's older, but we're trying to get closer."

The secretary nods knowingly. "That's great. Family is the most important thing. Well, he may be out there now."

"Okay." I head for the door, waving to Portia, who is deep in conversation. I hear the secretary call to me one more time as I exit the office.

"You're from Boston, right? Have you really hung out with Ben Affleck?"

I let the door close as I roll my eyes with my back turned to her. I walk out the front door of the school, my curiosity and my dread growing. I'm wondering whether I'm about to be kidnapped by the mob. Should I go back inside the school?

I stand on the curb and glance around the front parking lot, spotting a silver BMW parked alongside the curb, the engine running. As I move toward the vehicle, I'm unable to recognize the driver because of the sun's harsh glare on the dark windshield. I step up to the passenger side and lean forward as the tinted window rolls down. Sitting in the front seat is Frank Moretti, and he does not look happy.

Chapter 11

"Get in," Frank says.

I hesitate. On the one hand, I'm standing in front of a mobster—one who knows that I saw some extremely incriminating activities last night. This is also the guy I watched beat Iggy. On the other hand, Frank protected me from Gino, hiding me when he could have easily exposed me, and he kept Gino from harming Iggy too. At this point, I don't have much to lose either way. If I don't get into Frank's car now, Frank might tell Gino about my spying, and that could make the situation much worse. If the mob finds out that I've been watching them, my life is over anyway, sooner or later.

I open the door of the car and settle down gingerly on the black leather seat, which is hot from the August sun. I stare straight ahead, too nervous to look Frank in the face, and wondering whether I will make it out of this car alive. I had hoped we would chat in the school parking lot, but Frank quickly shifts the car into drive and leaves the school. My palms sweat as I feel my life is probably over.

"Where are we going?" I ask, strangely accepting my fate. I have never thought about my own death before. Fifteen seems like a very young age to die, but I don't know if I'm scared or sad. No matter what, I know I'll fight—I'm not going down without one. Then again, am I not the kid who just got into a mobster's car willingly? Maybe I deserve to die for sheer stupidity. I should never have climbed into this death trap.

"I'm taking you somewhere we can talk," Frank replies, his face expressionless.

"What do we need to talk about?" I ask, even though the answer is obvious.

"I believe you were somewhere you shouldn't have been last night. How did you find out about the diner, Danny?"

I stare at him, wondering what I should say. "It was by accident," I answer. *A very, very unfortunate accident.*

"No one told you the diner is a meeting place?" Frank asks sharply.

I shake my head. No one *told me* anything. I'm trying to figure out where Frank is taking me.

Frank seems to sense my nervousness. "It's okay, Danny."

"What's going to happen to me?" I ask, dreading the answer.

Frank chuckles. "I'm not going to kill you. You don't have to be afraid. I'm not even going to hurt you."

"I'm not afraid," I say, making an attempt to sound calm. I don't know whether to believe him.

Frank laughs in reply. "You're a pretty gutsy guy!" He starts to reach inside his jacket pocket, and I lean away, wondering if I can leap from the car if Frank pulls out a gun. But Frank brings out a leather wallet instead, and I relax slightly. Maybe Frank is going to try to pay me off. What should I do in that case? I don't want Frank to be suspicious that I will go to the cops, but I also can't take money in return for my silence.

But instead of offering me cash, Frank hands me the entire wallet. "Look inside," he directs.

I quickly open the thin bi-fold wallet and find myself looking at something I had not expected to ever see—FBI credentials. On the bottom fold is a picture of Frank Moretti, but on the top fold, the name underneath the "Federal Bureau of Investigation" is "Frank McCoy." And underneath the name is the title "Special Agent."

"You're not a mobster," I say, focusing on the picture.

"No, I'm not."

I study Frank closely. His hair is short and his face clean-shaven. Frank could pass for Italian, but he could certainly pass for an FBI agent too. His role as an agent makes his protection of me the night before easily explainable.

"What do you want with me?" I ask, my anxiety now replaced by curiosity.

"You're in real danger, Danny. You know what Gino does, but you're not part of his family. If he found out that you were there last night—"

"Gino wouldn't hurt me," I interrupt.

Frank frowns, but he doesn't argue with me. We pull up in front of a large building with a sign that identifies it as the Newcastle police station. Frank gets out of the car, as do I, and all the while I am wondering what the agent plans to do. Frank motions for me to follow him, and we climb the large cement stairs and enter through the glass doors.

The lobby is large and filled with people, mostly police officers. Frank leads me to the elevators, which we ride to the third floor. Once off the elevator, we walk to the end of a long hallway. I notice that the door to our right reads "Chief of Police" on it, and just as Frank opens the door on the left side of the hallway, the door on the right begins to open. Whatever Frank sees makes him push me through the half-open door on the opposite side, hiding us both from whoever is exiting the Chief's office.

"Thanks, Chief!" says a loud, hearty voice. "Please keep me posted!"

The door is cracked, so I can hear but not see what is happening on the other side of it.

"You got it, Mark, I'll let you know," says another voice, muffled by the door that is shutting.

"Mark, do you think he'll be able to find out?" a strident voice says, making me recoil in disgust. It belongs to Barb Kluwer, the DA's assistant. Frank keeps the door almost shut, but he is obviously listening to the conversation going on in the hall.

"Don't call me Mark around here," Mark says. "When we're in this building, you call me 'Mister Capriotti,' Barb."

My eyes widen, and Frank's hold on my arm tightens. He is clearly as interested in these two people as I am.

"Fine, but we should have talked more today about finding out who the undercover agent is!" she demands, her voice peeved.

Frank's face is angry as he waits for the two to move out of earshot, and then he takes my elbow and rushes me through a maze of cubicles to an office at the back.

"What was that all about?" I ask as Frank pushes me toward the office door.

Frank holds a finger to his lips again. He opens the office door and we step inside. Seated behind an enormous oak desk is a middle-aged man with short, gray hair and a mustache. He glances up from a stack of papers as we enter.

"We've got to talk," Frank says to the man as we enter. "Mark Capriotti is digging around the police department for information. He just came out of the Chief's office. And I've told you I must be warned if Capriotti is in the building! This is dangerous. If your guys can't communicate with me, it's the last time I'm coming here!"

"This is the kid?" the man asks, ignoring Frank's irritation and studying me, his blue eyes making me shift uncomfortably.

"This is Danny," Frank answers, taking a deep breath. "Gino's godson."

"He saw everything?"

"I'm not sure. Just when did you get to the diner last night, Danny?"

I consider the eager faces of both the men and decide that if any questions are going to be answered, mine are going to be answered first. "Before I tell you anything, I want to know what's going on. Frank, why are you helping Gino with mob stuff if you're an FBI agent? And who is *this* guy? And why did you kidnap me from school?"

Frank steps back as though he has been slapped. "I didn't kidnap you! You came with me willingly. I can't ask permission—who would I ask? I'm trying to protect you!"

"From what?" I shoot back, hoping I have caught Frank off-guard enough to get him to tell me exactly what is going on.

"From the Newcastle Mafia," the older man replies calmly.

"Danny, this is Detective Alvarez," Frank explains, motioning to the man behind the desk. "He and I are working on a joint task-force that's infiltrating the mob here."

Alvarez? The name rings a bell, but my need for information is crowding any other thoughts. "But I saw you beat someone up, Frank."

"What? When?" Frank demands.

Detective Alvarez smiles at me. "Agent McCoy does what he has to do to fit in. Otherwise he might be suspected as a UC."

I glance at Frank. "UC?"

"Undercover, Danny," Frank answers. "Unfortunately, you discovered me. You and someone else. Who was with you last night?"

I don't want to lie to him, but I've got to protect Reggie. "I saw you beat up Iggy," I accuse, changing the subject.

"You were there that night too?"

I flinch, realizing I have given up more information than I was asked. Then I nod. "Like I said before, it was an accident. I was in the back of the Lexus when you guys took off."

"Sometimes I have to do things to fit in," Frank explains. "As long as I don't kill anyone, it's for the greater good. Iggy got much less of a beating because I gave it to him. If a real mobster had beaten him, he might be in a coma—or worse."

"But you didn't do anything to help Chen!" I say, hearing the fury in my voice.

"We're so close to putting an end to the whole operation, Danny. I've been working on this for years! Chen knows the risks, and he's helping me anyway. I stepped in when I thought he couldn't handle any more.

But even so, I took a chance of compromising the case. I look at it this way—if I had tried to help Chen, I wouldn't be able to stop more men like him from getting beat up in the future. I must maintain my identity and then do what I can to lessen the violence. "

I shake my head, unwilling to agree that Chen had to suffer for the sake of others.

"We thought that if anyone were to discover Frank, it would be District Attorney Capriotti," the detective adds. "We've had a heck of a time convincing Frank's boss to let him stay undercover. So far, Capriotti has never seen Frank, and no one in this county besides me knows that Frank is the UC. Frank is from another state, so the Mafia wouldn't know him as law enforcement, but Capriotti is a recent development. We didn't know he was involved with the Mafia until just recently. Problem is, we don't really have any proof yet. Capriotti's never been spotted with the mob."

"But he's important to the mob, isn't he?" I say.

"He *does* know too much," Alvarez says to Frank.

Frank shrugs. "Then we need to get him out of there. We'll just have the county come in and say that the guardianship is under dispute and—"

"No!" I shout, much more loudly than I had intended. "No! I am not leaving the Vigliotti house. It's my home now. It's the only place I belong!"

"It's not safe there!" Frank counters. "Did you see what happened to Chen?"

"Yes," I answer, suddenly remembering that I still don't know how badly Tony's dad is hurt.

"These are not good men, Danny. They will protect each other above all else. Your life is in danger. Chen is only alive now because I was there to keep them from finishing him off. I was able to convince them that Chen needed to be alive to pay the extortion. But I still feel awful about what was done to an innocent man, and I know I couldn't stand by if they tried to hurt you."

"You see, Danny," Alvarez says, "we can't leave you with the Vigliottis. You'll compromise Frank's undercover work, or worse, he'll get killed if he tries to help you. We need you to give a statement as to what you saw last night, and then we will put you somewhere we can protect you."

"I won't leave," I say stubbornly. I know that, as dangerous as the situation may be, I'm not scared to stay with the Vigliottis, but I am afraid of where these men will put me. I'm afraid of having no control over my future.

"Danny, we cannot leave you in a dangerous situation," Frank states.

"You can't afford to take me out of it! I won't go quietly!" I threaten, wondering exactly what I mean by that. Then I suddenly have an idea. "But you could use me to help you," I offer.

Both men look at me skeptically.

"What do you mean?" Alvarez asks.

"Absolutely not," Franks says.

"I'll keep my eyes and ears open. If I hear anything important, especially anything about Frank, I'll let you know."

"No way," Frank replies. "That's too risky. We can't have a kid working for us."

"I'm not leaving the Vigliottis without creating a scene. And don't worry, I won't put myself in danger," I promise.

"Like you didn't put yourself in danger last night?" Frank shoots back.

"I won't go back to the diner. But I'll be alert at the house for anything that might help."

Neither man says anything for a moment, and I feel I'm making progress.

"How will you communicate with us?" Frank finally challenges.

"Actually, I might be able to help with that," Alvarez replies. "My daughter goes to Newcastle High."

"Evie?" I ask, finally connecting the last name to Portia's friend.

"Yes," Alvarez answers. "You know her, then?" he asks, with fatherly suspicion.

"She's a friend of a friend," I say. "She seems really nice."

Alvarez smiles. "I'm glad to hear that. She could get messages from you to me."

"No," Frank states emphatically. "It's too dangerous. It's not right to put a kid in this situation!"

"I'm not exactly a kid," I snap.

Frank scowls at me. "Yes, you are!"

"I think we should let him stay with the Vigliottis," Alvarez cuts in.

Frank turns to his colleague angrily. "Why are you so ready to put him in danger? You're talking about his life!"

"Because it may be more dangerous to move him out of the situation. You said you were the only one who saw him, right?"

"I think so," Frank answers. "But I don't know for sure."

"No one else saw me," I say. "Something would have been said. I can do this," I tell Frank, feeling the desperation so strongly inside me to convince this agent to let me stay where I am.

"Okay," Frank finally relents. "I can't believe I'm agreeing with this. But if anything happens that makes me think you're in danger, I'm taking you out of there. Deal?"

"Deal," I agree.

"All right, I'm going to go make sure the hallway is clear. Follow me in about two minutes." Frank strides out of the office, obviously bothered by my new role as a spy in the Vigliotti house.

Once he leaves, I turn to Alvarez one more time. "I need you to understand, there's not much chance I'm going to give you anything that will directly implicate Gino," I say. "Not unless he does something really terrible."

To my surprise, Alvarez simply smiles. "I understand, Danny. I think you're brave, but I also believe you are very loyal. Just do the right thing." Alvarez takes out a business card and scribbles a number on the back. "Keep this hidden, okay? The number on the card is a direct line to me."

I nod and take the card. The front has the name "Pete Alvarez" printed in black ink, and the number written on the back is the only other piece of information. This card won't get me in trouble if it is found—that is, until someone dials the number and reaches Detective Alvarez. I take out my own small leather bi-fold wallet and stick the card behind my student ID.

"Thanks," I say, and then I shut the office door and navigate the maze of cubicles to find Frank, all the while thinking that I may have just made the biggest mistake of my life.

* * * *

I return to school in time to attend my final class, which is, unfortunately, algebra with Mr. Doonesby. While I wait for Evie to come to class, I wonder what I will say to her once she sits down. I want to let her know that I met her dad, but I have to be careful not to let anyone overhear. Perhaps I should wait for her dad to tell her about this. Then again, do I really think I'll learn any more about the Newcastle Mob if I don't return to the diner?

Unfortunately, Evie rushes in just as class is starting, so we don't have time to chat. The class is painfully slow—algebra is a terrible subject on which to concentrate when my emotions are running wild. I can't believe what I have become involved with in just the last four days. Now, not only do I know I'm living with a real-life mobster, but I am spying for the FBI! If my movie watching with Vince has been any indication, spies (more commonly known as "rats" if they are part of the Mafia family) do not fare well if their deception is discovered. I have asked to stay in an extremely dangerous position, just so I can live in the house of the man on whom I will be spying.

I think about Vince's partiality for Mafia movies, and I have a sudden feeling in my gut that Gino's teenage son might suspect something about his father's late night activities. Then again, maybe Vince just likes the violence—but I can't shake the thought that the connection might be more than coincidental. I observe Evie out of the corner of my eye, and suddenly I wonder whether she has any idea that the Vigliottis are connected to the Mafia. Her interest in me as a member of the Vigliotti household certainly makes her suspect. At any rate, she is bound to find something out, at least from her father, if I pass her any messages.

Algebra eventually draws to an end. Mr. Doonesby has avoided any eye contact with me again, which is a definite relief. Perhaps Mr. Doonesby has come to terms with the fact that I might not want to be exactly honest about my background. Somehow, he must also realize that any connection between him and me might lead to some uncomfortable questions. Better to leave things as they are, I suppose.

As the bell rings, I heave my backpack onto my shoulders and glance at Evie. Maybe I should wait for her dad to talk to her, but I have an overwhelming desire to let her know I may be passing some messages her way. "Can I talk to you a moment?"

She smiles. "Of course, Danny," she replies pleasantly, standing next to her desk and gazing up at me with expressive dark brown eyes. She seems excited—what if she thinks I'm asking her out? Will she be disappointed? Looking in her eyes, I almost *want* to ask her out, but then I think of another pair of brown eyes, and the feeling passes.

"Um, maybe we could talk in the hall?" I say, wanting to escape the watchful eyes of Mr. Doonesby and have my conversation lost in the loud hum of voices outside the door.

"Okay." She collects her books and heads for the door as I follow behind her. As I pass through the doorway, I start to tell her to just meet me at my locker, but I'm stopped by a large hand wrapping itself around my neck and shoving me up against the wall.

"You haven't done what I asked!" Tommy growls at me. "Get ready to be humiliated!"

Chapter 12

I bring my hands up and move Tommy's thumbs away from my windpipe before wriggling free of his hold. "Get off me!" I shout angrily, drawing the curious stares and ears of nearby classmates.

Evie is glaring at Tommy. "Get away from him, Gallo," she says, her voice heavy with threat. Surprisingly, Tommy steps back from me, scowling at Evie with clear hatred.

"Just because Daddy's the long arm of the law doesn't give you any right to order me around!" Tommy snaps, but he makes no move toward her. He whips his head back to me. "What's it going to be, gutter-rat? You either do as I say, or I'll do what I told you I would do."

I study Tommy's face and almost laugh. Here I am, playing a dangerous game of cat and mouse between the FBI and Newcastle Mafia, and I'm worried about what kids will think about my hometown? I'm brave enough to put my life in danger, yet I'm scared of what a bully might tell people about me? I don't need to be ashamed of my town. Ridley might be the rat hole of New Jersey, but I guess I'm proud that I'm just as smart and athletic as these Newcastle snobs. How can I allow Tommy to force me to do something dishonest for such a small price?

Yet, Tommy will win whatever my choice, and I hate to see the kid triumph, especially now that I know Tommy's dad is as much a scumbag as his son. And in that moment, I smile, because I have a plan.

Tommy takes two steps toward me. "What's that? You're smiling? I wouldn't be smiling if I were you, gutter-rat. I'm about to ruin your life!"

I frown, trying to look more intimidated. "Fine, Tommy. I will take care of everything by tomorrow."

Tommy grins. "Good. I knew you'd come around." He nods toward Doonesby's classroom door. "You gonna take care of it now?"

I shake my head and begin to walk away. "In my own way, in my own time."

* * * *

I sit at the kitchen table making an attempt at my homework. The small, overly ornate desk in my bedroom just isn't working for me. Even though Ronnie is busy with dinner, I find I'm much less distracted in the kitchen. I always worked on my homework at the kitchen table in my old home, and it's one habit I can't break.

Besides, I have another reason to be in the kitchen. I want to be near the phone because Portia is supposed to call me within the hour. She is going to visit Tony and his family at the hospital where Mr. Chen is receiving care, and she has invited Evie and me to join her. I feel guilty about visiting a man I watched get beaten by the men Gino works with, but I want to offer Portia emotional support and also see with my own eyes that Mr. Chen is okay. In any case, this gives me an opportunity to speak with Evie. In fact, by this time, she may already know that I may be using her to deliver any messages I have for Detective Alvarez.

I tap my pencil on a complicated algebra problem.

Ronnie glances over at me. "Do you need any help, Danny? I was a whiz at math in high school."

"No," I say quickly and bend my head over my paper. I never had anyone help me with my homework before, and I wonder if *must-have-been-popular* Ronnie had really applied herself at math. Maybe I would learn more quickly if I had help, but I have a certain amount of pride in being able to figure things out for myself. In the past, that's the only option I had. Then again, I've never encountered the challenging high school homework like that at Newcastle High.

I really do try to focus, but I'm distracted by something else I need to do, something I'm dreading. I must speak to Julia, but I know she's going to be furious with what I will say, so I've avoided her so far this evening. But because I might get back from the hospital late, I should talk to her before I leave. For a few minutes, I watch Ronnie mix cake batter energetically (she told me she's making Gino's favorite—chocolate cake). I'm still curious as to whether Ronnie knows anything about the mob. Would Gino be able to hide that from her all these years? She does know that Ray is someone to fear, at least.

I finally coax myself out of the chair and up toward Julia's bedroom. I climb the stairs slowly and pass Vince's door, fighting the urge to go in and play video games with him. Somehow, I doubt that Vince is getting much homework accomplished, with the heavy metal music pulsing through the closed door. I pause in front of Julia's door and hear her chatting on the phone. Then I knock on her door, wondering if she will hear me.

"Who is it?" Julia shouts, her annoyance already obvious.

I open the door and find Julia stretched out on her bed, her cell phone nestled up under her hair next to her ear. Her wavy tresses fan across the bedspread much like they had when she distracted me from my homework just a few nights ago, and she is wearing her usual tight jeans and an extremely low-cut top. Baxter flies across the room with friendly yips and puts his two front paws on my leg. I scoop him up and pet his shaking, excited body.

Julia points to the phone and mouths, "I am on the phone."

"Duh," I reply, and start to back out of the room, but Julia shakes her head violently.

"Honey, I've got to go. Our exchange student is bothering me again!" she says sweetly. "I'll call you if everything works out tonight. You had better not be late!" She slaps her cell phone shut and throws it on the bed, and then she stares expectantly at me.

"Exchange student?" I ask.

"My boyfriend is *collegiate*. I think he's starting to get bored with me. Just trying to make life more exciting, maybe make him a little jealous," she replies, smiling coyly. "What do you want?"

I know I have no easy way to deliver the news, so I plunge ahead. "Tomorrow, everyone will know that I'm from Ridley, not Boston."

Julia's eyes widen. "How?"

"I'm telling them."

Her face twists in anger. "Whatever for? Do you want to ruin my journalistic reputation?"

"Maybe you should have thought about your 'journalistic reputation' before you lied in your article," I shoot back.

Her cheeks turn bright red. "I did it for you! Everyone will hate you if they know you're from Ridley!"

"I don't have a choice, Julia. If I don't tell everyone, Tommy Gallo will."

Her eyes narrow. "How does that creep know about you?"

I shake my head. "Beats me. But he threatened to expose me unless I do what he says. Besides, it's only a matter of time before someone Googles me and finds out I wrestled at Ridley Middle School."

"What does Tommy want you to do?" she asks, her anger momentarily distracted by the mention of something juicy like blackmail.

"Well, that's actually why I came to talk to you. I think we may be able to salvage your reputation and trap Tommy at the same time."

She scoots to the edge of her bed and studies me for a moment. "I'm interested," she says. "What do you want me to do?"

"First, I need you to write a retraction and tell people where I'm really from, but it can't be released until noon tomorrow. I need a chance to talk to my friends. Then meet me in the gym before third period. All you need to do is watch and listen. I think you'll be getting the scoop of the year."

Her eyes light up in excitement, but then she quickly wipes the eagerness from her face. "*Fine*. But I want a favor in return."

"The scoop of the year isn't enough?"

Julia crosses her arms. "I need to ride to the hospital with you."

"Why?" I ask, thinking that Julia could not have any reason to visit Tony's dad.

Julia shrugs. "A friend's mom is there. I want to visit her."

I glance at her cell phone and remember the words of her phone conversation—something about tonight. "I'm not helping you sneak out, Julia. I'm not lying for you. I'm trapped in enough lies as it is."

She glares at me. "I am visiting a friend, *okay*? That's all you need to know!"

I shake my head in disgust and reach for her cell phone. Julia tries to grab it first, but she's not quick enough. "What are you doing? Give it back!" she whines, lunging for it.

I hold it away from her and step back. "I just need to borrow it for a minute."

"No way!" she shrieks.

"Hey, you scratch my back, I'll scratch yours."

She looks at me with uncertainty. "What?"

I roll my eyes and turn to the door. "It's an expression, Julia. Don't get so excited."

She is infuriated by my jab. "Oh, shut up, Danny. Only in your dreams would I ever like you!"

I turn to her, smiling. "Only in my nightmares."

She throws a shoe at me, but misses.

"Nice shirt," I say, not able to help myself, "but you won't want to let your dad see you in that." Then I close the door and head back down the stairs.

* * * *

I take Julia's cell phone outside and sit on the step. Gino isn't home yet, so here on the porch I can talk to Reggie and keep a lookout for my godfather. I can't be certain that Gino's phones aren't bugged by the FBI or that Gino doesn't bug his own phones for any number of reasons. But I think Julia's cell phone should be a relatively safe way to get into contact with Reggie, who is my only advantage in this dangerous game I've decided to play. No one knows that Reggie has been at the diner—not Frank, not the Newcastle Mafia, nobody.

Reggie answers the phone on the second ring.

"Reggie, it's Danny."

"Finally! I almost had a heart-attack last night!" Reggie says.

"I know. That was a close call."

"So the plan—it must have worked, right? I mean, you're okay? I was worried, but my mom mentioned you called, so I figured you were breathing."

"I'm fine," I reply. "But I didn't exactly get out of there undiscovered."

Reggie sucks in air. "No way! What happened?"

"Someone knows about me," I continue, "but it's not the Newcastle Mafia. An undercover FBI agent covered for me."

"Does this 'agent' know about me?"

"No," I answer. "And I'm going to keep it that way. At least for the time being."

"Okay," Reggie agrees. "So what happens next?"

"Nothing. We wait and we watch."

"Shouldn't we—"

"No," I interrupt. "We'll wait."

* * * *

The ride to the hospital is extremely uncomfortable. Portia had come to the door, and when I answered, she had given me a big hug and thanked me for going to the hospital with her. "Tony needs my support, and I need yours," she had said. However, she quickly became guarded when she discovered Julia wanted to ride with us. Portia had nodded and smiled weakly when Julia made the request, but I know she is uneasy around Julia. Portia is a kind, sincere person who likes everyone except people who are exactly the opposite of her—fake, selfish people. Julia certainly fits into the second category, but I'm surprised at how both girls try to act pleasant toward each other. I decide that boys are much more straightforward than girls. That's why women are so frustrating—you never really know where you stand with them.

The car ride is quiet. Joe Saviano is at the wheel of the old Cadillac on which Portia was sunbathing when I first saw her. Portia is silent, although I wonder if this is due to Julia's uninvited presence and not due to Portia's lack of things to say. Portia sits up front next to her father, and Evie and Julia are sandwiching me in the middle seat. It's not a bad place to be, but I'd rather be sitting next to Portia than anyone else. The uncomfortable silence in the Saviano car finally wears on my nerves, which have already taken more abuse than I can stand for one day.

"Portia, did anyone find out what happened to Tony's dad?" I ask, wondering if Mr. Chen's mishap had been traced to the Newcastle Mafia yet.

Portia shakes her head. "I guess he told the police he couldn't identify the men who robbed and attacked him. It's so awful to think that those men might get away with doing such a terrible thing!"

I'm mildly surprised. So Mr. Chen did not alert the police to the Mafia's involvement? That seemed strange after his show of defiance last night. Had Ray frightened him enough to stay quiet?

I try to make small talk with Portia and Evie about various classmates, and I'm always impressed with how kind Portia is, even when gossiping about other people. She's certainly not a spoiled girl, even if she is an only child (as I found out from Vince). Julia snickers from time to time when certain names are mentioned, but for most of the ride, she remains silent. I can only guess what crazy scheme she has put together to sneak out of the house. I feel a little guilty about helping her, but she said she was visiting a friend's mother in the hospital and had thrown a long-sleeved T-shirt over her revealing top, so what else could I say? Ronnie had given her permission, and I have bigger things to worry about than Julia's underhanded schemes.

Julia deserts us the minute Joe puts the car in park. She says she will grab a ride home with her friend and then heads toward the hospital. I glare at her as she walks away because I don't believe her story for one moment. Portia obviously notices me watching Julia leave, because she says, in a resentful voice that is out of character for her, "Do you like her, Danny?"

"No, I think she's trouble," I say quickly. I smile at Portia. "Let's not worry about her. I'm here for *you*, and you're here for Tony. Let's go inside."

Portia returns my smile, and I'm proud of myself for turning a potentially sticky situation around so quickly. The truth is, I can't help but find Julia attractive, but I certainly don't want to do anything more than look at her. When it comes to wanting a girl with whom I could spend quality time, that girl is Portia. Outwardly, she is just as pretty as Julia, but Portia is far ahead in the personality department.

We enter the hospital and quickly find the intensive care unit where Tony's dad is currently undergoing treatment. I see the other three members of the Chen family before they see us. The family looks exhausted. Tony's mother has obviously been crying, and Tony's face is strained with worry. Tony's younger brother seems frightened by the doctors scurrying back and forth and the obvious distress of his mother and older brother.

And suddenly, looking at Mr. Chen's family, I know exactly why Mr. Chen didn't identify his attackers. Family is everything.

* * * *

I stretch out on my bed fully clothed at the Vigliotti house. It's already ten p.m., but I'm a long way off from being able to fall asleep. When I arrived back at the house, Ronnie had immediately asked me where Julia was. I had repeated what Julia had told me—that she would grab a ride home with her friend. I hadn't believed Julia, and now I could tell that Ronnie was regretting her decision to let Julia go out without obtaining any particulars about which friend she was visiting or when she planned to be home. I feel mildly guilty, but I can't take the blame for this one. Julia lied, Ronnie believed her, and whatever else happens is between the two of them—and possibly Gino, if Julia is unlucky.

I'm ridiculously behind on my schoolwork. This is very unlike me, as I have always breezed through my schoolwork and had excellent grades to show for it. The first week of school is almost over, and I have probably done less than a full hour of homework.

I may be able to get away with blowing off my work this week, but next week, if I don't crack down on myself, I'll start to fall even further behind. I'm not going to give the Vigliottis any unnecessary reasons to hand me back over to my mother. Gino's activities may be corrupt, but I cannot willingly let myself be kicked out of a house that is beginning to feel so much like a home. Gino has behaved fatherly toward me, Ronnie has already gone above and beyond my own mother, and Vince is beginning to feel like an older brother. The only Vigliotti who doesn't quite feel like family is Julia, and I know that's probably only because I find her attractive, and thinking of her like a sister, even though we are not related, just makes my attraction feel very wrong.

I think about the Chen family and how they have seemingly pulled together in a very rough situation. I didn't see Mr. Chen tonight, but Tony had described most of his injuries, which made me sick to my stomach all over again. The little brother was particularly difficult to watch—his young face so full of misery was more than enough to haunt me. And Mrs. Chen had appeared strong for her boys, but when she didn't think anyone was watching, her face fell into a look of such desperation that I had fought the urge to go and put my arm around her shoulders. Yet there they were, standing together as a family, and I knew that I had never known the love that these people held between them. The closest I have come to that is living in the Vigliotti house.

I know I will do everything I can to protect the Vigliottis. I don't want any more people to get hurt, but I begged Frank and Pete Alvarez to let me stay as much to help them as to keep an eye out for Gino and his family. My emotions are all twisted inside of me. On the one hand, I cannot ignore the terrible work in which

Gino is involved, but on the other hand, I don't want this family pulled apart in any way. Somehow, I hope that everything will work out so that Gino can get out of the mob, but that the mob itself will be destroyed. And yet, I know that having both of those outcomes is unlikely.

I get up to put my books in my backpack and get ready for bed, thinking about another missed opportunity to connect with Evie tonight. At no time did I have a chance to talk to her without making it look to Portia like I wanted to be alone with Evie for other reasons. I'm working hard to keep Portia from getting the wrong idea.

Lost in thought, I'm just slapping the biology book on top of the algebra book and wondering how I will ever zip my enormously overstuffed backpack, when the lights go out in my room, and a hand on my shoulder spins me around and slams me up against the closet door. In the darkness, my arms are trapped at my side in an iron grip.

Chapter 13

"Vince! What the heck?"

Vince's shadowy, furious face is just inches from my nose. His eyes are blazing, and I have no idea what has made him so angry. He looks like a kid who is ready to beat the crap out of me.

"Where did you go today?" Vince demands, holding me against the closet; although, to be fair, I have yet to struggle.

"What do you mean? You mean just now? I was at the hospital!"

Vince slams me against the closet door again, making a dangerous amount of noise. I'm thankful that Ronnie and Gino are busy worrying about Julia at the moment.

"Not tonight! I mean today! Where did you go during school?"

"Knock it off!" I say, pushing Vince back against the bed. He looks like he is going to rush me, but I put my finger to my lips and move to shut the guest room door, which is still ajar from Vince's abrupt entrance. Vince waits by the bed, his chest heaving and his fists curled into balls at his side.

I switch the light back on, shut the door, and then turn slowly, rubbing my neck. "Geez, Vince, you really should look into a sport like wrestling or something! Just calm down and I'll tell you whatever you want to know," I promise.

"I saw you digging around in Dad's office the other night," Vince accuses. "What were you looking for? What did you find?"

I step back, surprised. I had expected to talk my way out of this one, but now I realize that Vince has been keeping an eye on me. "Why are you watching me, Vince?"

"Answer my questions first!" Vince howls.

I quickly lift my finger to my lips again, but Vince is not settling down. "All right. I was looking for something," I whisper harshly.

We stare at each other, both of us waiting for the other to do something. Vince's obsession with mob movies and his disastrous trip to the diner flashes in my mind. And that's when I know that I'm not the only one who wants to protect Gino. I'm also not the only one in the house that knows Gino is involved in work that isn't just computer networking.

"Vince, I don't want anything to happen to your dad. I'm trying to protect him," I say, trying to feel Vince out.

The anger seems to drain instantly out of Vince. He collapses onto the bed, shaking his head slowly. "All this time, I didn't think anyone would ever find out. All this time Julia and I have been keeping a secret from everyone."

"Julia?" I ask, surprised that the shallow teen has time to worry about her dad's work.

Vince nods. "Yeah. And Mom does too. But I don't think she knows *exactly* what Dad does. And I don't think Dad started this until after they were married. All she knows is that he works for Ray Gallo, but she doesn't know exactly what that means." He glances up at me. "I shouldn't be telling you all this. I don't trust you."

"Someone else *does* know about your dad, Vince. But I'm going to protect him," I say, wondering if I will make good on that promise. I picture the worried faces of the Chen family again, and I don't know which side I'm on.

At that moment, the door opens. Gino stands in the open doorway, and I immediately wonder what he may have heard. I almost involuntarily shrink back, but Vince is immobile. "Is everything all right in here?" he asks us.

"It's fine," I reply quickly.

Gino's eyes narrows. "Even over Julia's whining, I could hear you guys yelling back here."

I think that Gino must also be noticing the strained looks on our faces. I glance at Vince and recognize a look on his face that I had worn on mine not too long ago. Vince wants desperately to please his father, but he doesn't know how to get close to him. I once felt that way about my dad; now I feel nothing toward Del after what he did to me.

But Vince loves Gino despite his mobster ties, perhaps even, to some extent, because of those ties. I don't feel the same way. Although I can't help but feel grateful that Gino saved me from the hands of Barb Kluwer and offered me a home, I also saw Tony's dad beaten almost to death while Gino stood idly by. I feel obligated to protect Gino as much as possible, and yet, my liking for my godfather has altered forever.

"You guys keep it down, okay?" Gino says. "We've got enough going on with Julia sneaking off tonight. She rode with you, didn't she, Danny?"

I put up my hand, as though fending off the accusation. "I got the same story Ronnie did," I say, a little guiltily, but truthfully.

Gino stays for several more silent seconds, as if judging the honesty in my story, and then he turns and leaves the room, shutting the door behind him.

"Who knows about Dad's real job, Danny?" Vince asks after several seconds, his eyes steely as he keeps them on the door.

"The FBI."

Vince appears panicked, as though he will run out of the room and warn his dad right now.

I catch his arm. "Don't tell him, Vince. We can protect him. Everything you guys have—your house, your life, your happiness—it doesn't have to change!"

We stare at each other tensely. Vince finally turns and walks to the door. "You keep me in the loop, okay? I want to help. If you don't, I'll warn my dad, and everything will disappear—for both of us."

I nod. "Well, on that note, I may need your help tomorrow."

Vince's head snaps back around toward me. "Something to do with my dad?"

I smile. "No. This is much more fun. We have a little appointment with an old friend."

* * * *

The next morning, I'm afraid that Julia will not be able to play her part in my little scheme—something Vince and I are calling "Operation Tommy Boy." In fact, Vince and I actually stayed up late last night as I outlined my plan and Vince excitedly endorsed it. Gino and Ronnie had been busy grilling a tired and grumpy Julia, who, as Vince and I had gathered, would be grounded for several weeks to come.

I didn't talk to Julia last night, but as I sit down to inhale a bowl of Cinnamon Swirlers (I have finally found a type of cereal that Vince doesn't particularly care for so that the box will last more than two days), I nudge her on the shoulder. "You still want that scoop?"

She glares at me with a look of pure death, and I take a few bites of sugary cinnamon clusters. After a while, though, I can't help myself. "So, how's your friend's mom?" I ask cheerfully.

I know I shouldn't provoke her, but I don't realize how angry Julia really is. She jumps out of her chair, grabs the half-full bag out of the cereal box, and then, glaring at me, proceeds to grind the sweet little clusters into a sugary cinnamon dust. She throws the bag on the floor and races up the stairs, and Baxter stands still for a moment of canine indecision, his beady little eyes moving from the bag of cereal on the floor to the figure of his mistress disappearing up the stairs. The food wins out, and I watch the dog lap up the tiny sugary crumbs where the bag had popped open on its way to the kitchen floor. Baxter and I enjoy our cereal in silence, although I regret that I will be forced to share Vince's Cocoa Nuggets tomorrow.

The ride to school is no better. Julia sits in the far back, ignoring Vince's teasing and my occasional pleas to still be a part of my plan. When we get to school and Vince drops us off in front, I grab Julia's arm. She struggles to be free of me, but I am much stronger than her.

"Stop it, Julia."

She quits squirming and glares at me. I suddenly notice Portia chatting with her usual group of girls a few yards away, and I quickly drop Julia's arm. "Come on, you need this story to make up for the fallout of me going public about where I'm really from. Just hide behind the bleachers in the gym before ten a.m., during third period, and you'll be able to hear everything."

She continues to glare at me as I walk away, hoping she will stop pouting and show up when she is supposed to. "Operation Tommy Boy" won't be the same without a little school media coverage. I stride toward the group of girls in which Portia and Evie are standing. A few weeks ago, a group of girls like this would have terrified me, but after the events of the past week, I know I have much bigger threats with which to deal.

This is the last day of the first week of school at Newcastle High. Most of the school is buzzing with pre-weekend excitement, but I'm just tired because I have had the most exhausting, most emotional week of my life.

I walk over to Portia. "Hey, how are you doing this morning?"

She glares at me. "Apparently, not as well as you. Seems like you have a little thing going on with Julia."

I roll my eyes. For as great as Portia is, she certainly has her jealous moments. But then I smile, trying a different tactic. A little friendly competition never hurt anyone, right? "What, you jealous?" I ask.

She frowns. "No. Why should I be? It's just—I don't really like her, Danny. She's pretty mean to my friends."

I laugh. "She's mean to everyone! I just need her to do me a favor—that's all."

"Maybe I could help you instead," Portia offers.

I notice Evie watching us with her sharp eyes. I still have not had a chance to speak with her. Then I realize Portia is watching me expectantly. "No. I prefer to keep you out of this." I put my hand on her shoulder as she starts to argue. "Portia, something is going to happen this morning that may make me an outcast here at school."

Evie laughs. "You? An outcast? Hardly! You're quickly becoming the most popular freshman here—especially since Tommy has been hinting he has some dirt on you. It adds to the intrigue."

I glance at Evie when she says this because she sounds like she is trying to warn me. The thing is, I already know what Tommy has on me, and although I might ruin my reputation for a while, revealing my true background will be better than living a lie. I think.

Portia puts her hand on mine, still on her shoulder. "Please, let me help you."

I shake my head. "Just promise you won't abandon me."

She nods. "Promise."

* * * *

After first period class, I make my way to the teachers' lounge, keeping my fingers crossed that a certain teacher, whom I had found out doesn't teach second period, will be in there. I spend the next half hour convincing this teacher to be involved in the plan. This is the most difficult part of my scheme, but it is also the most essential for getting Tommy into the kind of trouble he deserves. I tell the teacher where to meet us in the gym, and then I meet Vince at his locker.

As he and I start toward the gym, I feel almost giddy with relief. As much as I like the attention I'm getting at Newcastle High, I can't enjoy it because I know I'm hiding a very large part of who I am. Maybe the kids here look down on Ridley, but if they like me, then they may see that where I came from doesn't matter. Then again, because I lied, the other students may reject me as someone who tried to be something I'm not. I know it's my own fault for not setting the record straight from the beginning.

Vince and I walk into the deserted gym, our shoes squeaking on the spotless surface. I love being inside a gym. It reminds me of wrestling, a place where I could always prove myself, away from my parents and the gloomy life I had in Ridley. I wonder what wrestling at Newcastle would be like, and I hope I will make the team so I can have the chance to feel the thrill of competition that I love so much.

As we reach the center of the gym, Vince grabs my shoulder. "I hear them outside. What do you want me to do?"

I listen carefully and, sure enough, I can hear the voices of Tommy and one of his friends coming from the hall leading to the locker rooms. "I just need you to back me up. I think Tommy's going to get very angry."

Tommy struts into the gym with a triumphant smile on his face. He and Paul, the shorter teenager who has been involved in all our scuffles so far, walk to the center of the gym and face us. "So, Higgins, you ready to play the game my way?"

I glare at Tommy, but I try to appear defeated, as though I'm giving into his threat of blackmail. "I talked to Mr. Doonesby, Tommy."

"Yeah? And what did he say?" Tommy asks, smirking.

I consider my words carefully. In order for my plan to work, Tommy must admit to trying to cheat and blackmailing me to help him. "What kind of grade in math are you looking for?" I ask.

Tommy continues to smile. "I told you already. An 'A.' Only the best for the best, you know."

I try not to roll my eyes at Tommy's lame remark. "And how much work do you want to do?"

Tommy shakes his head, a look of annoyance passing over his arrogant face. "None! You stupid gutter-rat. I want an easy 'A.' I want a good-grade, no questions asked, no work expected of me. I want the same deal for Paul and Kurt—but Doonesby can give them 'B's for all I care." Paul starts to open his mouth to protest, but Tommy interrupts him. "Hey, you take what I give you, all right," he snaps at his accomplice. "Geez, the lack of gratitude is unbelievable. *I* put this deal together, and I don't want anyone to get too suspicious." He turns back to me. "So Doonesby will agree? He had better, for your sake and his!"

I'm silent for a moment, as if contemplating the terms of the deal. "And you won't tell anyone where I'm from?"

"That's right. As long as you continue to do what I ask," Tommy says, his eyes gleaming with mischief.

I tilt my head thoughtfully. "Hmm, that's what I thought. Somehow I knew you'd want more than one favor. What do you think, Vince? Is that a fair deal?"

Vince shakes his head. He is having trouble concealing his excitement at trapping Tommy in his own words. Tommy notices Vince's barely contained glee, and his eyes narrow. "What's gotten into him?" he asks me.

Right on cue, Mr. Doonesby and Lenny Capriotti, the English teacher, walk out from behind the bleachers, an exultant Julia following behind them.

"Tommy Gallo, I believe the game is up," I say smugly.

Paul is frozen in place as the men approach, but Tommy takes off across the gymnasium, heading for the exit leading to the outside. Vince doesn't hesitate. He races after Tommy and eats the distance between them at an alarming rate for someone so large. Mr. Doonesby races after them both, his long, gangly legs also making up the distance quickly. Vince reaches out to grab Tommy's arm, shouting, "Stop, Gallo!"

Tommy swings around and slams his fist into Vince's nose. Vince reels backward as blood spurts from his nose out onto the gym floor. Tommy is caught off-balance by his own punch, giving Mr. Doonesby the opportunity to grab him as he stumbles backward. Mr. Capriotti catches up with them both seconds later and helps Mr. Doonesby wrestle Tommy to the floor.

"That's enough!" Mr. Capriotti warns. "Hitting another student is grounds for suspension. You better behave yourself if you want to continue to be a student at Newcastle High!"

"I'm telling everyone. Everyone, Danny!" Tommy howls, struggling against the two teachers as they lift him to his feet. "I'm telling them all that you're a filthy gutter-rat!"

"Well, you'd better hurry," I reply. "Because within half an hour, everyone will be reading about it in the school paper."

Tommy momentarily quits thrashing. "What? Who told them?"

I smile at the look of defeat on Tommy's red face. "I did."

Tommy's glares at me, and his voice is deadly calm. "You haven't won, gutter-rat. Everything you have, that family of yours—" Tommy glances at Vince "—it's going down."

"Oh, come on, Gallo," Mr. Doonesby says. "Let's go. You've got enough suspension and detention to keep you occupied for a while. Only the best for the best!" he jokes, and I nod my head to him as a thank you for his help.

I chuckle as Tommy is led away. That is, until Vince points toward the gymnasium doors. Portia stands at the end of the hallway, glaring at me with hurt and anger written across her face, a school newspaper hanging from one hand. Then she turns and disappears from sight.

Chapter 14

"Portia!" I yell, taking off across the gym toward the doors through which Portia has just vanished. My moment of victory over Tommy Gallo is lost in my new desperation to explain my past to Portia before she reads about it in the school newspaper. I had made a deal with Julia for the paper containing my revelation not to be released until lunch, but I now realize I should have told Portia sooner. Much, much sooner.

I pause momentarily as I pass Julia. "I thought you said this was coming out at lunch!" I shout at her.

"It is," Julia replies. "She must have an early copy."

I shoot her a dirty look, knowing that Julia may be the reason Portia has an early copy. I suddenly realize that Portia may be jealous of Julia, but Julia may also be jealous of Portia, merely for the fact that I obviously like Portia. I don't think Julia really likes me, but I do believe she is extremely competitive, and my partiality for Portia seems to have brought her selfishness to a new low.

Third period has just ended, and students cluster in the hall around their lockers staring curiously at me as I rush by them. I am a little relieved to see that no one else seems to have an early copy of the newspaper. I don't catch up to Portia until I reach her locker, where, much to my dismay, she is being comforted by none other than Tony Chen. He has his hand on her shoulder, and she looks like she is about to cry. Tony was almost nice to me at the hospital, but any trace of that friendliness is now gone, replaced by a look of anger and disgust.

I waste no time trying to defend myself to Tony. That would be a useless cause. "Portia," I say softly. "I'm sorry for not telling you sooner. I wanted to, but I thought you'd hate me. Tommy said you would hate me; Julia said you would hate me. I felt like the whole school would look down on me at a time when I didn't think I could handle the teasing I would get as a kid from Ridley. You said you wouldn't abandon me, whatever happened today!"

Portia faces me and puts her hands on her hips. "You know, I thought you were different, Danny! I thought you didn't care what other people thought— that you were just yourself and that you'd look out for the 'little people.' But it turns out you were lying the whole time." Her furious face is inches from mine.

I suddenly have a strange urge to kiss her. Instead, I take a step back. "I just wanted you to like me."

"I did like you! Not because you were supposedly from Boston or because you beat up Tommy Gallo. I liked you because I thought you were a good person. But good people don't lie, Danny! And definitely not to their friends!"

Now I'm staring at the ground. "But I'm from Ridley, and—"

"Who cares?" Portia says, shouting. The stares from other students in the hallway have become even more curious. "I know I don't!" she continues. "Ridley wouldn't have hurt our friendship. But the lying, that ruins it."

Portia turns around and hurries down the hall, Tony following her quickly, after shooting me a disdainful glare. I can't think of anything else I can say to appease her. I feel someone come up behind me and I snap around, still edgy after my emotional showdown with Tommy. Vince stands at my shoulder, watching Portia and Tony continue down the hallway. "You did the right thing," he says.

"What? Lying to her?"

"No—making things right, telling the truth. It was really brave of you, especially with how much you like Portia."

I let out a long, frustrated breath. "Well, I couldn't have kept the act up for long. I don't know anything about Boston!" I pause. "Wait, how did you know I like her?"

"Oh, *please.* Everyone but Portia knows you like her." He turns and looks at the huddle of students watching us intently. He smiles and turns to me. "I feel like I'm a monkey at the zoo. You want to get out of here and go eat lunch?"

"Sure. But aren't you a little concerned I might destroy your reputation? I'm about to become the school outcast."

Vince chuckles. "My reputation? Really, Danny, you have no powers of observation at all. In case you hadn't noticed, I'm not that popular. Welcome to the club."

* * * *

My time as Newcastle High's outcast lasts a day. A long, embarrassing day, but only a day. By lunch, most of the school had learned I lied about the whole Boston thing, which took less than ten minutes after the first students got their hands on a fresh copy of the paper. Vince and I eat lunch together for the first time since I started school, and his humor helps me tune out the murmur of voices and ignore the many glares pointed in my direction.

Portia and Tony avoid me the rest of the day, even when we are in the same class. Evie is the one person who smiles at me, but I figure she may have already known about my past from talking to her dad. I give her credit for not spreading the news sooner. Timing was everything in my plot to trick Tommy.

In fact, my trap for Tommy quickly turns into my salvation. The next day, Julia's story about Tommy's blackmailing and my ingenious setup comes out in the online edition of the paper before first period, and by third period, I am the school hero. Many of the same kids who had whispered behind their hands yesterday actually come up and thank me for catching the "bully." I almost laugh as they congratulate me and give Vince nods of appreciation. The whole entire mess has come full circle in twenty-four hours. High school is a fickle place.

However, even after a few days, Portia continues to avoid me, and, compared with anyone's treatment of me, this hurts me the most. I see Tony and Portia glance up whenever I come to my locker, and then they hurry away before I have a chance to say anything. I am enjoying hanging out with some of the eleventh graders (because, despite Vince's claim of not being popular, he actually has some decent friends and is a persistent ladies man), but I miss my interaction with Portia. I'm depressed to think that I may never have the experience of chatting with her again.

Several weeks pass, but I have no opportunity to observe Gino's criminal activities. Gino goes out at night and gets back late in the morning, and I am busy trying to keep up with the high school workload. Gino is also making himself very likable to me in measurable ways. One day after school, I come home to find that Gino has bought me a new cell phone with a music player and unlimited text messaging. But it's not just the stuff that keeps coming my direction; even though we don't speak much, I always feel that my godfather is watching out for me and protecting me. He talks to me about school and checks up on me—just like a dad should.

In fact, I have almost convinced myself that my two trips to the diner were bad dreams and that Gino isn't doing the things I know he is. I find that I am definitely not making my role of being a spy in the Vigliotti house a priority. I have almost pushed the scenes from the diner out of my mind when I see Tony's dad pick Tony and Portia up from school one day and notice Mr. Chen's face is still black and blue from his brutal beating. The scene from the diner comes back like a blow to my head.

In an effort to distract myself from my conflicting emotions, I talk to Reggie on my new phone a few times a week and find that I miss my old friend as much as I enjoy hanging out with my new ones. I finally decide, on one Saturday a few weeks into September, to persuade Vince to drive over to Ridley with me to meet Reggie.

Unfortunately for me, Vince is not inclined to drive to Ridley, but he does want to make a trip to the mall. I call Reggie and convince him to meet us at the Newcastle Mall.

"But only rich kids shop there, Danny," he complains when I call.

"Come on, Reggie. I'll buy you something."

"I don't need your charity! Don't get all high and mighty on me!"

"Knock it off, Reggie. I was just kidding," I reply. "Just meet us there, okay? I promise, the scenery is great."

"You mean girls?" Reggie asks.

I smile into my phone. "Of course I mean girls."

* * * *

I don't know what I was expecting, but Vince and Reggie are not natural friends. Vince's burly Italian body and moody personality are a sharp contrast to the energetic and lanky Reggie. One has never known what it is like to want something and not get it, and the other has never been given anything he has not earned himself. But both teens make an effort to get along, at least for my sake, even though Vince is not helping the situation by constantly texting me.

"Stop texting me, Vince—I'm right here," I say irritably, even though I am just as guilty. We have been texting each other at the kitchen table for the past few weeks, much to Ronnie's consternation.

Vince scowls when I scold him yet again and pulls out a Snickers, which Reggie and I watch him devour. The mall is quiet, and we are soon bored with the lack of activity and "scenery." I talk Reggie into coming back to the house with Vince and me, although Vince grumbles something under his breath about Reggie's beetle, which is greatly outclassed by the Lexus. To my relief, Reggie doesn't let the older teenager's comment hurt his pride.

"Hey, you take what you can get when the only money you have is from your own piggy bank," Reggie replies.

Vince appears impressed. "You paid for your car by yourself?"

"Absolutely," Reggie says. "If I waited for my parents to help me, I'd be an old man before I got wheels!"

All three of us laugh, but I can tell that Reggie's comment has stirred in Vince a new-found respect for my less than wealthy friend. I ride with Reggie as he follows Vince back to the house, and I have to suppress a small surge of jealousy toward both of my friends; I don't have a car or access to one. Reggie has taught me to drive in a parking lot, but I'm sure I would be rusty by now. My dad has never had any reason to teach me to drive as there is only one car in the Higgins' family.

"Vince has never had to buy a thing for himself, has he?" Reggie asks, interrupting my thoughts.

"I don't think so," I answer and glance at my new cell phone in my hand, realizing I don't have much experience earning my own money either. My circumstances have changed because of whose house I am living in, not because I have worked to change them.

"Just be careful, Danny," Reggie warns. "It's easy to get comfortable with someone taking care of you. But if you let someone do everything for you, you'll never learn to be self sufficient. And besides, remember where all that 'stuff' comes from."

I know Reggie is referencing Gino's illegal activities, but instead of acknowledging the warning, I feel defensive for myself and my new family. "Take it easy, Reggie," I say. "It's not a big deal."

Reggie shoots me an irritated look, and we spend the rest of the trip in silence. As we pull into the Vigliotti driveway, Reggie exclaims over the size of the house, but I barely register my friend's amazement. I am staring at a very familiar BMW parked outside the Vigliotti house.

"Reggie, Frank's here."

Reggie's eyes widen. "The agent?"

I nod and am suddenly panicked. "We shouldn't have brought this car here! Frank and Gino didn't see it, I don't think, but if anyone else were to drop by—"

"Do other mobsters drop by often?" Reggie interrupts, his movements becoming agitated as he starts to put the key back in the ignition.

"No, no one else that I know of. Even so, maybe we should park this down the road," I reason.

"No, Danny. In this neighborhood? My car sticks out as much as I do!" He shakes his head. "No, I'm going home."

"You don't want to come in?" I ask, desperate to show my new home to Reggie. I realize I want someone from my old life to tell the others at Ridley how well I am doing, and I suddenly feel slightly ashamed of my motives.

"I can pretty much guess what it's like, Danny," Reggie answers quietly.

"Do you respect me at all? I feel like you're disappointed in me—both as a person and as a friend," I accuse, not even realizing I feel this way until I say it out loud.

"I *do* respect you, Danny. You've been thrown some real hardballs in your life," Reggie says, and I nod in agreement. It feels good to have someone acknowledge my challenges.

"But you've got to be careful," Reggie continues. "And you've got to stay true to yourself. The Danny I know has always done what's right, and he's always stood up for the people that need help defeating the bullies in this world. Don't let all this 'stuff' change that."

I nod again, but I don't respond. I get out of the car and shut the door, feeling that I have let my friend down. Reggie is right—having 'stuff' makes it harder for me to see the world as black and white like I did when I was poor. Now that my lifestyle is tied to Gino's livelihood, I'm not so ready to separate good and evil. But it is more than just the things; I like my new family. I still like Gino, even though I know what my godfather does is wrong. How can I betray the family who gave me a home when my life was falling apart? My world has become much more complicated.

* * * *

A few hours later, I sit in the kitchen, frustrated and bored. Frank and Gino left almost as soon as I walked into the house, and the house has been quiet now for several hours. Vince is sleeping on the sofa in the living room, and Ronnie and Julia (who has recently been released from her grounding) are now at the mall shopping.

I am about to go wake up Vince so we can play video games, when I hear the front door open. I wait to see who it is, but as soon as I hear several men's voices, I race to my bedroom. I don't want to come face to face with any of the mobsters I saw at the diner last month; I am afraid my face will betray me. I'm really not a great actor.

Standing in my bedroom, I crack the door. The living room lies to the side of the kitchen, and I can see Vince sprawled across the sofa, snoring loud enough that Baxter occasionally yaps at him and licks his hand, even though Vince doesn't respond to the small dog's attention. I step back as I see Gino enter the living room and shake Vince awake.

"Go upstairs if you're going to sleep. You're drooling on the sofa," Gino growls.

Vince grumpily heaves himself from the sofa and tromps up the stairs. When I see Gino head in my direction, I step away from the door and rush to the bed, leaping on it. I arrange my limbs haphazardly so that I look as though I have been sleeping, and then I turn my head away from the door and close my eyes.

Two seconds later, Gino sticks his head in the room. I can feel his presence as he stands in the doorway silently, and I hope that I can at least convince my godfather that I am asleep. My acting seems to work, because a couple of seconds later, Gino leaves the room, closing the door behind him.

This is it! I think excitedly. Maybe these guys are going to talk mob business. I creep to the door and open it the slightest crack, and when the door doesn't creak, I thank Ronnie silently for her impeccable homemaking skills. As my eyes find Gino at the kitchen table, I realize Frank is not with the group. The man Ray referred to as "Donny" is also sitting at the table across from Gino, but I am more surprised by the third man at the table—Joe Saviano.

What is Portia's dad doing here? I ask myself, thinking that Portia's gruff car salesman father has never seemed a likely member of the Mafia. But he certainly is hanging out with the right people—or the wrong people, I guess.

Against my better judgment, I decide I need to get closer. I scurry through my room into the bathroom, which has another entrance that leads into a room Ronnie has designated her "activity" space. She is a woman of many hobbies. Beaded napkin rings and fluffy pillows are just a few items I have noticed emerge from this room in the past week. But at the moment, Ronnie's room is serving as an alternate route for me. I slip through the room and into the hall and head to the foyer. From there, I pass Gino's office and creep near the kitchen.

As I reach the hall leading to the kitchen, I try to keep my breathing as quiet as possible. I can now hear the men's voices. I think for a brief moment that I may hide in the utility closet, but I want to be able to escape quickly, so I wait around the corner from the kitchen, listening to the muffled conversation.

"I hate meeting here," Donny says. "I don't think it's safe."

Gino huffs. "Shut up, Donny. This place is secure. It's your fancy apartment I'm worried about. So many girls go in and out of there, you have no idea if it's safe to talk business."

Donny starts to grumble, but he is interrupted by the low, gruff voice of Joe. "What's the deal, Gino? You going to leave Chen alone?"

Gino sighs. "I want to let this Chen thing go. I don't like beating up helpless old men who aren't scumbags. I'd have no problem hurting him if he were like half the riffraff we deal with on a daily basis—most of them are robbing their customers, so it's only fair we charge them in return. But Chen is a good man, and I'm tired of harassing him. Especially since he's your friend, Joe."

"I'm not tired of harassing him," Donny cuts in. "He owes us money, and he'd better pay. You've got a problem with being soft, Gino. I'd cut it out. Ray doesn't want a do-gooder workin' for him. Do-gooders don't make money."

"I agree with Gino," Joe says. "I need the money more than both of you, but Chen is a friend of my family, and I want him left alone. What happened the other night—that can't ever happen again."

Donny beats his fist on the kitchen table. "You don't call orders, Joe! Or did you forget? You're nobody! You're at the bottom of the food chain! I don't care who your friends are! I want my money, and I'll beat the living daylights out of anyone who stands in my way!"

"*Shut up*, Donny!" Gino says, keeping his voice low but firm. "Don't talk that way. Joe is a huge earner for us with that car lot. We work a lot of money through that place."

"I just don't want him telling me what I can do," Donny replies sullenly.

"Just keep it down, okay? Last thing I need is for one of my kids to hear you!" Gino says even more softly.

"Like Danny?" Donny asks. "Still can't believe he's Penny's son. She's a pretty gutsy babe to take off like she did."

"Shhhh! I said I don't want him to hear you! That kid has been through enough; he doesn't need to hear wiseguys reminiscing about his mother."

Donny laughs. "Kinda hard not to."

"Can we get back to the matter at hand?" Joe interjects. "Please, just leave Chen alone. There are plenty more fish in the sea."

"Yeah, I'm okay with that," Gino replies. "In fact, kudos to him for beating us at our own game. He's paid a big enough price already. We'll leave him be."

Donny clicks his tongue in frustration. "You're stupid for giving up good business. Ray will be angry."

"He won't find out for a while," Gino reasons.

"Maybe. But he will find out soon enough," Donny warns.

It's then that I realize the conversation is over. As I hear the chairs drag back from the table, I leap into motion and dash to my room, confusion and questions swirling in my head.

Chapter 15

Over the next week, I go through the motions at school, getting my work completed and hanging out with Vince at lunch. I visit the workout room after school to prepare for the wrestling tryouts being held at the end of the month, and Vince usually joins me, even though he only tried wrestling for one season in middle school and doesn't care about making the team. I know I have a big hurdle to overcome—Tommy Gallo is in my same weight class, and although he is in detention nearly every day now, he is a state championship wrestler and still favored by the coach.

The words that were spoken about my mother haunt me. I find my mind drifting off in class, wondering how my mom is known not only to Gino, but also to the other wiseguys in the Newcastle Mafia. I wish my mom would visit now; I would demand that she tell me how she is involved in all this. I momentarily speculate that my dad may have had some Mafia ties, but when I think about my dad's job at Save-Much and our family's poor living conditions, I quickly rule out any association with the mob.

On Friday, I trudge to my locker after algebra and am pleasantly surprised to see Portia standing next to it. I have heard from Julia that neither she nor Portia won the role of Juliet. Knowing how disappointed Portia must be, I have wanted to cheer her up. I miss her. But Portia still hasn't spoken two words to me since my public exposure. She isn't smiling, but she doesn't appear angry either. She looks worried.

"Hi, Danny," she says.

"Hey, how are you doing?" I ask, elated that she has actually sought me out.

"I'm fine," she replies, pausing for a moment, as if struggling with what to say. "Look, I'm still really angry with you, and I still don't want to hang out." My smile falters at her words. "But I had to tell you something," she continues. "I saw Tommy at your locker a few minutes ago. I think he robbed you."

"Tommy Gallo was in my locker? That's not possible! It's got a key lock!" I motion to my padlock in frustration.

Portia steps back from me. "Don't yell at me! I'm only telling you what I saw!"

I quickly adjust the tone of my voice. "I'm sorry— I didn't mean I didn't believe you. I'm just not sure how he could do it."

She motions to my locker. "You better check to make sure everything is there."

A pang of anxiety hits my stomach instantly. "My wallet!"

"You left your wallet in your locker?"

"I know—it's stupid!" I say as I move to my locker. "But Vince likes to take it when I'm not looking and steal my money, which he says is really his money, and, well, never mind." I pull the key out of my backpack, but I quickly realize I don't need it; the lock has been picked open. I quickly fling the door open and search the spot where I usually stuff my wallet. My heart sinks.

"Is it gone?" Portia asks.

I stare at her blankly. I'm not worried about the forty dollars or the credit card that Tommy probably won't use. I'm thinking about a sensitive business card that was handed to me by Detective Alvarez.

"Danny, is it gone?" Portia asks more forcefully.

I finally focus my eyes and nod.

"Then you had better go report it. I'll go with you and tell them what I saw." She starts to walk past me toward the principal's office, but I reach out and grab her arm.

"No, Portia."

Portia jerks away from me. "What?"

"No, I'm going to handle this myself."

"Are you kidding me?" she asks. "You'll handle it? You'll *handle* it? You are such an idiot, Danny! I don't know what I ever saw in you!" She stalks away from me, but not before I see tears coming down her face.

"I'm sorry, Portia. For everything," I call, not knowing what else I can say.

She continues down the hall, not acknowledging my apology. I want to chase her down, but I can't now. I have a huge problem, and once again, it starts with the name Tommy Gallo.

* * * *

Vince drives the Lexus slowly down the road, peering into the darkness because we have decided to leave the headlights off. I can't believe we are creeping along in the Gallo's neighborhood at one a.m. in the morning, but sure enough, a few rash decisions have led me quickly to this point. I decided to tell Vince about the robbery; however, I want to get the wallet back myself.

"So your wallet has something in it that might compromise my dad?" Vince asks me for the tenth time that evening. He is angry.

"I told you, Tommy will never figure out anything unless he finds the card behind my ID, and then he actually has to call that number. The only person it could possibly compromise is me, but because I'm connected to your dad, I don't want to take the chance."

"And you don't want my dad to find out you're a rat."

I glare at Vince. This is the first time he has called me that name. I have tried to not consider myself a rat, despite the circumstances, but Vince's accusation frustrates me.

"Don't call me that! I'm caught in a tough situation right now. I'm trying to protect your dad!"

Vince shakes his head. "Well, you're doing a terrible job."

"Just shut up and drive," I say, wishing I could keep my emotions under control. I need Vince's help right now.

"*Fine*," Vince answers. "Whatever you want, *boss*."

I can't help but recognize Vince's sarcastic reference to the mob, but I keep my angry comeback to myself and instead try to figure out which gigantic house belongs to the Gallos. I look up from the paper I hold in my lap. "I think we're almost there—just a few more houses."

"You're sure no one's home?" Vince asks, the first indication that he is uneasy about this scheme.

"I'm positive. I asked Tommy's friend Paul where he was because I needed to speak with Tommy. He said they were going to Tommy's grandmother's house for the weekend."

"Maybe it's a trap," Vince offers.

I shake my head. "I don't think so. You're giving Paul too much credit."

"And you're breaking and entering how?"

"I don't have to." I hold up a key.

"You have a key?" Vince asks in disbelief. "And how about an alarm?"

I hold up a piece of paper in my other hand. "I got really, really lucky. I saw this stuff in a plastic baggie when I was snooping in your dad's office last month. I don't know what your dad does for this guy, but Ray must really trust him. They were in a locked box under the desk, which I opened with a key in a drawer. People never hide keys very well. I remembered the baggie today when Portia told me about the robbery."

Vince shakes his head and chuckles. "Sometimes I don't like you, Danny. But man, you are crafty. Better not let my dad catch you pinching stuff from his office, though."

"Yeah, I wouldn't want to have to explain *that* to him."

We both laugh, easing the tension between us.

"Let me help you," Vince says finally.

"No, I need you to be a lookout and call me on my cell phone if you see anyone. I'm not dragging you or Gino into this any further."

"In a way, we may have dragged you into this," Vince counters, strangely thoughtful.

"Maybe," I reply. "But like I said, I'm doing my best to protect you." I point to a large brick colonial house on the left. "There it is. Stop here."

* * * *

I creep up to the front door and listen carefully. This plan is crazy, and I'm starting to lose some of my nerve. A dog in the backyard lets out a few half-hearted barks, but the house seems deserted. I punch the Gallo's number into my cell phone and wait. I can hear the phone ringing in the house, but after the fifth jingle, the answer machine picks up.

I snap my phone shut and insert the key in the lock, apprehensively wondering if it will open the door. I breathe easier as the key turns first the knob lock and then the bolt lock, and I take a deep breath and open the door, immediately scanning the foyer for the alarm security box. I find it to my right, the red light blinking in warning. Taking two steps toward it, I quickly punch in the security code. The light stops flashing but remains red. A prompt comes up on the digital screen: "Please type password."

I immediately panic. Here I am, breaking the law, and if I don't think of something quickly, I might get caught. My brain races, making me wonder how many password tries I will get before the alarm goes off and I have to run for the Lexus. I take another deep breath and punch the only word I can think of at that moment: "T-O-M-M-Y."

I must be on a lucky streak. The light changes to green and the words "Thank you" drift across the digital screen. I fall back against the wall, relieved and surprised that Ray Gallo would pick such a weak password.

"Well, well, nice guess. I'll have to tell Ray Gallo that his password is inadequate."

I flinch at the sound of a familiar and unwelcome voice and quickly flick the light switch next to my hand. The brightness illuminates the unpleasantly bird-like face of Barb Kluwer.

"What's going on?" I ask, angry and defeated all at once.

"Perhaps *you* should tell *me* what's going on. Ray invited me to his home. I don't believe you were invited."

"Tommy stole my wallet. I need it back." I pause when I see the pleased look on her face. "But you knew that already."

"Perhaps," she replies, not a hint of surprise in her voice, "a little bird told me. You played right into our hands, Danny. Why not just tell an adult about the wallet?"

"This is between me and Tommy," I say furiously.

"Oh, really?" Barb laughs in a way that makes me again want to shove her. "I thought it might have been because of this." She holds up a small business card with the name "Pete Alvarez" on it. I grimace, knowing that my connection to the Newcastle police has been discovered.

"Tommy's a good boy—he showed his father this card in your wallet because they know Pete's a cop. Ray contacted me to see if it might just be something from your little scuffle at home. You see, the Gallos have been very interested in your arrival at the Vigliottis. I told them I would talk to you, but I knew that you didn't have any interaction with the police, by your own choice, of course. Besides, Alvarez is a Newcastle man, not a Ridley man." She sighs and narrows her eyes. "I'm very interested by what appears to be a little espionage," she continues, her strident voice crooning with triumph. "Here I was, thinking you were such a lucky boy to be rescued by a well-to-do family like the Vigliottis, and yet I find that you are ratting on them, betraying their kindness to the police."

"I am not betraying them!" I exclaim, my rage now almost completely out of control. "They want information, but I won't betray Gino!"

"They?" she asks innocently.

I fall silent, aware that I have confirmed her accusation.

"Oh, don't worry," she says cheerfully. "We already know that there's an undercover cop somewhere within the organization. There are so many new associates, it's hard to tell who he may be, but we're getting closer. Perhaps you know?"

"I don't know," I lie. "They didn't tell me."

"Hmm, I think you're lying, Danny," she says, her eyes narrowing on my face. "I hear you've been doing an awful lot of that these days."

I want to say something really nasty to her, but I catch myself. I'm playing right into her game—she is trying to make me angry. If I want to win this battle of wills, I need to play it smart. "I don't know who the undercover is, but I'm trying to find out so I can protect Gino."

"If you're not careful, you're the one who is going to need protection," she says, smiling. "I hear Gino was responsible for taking care of a rat not too long ago. He takes tattlers very seriously. So does Ray Gallo."

I try not to show her my uneasiness. I wonder if she is telling the truth about Gino killing a rat. I change the subject. "So, I see you've got plenty to hide as well. I knew Capriotti was dirty, but now I see you're involved in all this too. I could tell them, you know."

She chuckles. "Well, you could. But then I would be forced to inform Gino of your true loyalties. I'm afraid he would be very disappointed in his godson."

"He would never hurt me."

"Really? I wouldn't be so sure. His allegiance is to his family and the Mafia. And you haven't exactly proven yourself trustworthy." She motions to the paper and key in my hands. "I'm pretty sure he didn't exactly hand those over to you. Although, I must say, even though we expected you to show up after you questioned Paul, I had no idea that you would take Gino's private items to get in here."

I shake my head in frustration, ashamed of myself but not wanting to show it. "What do you want from me?"

She eyes me intently. This is the question for which she has obviously been waiting. "So many things, Danny. You're an important key to this whole organization. But for the moment, my silence can be bought with two items. Two items that will keep me and my boss from saying anything 'unfortunate' about you to Ray or, more importantly, Gino, whom Ray still trusts completely."

I say nothing. I feel helpless, as though the door I have chosen has opened into a gaping, black hole from which I can't escape.

"I need you to find out who the undercover person is from your little friends at the police department," Barb says. "And then, I want you to get us Tony Chen's laptop."

"What?"

"Yes. You see, it seems as though Mister Chen is selling his son's protection software to some of Ray's clients. We need Tony's laptop. If you don't help us, we'll just take it ourselves—and maybe take the whole family out while we're at it."

I stare at her in disbelief. "Why? Why would you kill an entire family?"

"This is big money," Barb replies. "More than your tiny brain could ever imagine. We're not letting one little family stand in our way." She sneers at me. "And we're not letting you stand in our way either." Next she pulls my wallet out of her pocket and puts the business card back behind my ID. "You've got three days, Danny. That's it. Then I'll tell Gino and Ray you're a rat. On Tuesday morning you will meet me at the Newcastle Mall and turn over both the computer and the name of the undercover."

I glare at her, agreeing to nothing.

She holds out my wallet. "Do what you're told, Danny. Stop trying to be a hero. It didn't work for your dad, and it won't work for you."

"My dad's not a hero, not even close," I counter, snatching the wallet from her claw-like fingers.

"Not that one," she says, and then she cackles at the look of confusion crossing my face. "You had better go—I don't want your buddy to get suspicious."

I don't move. "What did you mean about my dad?"

Her face contorts unattractively. "All these father figures—and not one of them good. Poor boy."

I wait for her to say more, but she just leans quietly up against the stair rail and grins at me. "This is not over. I won't let you win," I tell her bitterly.

"Oh, you're right about that, Danny. It's not over. We will use you however we see fit. You may have escaped me once, but it won't happen again."

"Why won't you leave me alone?"

She sneers. "We will—eventually. When you are of no further worth."

I scowl at her and then hurry out the door, desperate to get away from a mess I may never escape.

Chapter 16

I climb into the Lexus, feeling like I have just been shot.

"Well?" Vince asks, his face as serious as the night he tried to attack me.

"I got it," I reply, holding up the wallet.

Vince nods, but he doesn't fire up the SUV. "You're awfully serious for someone who just had a successful break-in. I thought you'd be all excited. What's up?"

"Nothing," I snap; I'm spinning out of control.

"Did you run into their Rottweiler?"

I spin around to face him. "They have a Rottweiler? That might have been important information for me to know!" I am definitely overreacting, but the truth is, I can't check my emotions at the moment.

"Hey, take it easy!" Vince snaps back. "You didn't run into any trouble, right?"

I shake my head and turn to look out the window, making myself live yet another lie. "No, it's fine. I'm just—I'm just tired of all this nonsense with Tommy."

Vince puts the SUV in drive and speeds quickly out of the neighborhood, seemingly oblivious to our earlier goal to not raise suspicion with the neighbors. But I don't care at the moment. The truth is, I did run into trouble, and I think an encounter with the Gallo's vicious dog might have been preferable to the meeting I had just had with Barb Kluwer.

I can't believe that I am getting blackmailed for the second time in less than a month, and I can't tell

Vince because I know his loyalties are to his dad first. If I tell Vince what Barb wants, Vince will urge me to divulge the undercover's name and take the computer just to make sure Gino doesn't get into any trouble with the mob underboss. But I know I can never give up Frank's name to that woman. Not only would Frank be as good as dead, Gino might die too because he brought Frank under his wing. I'm relieved that Barb and the others think the undercover is a cop; however, someone may suspect Frank. And I know I must warn him before the wiseguys figure out who the spy is among them.

* * * *

Finding a way to contact Pete Alvarez on Sunday is more difficult than I thought it would be. Julia's cell phone is practically an extension of her ear, and I don't want to ask Vince because this might raise a bunch of questions I won't be able to answer. I can't use the house phone or my phone because I don't know who might be listening to my call. It's possible, maybe unlikely, but possible. Eventually, I decide to go to a pay phone, but by the time I go with the Vigliottis to church and have Sunday dinner, I have already lost a decent portion of the afternoon. Finally, I use my cell phone to call the one person I had really hoped to avoid until I figured this whole mess out.

Reggie picks up on the third ring.

"You guys are really dropping the ball. I've never waited for three rings before," I joke.

"Hey, Danny," Reggie says, his voice lacking enthusiasm. "What's up?"

"I need your help."

Reggie sighs. "What is it this time? I was grounded for three weeks last time you needed my help. And what could you possibly want from me? I've seen your place, Danny. Remember? You've got everything you want."

"Knock it off, Reggie. I really, really need a friend right now," I say, trying to express in the tone of my voice everything I can't say out loud. "Please come get me."

Reggie groans. "Fine. But I'm taking my mom's car. I don't need to get knocked off by the mob."

I mildly control my frustration. "Just come get me. I'll reimburse you for gas."

"How about my homework? Will you do that too?" Reggie's voice is oozing sarcasm.

"Just come get me." I snap my cell phone shut with more force than necessary and glare at Baxter, who wags his tail happily, despite my scowl.

"Baxter, I feel like I'm you and everyone else is Tommy Gallo's Rottweiler." I pat his tiny head then walk outside to wait for Reggie.

Thirty minutes later, my friend arrives in an old Toyota Camry. He is in no better mood than he was on the phone. "Where are we going?" Reggie asks. "The mall? Are you going to buy me something nice?"

I slam the door, my anger starting to spill over despite my determination to control it. "Gas station on the corner."

"I came all the way here just to drive you to the gas station?" Reggie complains bitterly as he pulls away from the curb and starts down the street. "Couldn't you get your spoiled 'brother' to take you?"

I've finally had it. "Enough, Reggie! I am asking you as a friend to help me. I'm in a lot of trouble, and I need it to look like I'm out with a friend. You *are* my friend, right?"

Reggie rolls his eyes. "You tell me. You're the one who left, Danny. You left and now you're all wrapped up in your new life as the son of a mobster."

"Gino's not my dad. And now I'm in a big mess." I pause, trying to figure out what I should tell Reggie. "The district attorney's assistant knows about the undercover agent, except she wants to expose him to Ray Gallo. She wants me to help her do that in addition to doing some other things for her."

"Other things?"

"She wants me to steal a laptop, too. If I don't, she's going to tell Gino and Ray about my connection to the police. Reggie, I don't know what they will do! Well, scratch that—I have a feeling I know what Ray will do."

Reggie smashes his hands angrily against the steering wheel. "Are you kidding me? What is wrong with you, Danny? You've got to get out of this!"

"What do you mean?"

Reggie slams on his brakes in front of the gas station. "Just tell the agent you're in trouble and you need to get out of the Vigliotti house."

"Are you joking? I'm not leaving the Vigliottis. I need to protect Gino, like he protected me!" I counter.

"No, Danny. You need to protect yourself *and* do what's right. Get out of there!"

I want to beat the dashboard. "You don't understand! If they take me away from here, I won't see anyone again, including you!"

"Well, that won't be much different from how things are now, will it?" Reggie retorts. "You're becoming just like them, Danny. You're practically one of them."

"What? A mobster? How can you even say that? I've always done the right thing!"

"Really? Take a good look at who you're protecting, Danny. Whether by accident or not, you're now a part of the Newcastle Mob."

"That's not true," I shoot back, but I don't know what else I can say to defend myself.

We glare at each other for a few minutes. I am furious with Reggie's lack of support, and I don't feel like I can count on anyone now. I decide to do what I had planned to do, even though I'm losing trust in my friend. I pull a piece of paper out of my wallet.

"What are you doing?" Reggie asks suspiciously.

I place the piece of paper in his cup holder. "It's a phone number. If anything happens to me, I want you to call this person and tell him everything you saw that night you joined me in the diner. But only if I disappear, okay? Not before that."

He shrugs. "Why shouldn't I call it now?"

"Because, if you've stopped being my friend, at least be loyal enough to help me one last time." Opening the door, I climb out quickly. "Just go home, Reggie. I guess I'm on my own." I slam the door and walk away, and my one-time best friend drives away.

* * * *

Reaching Agent Frank McCoy turns out to be much easier than I had expected. I call Pete Alvarez from the pay phone at the gas station, only to find out that Frank is in his office. The hard part is getting Frank to listen to me.

"Frank, you've got to get out. Ray knows there's an undercover."

"Really? This is bad news."

"I know," I agree. "You've got to get out."

"Get out? Now? They don't suspect it's me, do they? I've been in a while."

"They suspect everybody," I answer. "They don't know who it is. But they want me to tell them."

"Then you've got to leave," Frank states.

I feared this would be his reaction. "I'm not leaving. I told them I don't know who it is."

"It's too dangerous, Danny. You're leaving."

"No! I'm not."

"If I have to kidnap you myself, I'm getting you out of there," Frank warns.

I think fast. If I want to stay with the Vigliottis, I'll have to come up with another plan. "All right! Fine!" I say, making my voice sound angry. At this point, it's not difficult. "I'll leave. You can pick me up Wednesday after school."

"No, I'll pick you up tomorrow."

"Wednesday—or I'm running away," I threaten.

"You're such a brat, Danny. Fine, I'll pick you up Wednesday."

I hang up the phone. Another pointless conversation, and now I am running out of time and allies. I need help, and I can't turn to the Vigliottis, my law enforcement contacts, or my best friend. I'm trapped.

"Hey, Danny. What are you doing here? I thought you were going somewhere with your friend."

I spin to find Gino behind me and plaster a smile on my face. "Oh, he got a call from his mom to come home and finish his homework," I explain. "I told him to drop me here. I was trying to call Vince to come take me home because I left my cell phone at the house." I almost shake my head. I am getting so good at lying that I am starting to convince myself my made-up stories are true.

"Well, then, I guess it's your lucky day," Gino says, pointing to the Lexus. "'Cause I'm headed that way myself."

I can't help but grin, and I follow Gino to the SUV. I feel content when I'm around Gino. Despite everything I now know about my godfather, I have to admit that I like being around him, and maybe, he actually likes having me around too. This is such a good feeling for me; I never felt wanted by my dad. That's why I feel so strongly about protecting Gino. Above everything else, I owe him for giving me a family.

I lean back on the seat and sigh.

"What is it?" Gino asks, smiling at me.

I grin back. "I love this car. Especially when I don't have to worry about a bloody head."

Gino chuckles. "That was an interesting night."

All of a sudden I feel brave. "Barb Kluwer was terrible. I wonder what ever happened to her," I say casually.

But Gino's face is unreadable. "I don't know. She wasn't my favorite person either. Thankfully, her claim on you wasn't as good as mine." He smiles again. "Are you going to try out for wrestling at Newcastle High?" he asks, changing the subject abruptly.

"Yeah, I think so. Practice begins next week. It's too bad Vince—"

"Vince doesn't like sports," Gino interjects. "There's nothing we can do about that." His voice is tinged with irritation.

"I know. I just think he could be good—he's amazingly fast and has great fighting skills," I say, but I notice that Gino's face is still hard. I pause for a moment, wanting to change the subject and wondering how I can bring up something that has been on my mind since the day I saw Gino, Joe, and Donny in the Vigliotti kitchen. I try an angle I think might get me there. "Do you know what's going on with my parents?"

Gino shakes his head. "I don't really." He pauses. "I'm going to be straight with you, Danny, because I know you're old enough to understand this. I want to warn you that your parents may not stay together."

I don't mean to laugh, but I can't help myself.

Gino scrutinizes me carefully.

"I'm sorry," I say. "It's not funny. It's just, they were never a good match—I'm almost relieved it's over." I choose my next words carefully. "Mom was never happy with him. I think she must have had another life before that one."

Gino nods. "Your mom was very different before she met Del. I think he was an escape for her."

"An escape from what?" I ask quickly.

Gino scowls, as if knowing he may have revealed too much. "A life she wasn't sure she wanted," he answers carefully.

"Well, she didn't end up wanting Dad. But, with the way he's treated me, he's not really my dad."

"No, he's not really, is he?" Gino asks rhetorically as he pulls the Lexus into the driveway. Before I have a chance to say more, Gino is out of the car and headed for the door.

"You have to tell me about her eventually," I say to the empty car.

Penny Higgins has a hidden past, and as her son, I want to know what that is.

Chapter 17

Monday morning brings no answers for me. I have less than two days to figure out how to handle Barb's blackmailing. I'm not giving her or Ray Gallo what they want, but if I don't, Gino might kick me out for good. And the Chen family will be dead. My options are so limited; I can't trust any Vigliotti with this information, Reggie has disentangled himself from the sticky situation, and Frank is ignoring his own danger and my desires to stay put. For the first time since my dad attacked Mr. Doonesby, I feel completely, hopelessly alone.

Second period is usually a high point in my day. Mr. Capriotti's English class is fun because I often find myself enjoying the class discussions. I'm even finding that I like to write because it helps me cope with some of the anger I feel every day because my parents don't seem to care whether I'm around or not. Not that I want to be with them; my new life, even with all of its drama, is great. I just want to make sure it stays that way.

But today, I'm having trouble concentrating, and by the end of class, Mr. Capriotti is somehow aware of my struggle. "Danny," the teacher calls as students gather their items and leave the room. "Can I see you a moment?"

I instantly regret my lack of focus. I don't need trouble now—my plate is well beyond full already. I trudge to the front of the room, trying not to show my frustration.

"What's up, Danny?" Lenny Capriotti asks, his dark eyebrows arching questioningly. "You're usually right in the middle of our class debates. Today you're a zombie."

I shake my head. "Sorry. It's been a tough week."

"It's Monday, Danny."

I shrug. "I know. And it's been a tough week," I repeat, aggravated that Mr. Capriotti feels the need to interrogate me.

Mr. Capriotti leans back in his chair and studies me thoughtfully. "Do you know my brother?"

I try not to jerk with surprise. I'm definitely not expecting the question, and right now, the issue is a little sensitive. His brother's assistant is blackmailing me, so I don't exactly have warm, cuddly feelings toward Mark Capriotti at the moment. "What? Why?"

"I stopped by my brother's house on the way home last night. I've been trying to have a better relationship with him, although right now the effort is all one-sided. But I could have sworn I heard him mention your name when he was on the phone."

"Really? How strange," I say, not thinking this was strange at all.

"Yeah, maybe I misunderstood him," Mr. Capriotti says. "He blew off our plans to go to a game tonight to go to a business dinner instead. Typical."

I'm beginning to feel uncomfortable with Mr. Capriotti's personal sharing. I'm sure he's doing it to draw me out, but I wish he'd leave me alone. "That sucks. Too bad, since you're trying so hard to get to know him."

"Yeah, it stinks," Mr. Capriotti agrees, and then he laughs harshly. "Apparently, he'd rather spend time with Tommy Gallo's dad than his own brother. How's that for cruel justice?"

I stare at Mr. Capriotti with an intensity I can't hide. "What? He's getting together with Mister Gallo tonight?" My voice seems to have traveled up an entire octave, but I'm too focused to care.

Mr. Capriotti shrugs. "Oh, I don't know. That's what it sounded like. Of all the people! He'd rather go to a dinky diner than to a baseball game with me!"

I start to back away. "I gotta go. I promise I'll try to do better next time."

"Yeah, okay. Sorry for the whining. I'm sure you've got plenty of other things to worry about."

"It's okay. Don't worry about it. We all have our family issues." I try to sound reassuring while at the same time backing out of the room. I finally reach the door and hurry out, relieved to be away from my teacher so I can think about the new information I stumbled on.

Mark Capriotti and Ray are going to meet. This is a big deal—something I'm sure the district attorney had never meant for his brother to overhear. And my teacher, Mr. Capriotti, had probably no idea how important this information is. I can almost hear Reggie urging me to tell Frank about the meeting so the FBI and police could catch Mark Capriotti in the act. But what if Gino is there? He could be caught too, and although my godfather might deserve to be arrested, I can't be the reason Gino is caught. Gino saved me from Barb Kluwer; I owe him my life, in a way. I can't betray him—right or wrong. Debts like that can't be forgotten.

The information is enough for me to design a new game plan. True, most of the people I would have trusted in my present crises are now unavailable to me or unwilling to help me do what I want to do—that is, protect Gino, Frank, and the Chen family all at once. But I don't have time to sit and feel sorry for myself. My time is short, and I must work quickly. That leaves only one option—resurrecting old friendships and taking on the Newcastle Mafia's underboss with a small advantage—the element of surprise.

After third period ends, I stand next to Portia's locker, knowing she and Tony swap their books after their first three classes. I must talk to them both, but I'm not expecting any miracles. And their helping me would be just that—a miracle.

Sure enough, Portia and Tony are headed in my direction less than a minute later. When they see me, neither looks pleased. I know if they hadn't needed to change their books they would have turned and walked away from me, but at the moment, they are trapped. They walk slowly toward me, Tony scowling and Portia's expression worried and angry. As they come closer, Portia confronts me. "What do you want, Danny?"

"Hey, Portia, I'm going to get a drink of water. I'll come back when he leaves," Tony announces ungraciously.

"No. I need to talk to both of you. Alone. Now." I hope they will agree without a fight, but I wouldn't be surprised if they push me out of the way and ignore me.

"Right now?" Portia asks.

"No way," says Tony. "I'm not being late to class for you. That would be a total waste of our time."

I hate the way he says *our,* but I still need his help. Tony will never listen to me unless I offer him something he can't resist. "Tony," I say quietly, so that only Portia and he can hear me. "I know who hurt your father. And if you don't listen to me—if you don't help me—they're going to hurt your whole family too."

Portia gasps, but Tony moves forward and stands face to face with me. "What the hell are you talking about?" he spits, careful to keep his voice low. "Are you threatening me?"

His nose is inches from mine and my temper surges. I push Tony back, and he stumbles into Portia.

"Danny, what is going on?" she demands, her cheeks turning red with fury.

Tony regains his balance and glares at me as though ready to try his luck in a fight. I hold up my hand. "I'm talking about an issue of life or death. Please talk to me. I don't have anyone else to turn to. If you don't help me, Tony's family will be hurt, and I may disappear forever."

* * * *

Convincing Tony Chen to help me is as difficult as I imagined it would be. He's irate that I saw the men who had beaten his dad and yet said nothing.

"My life was in danger, because if I said anything, the mob would kill me," I explain, snapping a leaf off one of the smallish trees shielding us from the school. We are standing outside, knowing we could all be in trouble if someone sees us out of class.

"I couldn't care less about your life," Tony retorts.

"Oh, come on, Tony, just listen to him." Portia is turning into my best ally, even though she is still obviously distrustful of me. "Why didn't you go to the cops, Danny?"

Because I needed to protect Gino, I think. "I told you, I was discovered by an undercover cop."

"And you were there, why?" Tony asks, his tone accusing.

"I saw your dad being roughly pulled into the diner. I was out with another friend, and we were worried about him, so we checked it out," I say, trying to keep the story as close to the truth as possible, yet not wanting to tip them off to the Vigliotti connection. "I was discovered but, thankfully, not by a mobster."

"No kidding," Portia says. "You could have been killed!" I am momentarily distracted by her concern for me. I feel my attraction to her washing over me all over again—I'm not sure it ever went away.

However, Tony quickly brings me back to the moment. "So it's either my family or this undercover guy? Just tell them who the undercover is and be done with it."

"Tony! Are you serious? You'd let another innocent person die?" Portia is livid.

"Over my family? You better believe it!" he shoots back. I've never heard Tony raise his voice to her. He certainly cares deeply for his family.

"Tony, I'm not giving up the name of the undercover. Besides, that's not the only thing they want. They also demanded that I steal your laptop."

Both Portia and Tony look confused. "My laptop?" Tony asks doubtfully. "What's going on here, Danny? Are you jerking us around or something? I know you're not the most honest guy."

I know I deserve that comment, but I try to ignore it. "They want to hack into your system. You're hurting their business, Tony. They want your computer, and they want you gone."

Tony glances anxiously at Portia, then back at me. "That's impossible. I'm just a teenager."

"Well, you're keeping them from making money. That's an offense people get killed for when it comes to the Mafia."

"Why tell us?" Tony asks. "Why not go to the police?"

I sigh. "If I go to the police, they'll still go after your family."

Portia studies me. "But how did the mob find out about *you* if you were discovered by an undercover? How do they know you know who the undercover is?"

"Tommy Gallo."

"Tommy?" Tony asks doubtfully.

"Stupid kid steals my wallet and finds a business card leading to a detective."

"But how do they know that's not for something else?"

I bite my lip. I can't tell them I'm staying with an important mob leader, which makes my having a policeman's card a crime against the Newcastle Mafia. "Apparently an assistant district attorney—not a good one—found out about me," I answer truthfully.

Portia and Tony sit quietly, as though unable to take in everything I have shared. I can't blame them—I myself barely believe everything I have experienced over the last month. But I desperately need their trust now because they are all I have.

After a long silence, Tony sighs in frustration and looks directly into my eyes. "What do you need me to do?"

Portia nods. "Yeah, Danny, how can we help you?"

I glance between the two, relieved to have them on my side. "It's going to be a lot of work, but I think we can get these guys to hang themselves."

* * * *

Baxter is asleep on the bed as I begin to pack the items I have casually collected over the course of the evening. I place a flashlight, a notepad, and a kitchen knife in my backpack and stuff my cell phone in my pocket. I don't really know what I need beside an extra dose of courage. I'm beyond nervous. What we are doing tonight could cost us our lives. But I don't see any other option. Frank has offered me a way out, but I can't just run away.

Tony and Portia are going to meet me down the street with a van Portia is "borrowing" from her dad's lot. I'm surprised she would do anything that could get her in trouble, but she is committed to our plan and has promised to do anything to help. Tony, with just a learner's permit, is doing the driving, a risk we agreed had to be taken. Am I putting them both in danger for Gino's sake? I know that would be wrong. But if I simply go to the police, I have no guarantee that the mob won't hurt the Chens. This plan may be the only way to protect them.

Gino left earlier this evening, and I'm worried my godfather will be at the meeting tonight. But if everything goes as planned, I will get Capriotti and Ray on tape and in a picture together. Tony has a technically flawless strategy that will allow me to protect Gino even as I gain evidence to put Capriotti, Kluwer, and Ray in the hands of the FBI.

The clock next to my bed reads eight-thirty p.m., and I know I need to get down to the corner. The house is strangely quiet as I leave, but I think Ronnie and Julia have gone out and Vince is upstairs, as always, playing video games at the expense of his homework. I creep through the back door and down the driveway. I figure my black garb will keep me concealed from any curious neighbors. I can see the van next to the curb just several houses down, and I speed up as soon as I reach the street. As I come closer to the vehicle, I see Tony sitting in the driver's seat, his face tight with anxiety.

I open the passenger side door. "You ready? Where's Portia?"

Tony shakes his head and motions to the backseat. At that moment, the sliding door of the van opens, and I'm face to face with two unwelcome visitors: Vince and Julia. I groan. Will nothing go right for me?

"Well, well. Here I am, driving back from the gas station with my little sister, when all of a sudden I see a very interesting sight. Nerd boy and Prissy Saviano are sitting in a van just down the street from my house. Didn't you think that was odd, Julia?" Vince asks, his sarcasm unmistakable.

"Why, yes, I did!" Julia exclaims, her voice innocently surprised. I notice Portia sitting in the back seat, her arms across her chest and her face like stone.

"You're a sneaky little bastard, Danny. I've helped you over and over again, and Julia has too," Vince says, motioning to his smug sister. "And what do you do? You go behind my back and recruit these psychos for whatever little espionage you've got planned."

Julia crinkles her nose. "Do you smell that stench? I think it's rotten cheese. There's a rat around here—three of them!"

The two Vigliotti siblings glare at me, no hint of family affection showing on their angry faces. I know Portia and Tony have no idea what is going on, but I can't worry about keeping them out of the loop any longer. I'm going to be completely honest—with everyone. "Okay, you got me. I'm stuck. Either Tony's family will be murdered and I'll be kicked out on the streets or worse, or I'll be taken away and your father put in prison. Those are my choices."

Everyone is stunned. Julia is the first to break the shocked silence. "So which one are you going with—let me guess, since the nerdy one is sitting in this car, I'm guessing you're squealing and leaving," Julia snaps.

I shake my head. "No, I'm picking option three. I'm taking down Ray Gallo and saving your dad and the Chens at the same time."

"Wait a minute—how's your dad involved with this?" Tony asks Vince, his voice edged with suspicion.

Vince moves in quickly and grabs Tony by the neck. "None of your business, egghead."

"Oh, for God's sake, just knock it off!" I say, physically removing Vince from Tony.

Tony glares at me. "I'm not helping you if Gino was involved in hurting my dad!"

"Gino's trying to protect your dad!" I say, almost shouting in aggravation.

"No, he's right, Danny," says Portia. "I'm not helping you if you're trying to protect a mobster!" She looks at Julia. "I can't believe your dad's in the mob!"

My anger gets the best of me. I'm tired of Portia's righteous indignation, even though she doesn't know any better. I'm about to change that.

"You want the truth, Portia? I only hid it from you because I didn't want you to get hurt. But just so I won't be the liar you hate so much, here it is! Your dad's a mobster just like Gino! *Just like Gino!*" I repeat.

Portia sits back as though slapped. "You're lying. That's ridiculous!" Yet her face contradicts her. She looks like she has been caught doing something wrong.

"You already guessed that, didn't you?" I say, surprised.

Portia buries her head in her arms.

Julia glares at her coldly. "Oh, please! Get over it! You can't wear your little halo forever."

Everyone is angry and confused, but I don't have time to play peacemaker—or therapist for that matter. Hurt feelings can be sorted out later. I have too much to accomplish, and my window of opportunity is getting smaller by the moment.

"Fine. Guess what? Now you get to help me, too," I say to the Vigliotti siblings. "Tony, let's go. I'll bring these guys up to speed."

Chapter 18

I smooth my button-up shirt for the fifth time, realizing that the motion is my nerves getting the better of me. I tried to dress a little more grown-up tonight in a black shirt with my blue jeans. The last thing I want is to feel like a kid when I need every ounce of nerve I can muster.

The Vigliotti siblings and I are standing in the shadows of the dusty parking lot behind the diner. Julia shifts uneasily beside me, and Vince is hopelessly in motion, swaying from side to side in a frantic manner that I know won't stop until we're inside the diner. But for the moment, we are captives of Tony's lecture about hidden wireless transmitters.

"This is a wireless headpiece that will transmit back to me in the van," he says, holding up a tiny earpiece. "I'm glad Julia is going with you guys. She can wear this and no one will see it because of her hair."

"I'm not letting my hair out of this ponytail," Julia replies. "I don't do 'dent head.'"

Vince rolls his eyes and pushes his sister roughly.

"Hey!" she snaps, then covers her mouth. Even she knows she was too loud.

"Just do what he says!" Vince orders, the strain in his voice unmistakable.

"Hey, Vince, are you sure you can do this?" I ask doubtfully, knowing that any slipups on our part might mean the end for all of us.

"Yes—but let's get on with it!" Vince replies, continuing his anxious sway.

Julia reluctantly lets down her hair and puts the earpiece behind the waves framing her worried face. "It's too big. It might fall off."

"As long as you don't start prancing around like usual, you'll be fine," Tony says sharply, getting a giggle out of Portia in the process.

Julia glares sourly at them both.

Tony hands a phone to me. "When they ask you for the name, tell them you'll give them the address and say it's in the phone. Take pictures while they are concentrating on the address you're telling them. The sound on the phone is off, so it shouldn't clue them in to what you are doing. Then you'll give them this computer—okay?" He hands me a laptop.

I'm impressed with Tony's calmness when we are in so much danger. "Where'd you get this?"

"Just one of the old ones we've got sitting around."

"Man, I hate to give this up," I joke, knowing that one thing I'd still love to have is my own computer.

Tony's doesn't laugh. "If you help catch the men who beat up my dad, I'll get you one that's even better," he says in a moment of pure generosity.

I immediately feel guilty and shake my head. "You don't have to do that. I just want things to go right so everyone is safe."

"Then for God's sake let's go!" Vince urges.

"Wait a minute. What am *I* doing?" Portia asks, her arms folded across her stomach. She has barely spoken a word since I named her dad as a mobster.

"You're the lookout," Tony answers.

"Like hell I am!" she snaps, somehow able to glare at everyone at once.

"Yes, you are," Tony says. "You agreed to follow my plan, Portia. Now, start doing your job! Who's in the parking lot? You know the cars."

Portia frowns for a few seconds, then she sighs, and with little enthusiasm, starts identifying cars. "Ray is here. Donny is here. Lou and Johnny are here. Gino is here—"

"What?" Vince cut in. "My dad's not here."

"Yes, he is," Portia said. "My dad sold him a black pickup last month. You've just probably never seen it before because he keeps it at the car lot."

I glare at her because I'm upset that she has been holding me to such a high standard when she's obviously been living a double life herself. Then I feel my courage draining at the thought of confronting the mobsters with Gino in the mix. "That's going to make this much more difficult."

"It makes things better," Portia asserts. "No one will hurt Gino's kids or godson while he's there."

"Or he might get hurt because of us," Julia adds, her anxiety evident in the way she is now wringing her hands.

"I told you, Tony, I'm not implicating Gino!" I warn.

"You won't need to. Julia can stay close to Ray and Capriotti, and you need to take pictures only of them," Tony says.

I study him, wondering whether he will find a way to implicate Gino anyway because he was involved in hurting his father, but I don't have time to worry about that now.

"Okay, Portia, keep going," I say.

"So, Gino is there," she continues quietly. "The beamer is most likely Capriotti's. Oh yeah, and that young guy—Frank."

I try to keep any expression from my face as Portia unknowingly mentions the FBI agent. I can't tell any of them who the agent is—that would only present more danger. But I don't know what Frank will do when he sees me and the Vigliottis in the diner. I hope he will let us execute our plan to gather evidence on both the district attorney and Ray and then get out.

I survey this group of teenagers—people I didn't even know two months ago. Now my life is in their hands. And in this moment, I feel I'm ready to face anything. "Let's go."

* * * *

"What the hell is going on? Who let these kids in here?"

Ray Gallo's face is beaming a bright red. He stares at us, three teens who walked into the diner, unannounced, and who are, by the furious expression on his face, definitely unwelcome.

The diner door had been locked when the Vigliottis and I had tried to open it. When we settled for knocking instead, an enormous wiseguy answered, taking all three of us in with a cool glare. I had quickly identified us as "Gino's kids," which kept the man from beating us up right there on the doorstep. He had paused for a moment thoughtfully, and then as recognition had crossed his face (at least when he looked at Vince), he had stepped back and let us past. Based on Ray's expression, that decision was almost certainly one the wiseguy would soon regret.

Nevertheless, we have made it into the lion's den. I attempt to ignore Frank, whom I can see out of the corner of my eye. I don't want to give any indication that I'm familiar with Frank and blow his cover. I also try not to acknowledge Gino; however, Gino makes this impossible.

"What are you doing here?" he demands, but I can hear the panic in his gruff voice.

"Lou, you stupid buffoon! I told you no one was allowed in here!" Ray looks like he is ready to snap—if he hasn't already. He motions to Donny, who slams Lou into the wall and knees him in the stomach until Lou is gasping for air.

I glance at the Vigliotti siblings. Julia looks like she is ready to bolt, but Vince is oddly cool. Maybe all those mob movies have desensitized him.

"Donny, stop. My kids are here!" Gino says, his voice edging on desperate.

"Yes, why is that exactly?"

I search the room for the man that belongs to the smooth, strong voice that just spoke. A tall, well-built man in an immaculate black suit is seated just to the right of Ray, not far from where Frank is watching the scene with an expression of fury and alarm.

"Mister Capriotti," I say without a moment's hesitation.

Capriotti leans back in his chair and scrutinizes me. "Yes, that's right." He smiles, but the expression isn't pleasant at all. "You're Barb Kluwer's little project."

"Get these stupid kids out of here," Ray demands, but Capriotti lifts his hand.

"Wait one moment," he says coolly.

Frank and Gino are frowning at me, both probably trying to figure out my motive for being here. I take comfort in the fact that the Vigliottis are standing on either side of me, their silent support boosting my confidence. Why did I ever think I could face all these men alone?

"I'm not a big fan of Barb Kluwer," I say, directing my comment to Gino and Frank. "But she certainly enjoys blackmailing me."

Capriotti laughs, but he is the only one. Everyone else in the room has faces of stone, with the exception of Gino, whose distress is now obvious. I can't blame him. Two of the people he cares about most are standing in a room surrounded by hostile mobsters. And I'm sure he hates me now if he thinks his kids are here because of me.

"You were supposed to meet Barb tomorrow," Capriotti reminds me, as though I have forgotten the place and time chosen for the exchange of information.

Ray scowls. "How in the world did you come to find us here?" he asks, his face beginning to take on a more normal color, even as his eyes harden to steel.

"I have my sources—at school, you know?" I say, hoping that they might think I tricked Tommy into spilling information. I couldn't care less if Tommy gets in trouble. "So I decided to give you the information on my terms."

Ray eyes me coolly, but the hungry expression on Capriotti's face intensifies. "You have the information for me? The laptop?"

Vince holds out the laptop, which Capriotti snatches greedily and hands to Ray.

"Tony Chen's laptop—that should solve some problems for you. You owe me for this favor," I say grandly.

I can see the looks of disapproval on both Frank and Gino's faces. I hate for them to think I'm a thief, but I must convince everyone right now that I'm as sneaky and corrupt as the rest of them. Frank makes me feel the most ashamed—he's the only truly good person in this room.

"And the name of the undercover?" asks Capriotti, and this time I notice that Frank flinches. Will he make a run for it? I know that would ruin everything. I must get my next words out quickly.

"Yes, but I'm not giving you his name," I say slyly and notice Frank relax slightly. "I put his true address in my phone. That way you can find him at his house, and then you will know who he is." Frank tenses. I have no idea if the agent has a family, but I'm sure Frank is worried that I may still betray him.

"He lives in Delaware," I say casually, wondering if, by any chance, Frank actually does live in Delaware. But he must not, because he relaxes again when I mention the small state to the south. Hopefully, now Frank will know I'm not actually giving the district attorney and the mobsters the information they want.

"Really? That seems odd," Ray says, his voice skeptical.

"Couldn't take a chance of someone local, you know. Too much chance of him getting recognized," Vince cuts in, lending me a hand in the ruse.

Ray doesn't answer, but his expression becomes less suspicious and more interested. "Well, what's the address?"

I pull out my cell phone, holding it up to take a picture of Capriotti and Ray sitting side by side, their faces watching me eagerly. Glad that no one is standing directly behind me and that the Vigliottis should block any side views of the cell phone screen, I take several snapshots, being careful to make sure Gino is not in the background. "Hold on just a second," I say slowly, "I put it in my address book."

Capriotti grabs a sheet of paper and pulls a stylish pen from his suit pocket. "I'm ready."

"Two-two-five-five West Worthington Street, Littleton, Delaware," I say, drawing each word out slowly so that I can snap a few more pictures.

"What? Littleton, Delaware? I've never heard of such a town." Donny stands close to us, his expression confused. "And I grew up in Wilmington."

Before I have a chance to dodge him, Donny snatches the phone from my hand.

"Hey! There's no address on here. Just a picture of you, Ray, and the DA!" he bellows. I exchange panicked glances with the Vigliottis, hoping one of them can think of any excuse, because not one is coming to me.

"What the hell!" If Ray was angry before, he is enraged now. He heaves himself out of his chair rather awkwardly and grabs the phone from Donny. He takes one look at it and then glares at me. "What's going on, boy?" he demands, shoving the phone back into Donny's hand.

I'm frozen in place, not knowing what to say or do. Hopefully, Tony and Portia will realize the plan has gone terribly wrong. I gaze at the cell phone blankly and then try to defend myself as best as I can. "I must have accidentally pressed a button. I can bring the address back up. Geez, just take it easy! The picture was an accident. It happens to me all the time." I stare into Ray's cold eyes. I can't believe I'm attempting to deceive a man who has probably killed many men for just that. I'm trying to hide my fear, but I can feel the adrenaline pumping through my limbs, a sure sign that I'm scared.

Julia comes to my rescue. "Yeah, you guys are idiots. Leave it to old men to not understand technology."

"Be quiet, Julia," Gino warns, but too late.

Ray turns his anger on Julia, grabbing her arm and pulling her within an inch of his big, bullish face.

"You better be glad your dad's a *capo,* young lady, or you'd be in more trouble than you can imagine," he says cruelly, his white teeth flashing under heavy lips. He pauses for a long moment, staring into her frightened eyes. Suddenly, his eyes narrow in on her ear and his lips curl in a snarl. "What's this?"

When Ray grabbed Julia, her hair had fallen away from her face, revealing the earpiece. I groan—our plan is demolished, and we have no plan B or C to fall back on. Ray rips the earpiece from Julia's ear and throws it on the floor. He stomps his foot down, crunching the small device against the wood floor.

"Lou! Get outside! This couldn't have been transmitting far. I can't believe it—stupid teenagers are trying to trap me. I knew I should never have come here." Ray's eyes are blazing.

Gino is motionless, but appears ready to spring— toward what, I don't know.

Capriotti sits back in his chair, watching the scene with intense interest, as though it were nothing more than a fascinating play. "I thought you were more efficient than this," Capriotti taunts, as though his own life isn't in jeopardy by being caught with a mobster.

"I can't help it if my own men are betraying me!" Ray almost shouts. "But I can help it now."

"I told you Gino was dirty," Donny says to Ray. "You should have let me take care of him a long time ago."

Gino's face fills with dread, a look I have never seen before. "What are you talking about?" he gasps.

Ray scowls at Gino. "To think my own captain was betraying me, snitching on me! Using your children, no less." Ray walks toward Gino, his gestures emphasizing his words. "And that—that filthy boy! Using Mike and Penny Esposito's son against me? Traitor!"

Gino is completely still, even as Ray advances, but his voice trembles when he speaks, and his anguish for the safety of his children is plain. "That's ridiculous, Ray," he says, almost pleading. "I have been a true member and a good *capo*. I would never betray you. And this has no connection with Mike. I don't know what's going on here, but if you calm down, we can figure it out."

I should be frightened—my life is on very shaky ground at the moment. But I'm stuck on what Ray just said. "Who is Mike's son? Are you talking about me? That's not my dad."

Ray spins, his fierce eyes burning. "Oh, don't you dare lie to me, you stupid kid. There's no question about it. I know who you are. You're Mike's filthy offspring."

I shake my head. "Tell him, Gino. He's wrong. I don't know anyone named Mike." I turn to my godfather, but Gino says nothing.

"You're just like him," Ray accuses. "Coming here like you want to help, but betraying us instead. Gino should have killed him when he had a chance. And your mom wasn't much better—just the thought of trouble sent her running, taking you with her and any chance we had of 'persuading' Mike to come back and take his punishment like a man. Too bad Barb Kluwer didn't get you when she had the chance. We could have tied up some loose ends."

My knees are going to buckle. The information, true or not, is too much for me. I'm relieved to feel Vince put his arm under my elbow, steadying me. With the crazed look on Ray's face, I know the Vigliotti siblings must be as terrified as I am.

"That's enough, Ray," Gino cuts in. "Like I said, just calm down, and we'll get this thing sorted out."

Ray explodes. "Calm down? Calm down? Donny was right about you. And I've trusted you with everything. Everything! You filthy Rat! Don't worry, I'll take care of your stupid kids. But your job at the Newcastle Mafia has been terminated! And pretty soon, you will be too!"

I turn to Capriotti. "Stop this—stop this now! You're the only one who can calm him down!"

But before anyone can say another word, a gunshot rips through the room. Julia screams. Ray is holding a gun—and it's pointed at Gino.

Chapter 19

I hear Vince wail and see him charge Ray, only to have Ray's gun pointed at his head. I try to run to Gino, who has crumpled to the floor clutching his rib cage; the gunshot from Ray hit him square in the torso. But Lou grabs me, forcing me to leave Gino abandoned on the floor.

Mark Capriotti leaps out of his seat and is at the door to the diner in less than five seconds. "Gallo!" he yells. "How dare you! I don't want to be part of this! We're through!"

Ray twists from an infuriated Vince to the fleeing Capriotti and aims the handgun at the district attorney's head. "Oh yeah? You're going nowhere."

Capriotti removes his hand from the door handle, but continues to stand next to it, as if hoping he could wish himself out of the room.

"Sit down!" Ray screams at him. Capriotti sits in the chair nearest to the door, his horrified eyes fixed on the blood streaming from Gino's chest. But Ray's momentary distraction is enough to give Vince the opening he needs. He plows into Ray's stomach as Donny pulls out his own gun and takes aim at the burly teenager struggling to take Ray's weapon.

Frank leaps across the fallen Gino and punches Donny in the jaw. Donny's shot zips past Ray's shoulder instead of into Vince's back, but Donny is ready for Frank's kick to the groin; he backs out of the way and catches Frank's leg, trying to knock him to the floor. Frank jerks his foot out of Donny's hand before he topples over, but not before Donny fires and misses a shot at Frank's head. Frank dives for the floor as Donny fires again, his bullet catching Frank's foot.

Frank won't last long if I don't help. Lou has both his beefy arms around me, but I know I must escape. I leap up and slam the back of my head into his chin, and his arms loosen, allowing me to struggle free. I expect Lou to chase me, but when I turn to look over my shoulder, I see him eyeing the room and backing away. First smart thing he's done all night, I think.

I quickly realize that Donny is trying to finish Frank off, so I rush forward, grab the mobster's hand, and push it toward the ceiling. In retaliation, Donny wraps a beefy arm around my neck, and despite all of my wrestling experience, I can't escape the iron headlock. With my windpipe cut off, my vision starts to go black. I'm going to pass out.

Just as I feel everything going black, the hold around my neck releases abruptly. I crash to the floor on top of Donny and scramble away from the mobster, struggling to catch my breath. But Donny isn't moving. I glance behind me and find Julia standing there, a broken bottle in her hand.

"You're awesome, Julia," I gasp, but then I see my godfather lying on the floor across the room. "We've got to help your dad!"

I fish my phone out of Donny's pocket. As Julia and I rush across the room, I frantically do the only thing I can think may save us. I push "2," the speed-dial for Reggie. I wait for one ring and then hope the noise on the other end is his picking up.

"Help! Call Alvarez! We're at the diner—" I begin to say.

We're almost to Gino, but the boom of another gunshot causes Julia to stumble into me, and I drop the phone and whirl around to see who fired the shot. Even with Vince attacking him, Ray was able to shoot at the fleeing Capriotti, who, finding the front door blocked by Lou, must have scampered to the back door of the dining room. The shot did not hit its mark, because Capriotti disappears behind the door a moment later.

Ray continues to wave the gun around and scream profanities as several mobsters roughly pull Vince off Ray. I want to help Vince, but I quickly realize that Julia and I will not even be able to make it to Gino. The remaining mobsters are circling us like hungry dogs. I glance around—but no one can help us. Frank is being pummeled by three of Ray's men. *Cowards,* I think. *It takes three of you to even bring him down.* We are defeated.

A small, steely-eyed mobster reaches out to grab Julia's arm. She shrieks and jumps back as he leaps after her. She backs into another mobster who jerks her arms behind her back and starts dragging her toward Gino. Two other mobsters grab me, and although I struggle and manage to kick one of them hard in the knee, I can't escape as they drag me toward Gino as well. Three men are needed to control the thrashing Vince. The three of us are thrown on the floor next to Gino. I see tears streaming down Julia's face, and Vince stops struggling as he kneels by Gino's head. I'm terrified that Gino might already be dead. What have I done?

Ray, his face cut and bleeding, stands before us, his eyes murderous. I instinctively know what is coming. I prepare myself for what may be my last moments of life.

"That's it, I'm finishing him off," Ray snarls, pointing the gun at Gino's head.

"No!" I yell, jumping in front of Gino.

Ray studies me, his eyes glinting. "I prefer for others to do the dirty work around here. That's the way the mob is supposed to work. Even a small one like we have here in Newcastle. But I believe you deserve my 'special' attention. I might have let you live had you accepted your godfather's execution with dignity, but you're as stupid as he is. So, if I've got to get my hands dirty, who better to start with than the son of the man I want dead more than any other."

Ray trains the gun on my head, pointing it between my eyes. I feel my body go rigid with horror. I can't survive this shot. It's over.

But Ray never fires. The walls of the diner explode inward. Bricks fly through the air, striking mobsters like bowling pins. The Vigliottis and I duck down, covering our heads and shielding Gino from the onslaught. I'm struck on the shoulder by flying debris, and I gasp in pain. I turn my head to see the cause of the destruction and discover Tony and Portia scrambling out of the van that just smashed into the front of the diner.

The crash is enough to make most of the mobsters bolt. They scatter like ants in a hundred directions, leaving behind their flustered leader, who has been pinned by a table, and the unconscious Donny.

"Get back here," Ray screams at their fleeing backs, but not one of them even slows at the sound of his infuriated voice. Ray howls in frustration and points his gun at Gino. "This is all your fault!" he shrieks.

Ray aims at Gino's head this time, but I'm ready. I leap from the floor and slam my body into the trapped underboss. Ray fires but misses Gino's head by several feet, his bullet puncturing a chair. Vince is at my side, and before Ray can regroup, he stomps on Ray's hand, forcing him to let go of his gun. Vince snatches the gun and points it at Ray's head.

I immediately see the danger in what Vince is thinking. "Hey, Vince. Why don't you hand me that?" I say as calmly as I can manage.

"He shot my dad. Ray Gallo deserves to die," Vince responds, his voice hard, unforgiving.

"This is not the way, Vince. Let him pay by being humiliated. Let him know what it's like to be a nobody," I plead.

"Come on, Vince. Just give the gun to Danny and we can go home!" Portia says, now beside us. Tony is across the room, surveying the damage from the van, and Julia is kneeling next to Gino.

Vince glares down at the fallen underboss, and I think that perhaps he is not acting out of emotion. Instead, Vince seems to be enjoying this moment, as though playing a part in the mob stories he loves so much. He moves the barrel slightly to the right and fires, causing Ray, and everyone else, to jump. Vince laughs like a lunatic and hands the pistol to Portia. "Gallo, you big chicken. You're through!"

Portia shoots Vince the *you're crazy* look and turns to me. "Sorry about the van. We didn't know what else to do. But we heard everything before the transmitter was destroyed, and then, as we tried to figure out what to do, we heard that horrible gunshot—and we had to do something!"

"It was a risk, but you did the right thing. We still need help though!" I say desperately, turning toward Gino.

"We called the police, but I'm not sure they thought we were serious. I'm going to run down to the convenience store and try to get an ambulance here!" Tony says as he comes up beside us, glancing at Gino. Julia is holding her sweatshirt to her father's side. The amount of blood is alarming. Vince is now beside her, his hand on his father's shoulder.

Frank limps over, his face scratched and bleeding. "Let me see what I can do until they get here," he says, moving toward Gino.

But before Tony can take two steps toward the door, a commotion in front of the diner causes us to cringe, preparing ourselves for another onslaught of mob fury. I also hear noise coming from the door behind us. Is Capriotti still here? Surely he must have escaped by now.

We wait anxiously, but instead of angry mobsters, men in helmets and shields file into the diner through the hole the van created. I see the words SWAT splashed across a bulletproof vest.

"Cavalry's arrived," Vince says, moving his body between the formidable newcomers and his fading father. I hear Frank yelling directions to the SWAT team. The men surround us, but Frank limps over and shoves them aside. "Get out of the way! Make room for the paramedics!"

The men from SWAT move to take charge of Ray and Donny as paramedics flow through the door and hurry to Gino, pushing us out of the way. I work my way toward Frank and motion to the back room. "I think Capriotti's still here!"

Frank doesn't hesitate for a moment. He limps through the growing crowd of federal agents, cops, and paramedics to the back door. I follow, looking for any distraction from the cold reality that my godfather might be dying—and knowing it's my fault.

Frank bursts through the back door, and I almost plow right into him as I follow. The agent has stopped just a few feet into the room because the area is shrouded in darkness, except for a sliver of light escaping from the dining room through the slats in the bathroom. I brush past Frank, who whips toward me with his gun.

"Frank, it's me—Danny!" I say quickly, backing away from the agent. "Hold on—there's a light over here." I shuffle through the room toward the light switch at the back.

"Danny! I could have shot you. You shouldn't be back here."

"It's no big deal," I reply, reaching for the switch. I flick it up and find myself staring into the barrel of a small handgun, which extends from an agitated Mark Capriotti.

Chapter 20

"Put it down, Mark," Frank warns, his gun trained on Capriotti's head.

"No way. He's my ticket out of here."

"How's that?" Frank answers, moving closer.

"Stay away!" Capriotti yells, glancing nervously at the advancing agent. I glance nervously too—doesn't Frank care if I die?

"You're not going to shoot him," Frank states. "Right now the charges against you will only keep you penned up for a few years. A murder charge, however, might go another way."

Capriotti sneers at me. "This kid has messed up everything. I want him dead." His finger moves imperceptibly on the trigger.

"I'd hoped to see you in court, but I'm not that particular about how I take you down," Frank threatens. Capriotti screws up his face angrily and starts to pull back the trigger.

In less than an instant, I am struck by something heavy and melt into the ground. As I hit the floor, my head explodes with pain. And then, everything is black.

* * * *

The hospital in Newcastle smells like antiseptic and lime jello. At least, that's what I think as I survey the too white room with a large window, a tiny television, and an awkwardly hung picture of random flowers. I lean back in my wheelchair in which the nurse has forced me to sit because of my injury. But I almost jump out of it when I'm startled by a familiar voice.

"Well, you're doing better than expected. Always knew you were a fighter." Gino has just awoken in his hospital bed. Even though I've been waiting for him to wake, I find that I am afraid to speak to him.

"Hi, Gino."

"Hey," he answers as I wheel my chair closer to his bed. I feel exposed in my blue hospital gown.

"How are you?" I ask.

"Feeling better every minute. I heard you had quite the time, though."

"Who told you?"

"Frank. He said he had to shoot Capriotti to save you, but the DA took you down with him as he fell. You would have been fine had you not hit your head on a crate," Gino summarizes.

I nod and hold back a laugh. That stupid crate had found yet another way to cause me pain.

"But you're okay?" I ask, overwhelmed that this man sitting in front of me had been on the verge of death. I have already spoken to the other Vigliottis. Ronnie still doesn't understand quite what happened at the diner that night, but something tells me she is just grateful that her family survived whatever it was. She hasn't been too intent on grilling us for details, which makes me think she suspects we just barely escaped criminal activity that we may or may not have been a part of. However, this is the first time I have been allowed to talk to Gino, three days after *that* night.

"Well, I'm alive," Gino replies. "Ray must have been really off his game to take a shot like that. The bullet just missed my heart, but I lost a lot of blood and broke two ribs."

"Thanks to me," I say glumly.

"Thanks to you, I didn't get shot in the head. Vince told me you saved my life."

"Did he say anything else?" I ask, wondering whether Vince told his father I had been talking to law enforcement. Vince had yet to speak to me, treating me with atypical coolness.

Gino sighs. "Danny, you just happened to be in the wrong place at the wrong time. Frank told me everything. You became a little mobster yourself—manipulating everyone—quite by accident, it seems."

I cringe at being compared with a mobster. "I didn't realize you already spoke to Frank. So I guess the FBI will take me away now. And I bet you'll be glad."

"Danny, Frank's not charging me. He said he got what the FBI wanted, and he said he owed you a favor for not turning him over to Capriotti. I'm guessing I'm that favor, and for that, I owe you. You're staying with us—unless you want to leave."

I straighten in my chair. "No, I don't want to leave. But you'll never trust me again. You hate rats."

"I despise rats, Danny. But, I trust you with my life—and I owe your father and mother, who by the way, was here just a few minutes ago. She ran down to the cafeteria to grab coffee. She's very nervous to see you."

"She said I could stay? Even after all this?" I ask.

"She doesn't have a place for you. Del is living at your old house, and Penny is with a friend. She could stay with us, but she doesn't want to live in Newcastle. Too much history for her, I think. Plus, she said she's started seeing someone again, and she thinks you'll be upset about it."

Doonesby, I think. Mom's seeing him again? I'm not sure how I feel about it now—I have a new sense of what my mom has gone through in her life.

"Your parents are getting divorced, Danny," Gino says softly.

"But Del's not really my dad, is he," I say. It's not a question.

"No, Danny. He isn't."

"My dad was a mobster."

Gino sighs again and stares out the window. "Your father, Mike Esposito, was a good man. And I wasn't a good enough friend. So I've got to make it up to him by taking care of you. And the thing is—I like having you around because you remind me of him—so it doesn't feel like I'm doing him a favor at all."

I turn my head away and try to contain all the emotions churning in me. "What happened to my dad?"

Gino stares at the ceiling. "I don't know. Nobody knows if he's dead or alive. As for what happened before he disappeared, that's between him and me." His jaw is hard and his voice tight. I know I won't get the information I so desperately want to hear.

Another thought occurs to me. "You didn't take me in to see if it would lead you to him, did you?" I ask, wondering whether Gino's good nature had an underlying, darker motive.

Gino seems taken aback by my insinuation. "Danny, you're with us because I need to do something right by your parents. But you're more than a favor—I like having you with us," his voice is low, struggling against some strong emotion. I know these words are hard for a tough guy like Gino.

"So what happens for you now?" I ask, changing the subject.

"Well, I don't know," Gino says, shrugging. I look at him sharply and wonder whether Gino is going to use his free pass to get out of the mob lifestyle. Is he in danger because he was connected to the undercover? Do the others consider him a rat? Will he survive all of this? I'm smart enough to know that Gino would never tell me one way or another.

"How about Ronnie?" I ask. "Are you going to come clean with her about all this?"

Gino's eyes narrow. "She knows as much as she needs—and wants—to know," he replies vaguely. "Hey, I have some news about some folks that I think you'll really like," he says abruptly.

"Yeah?" I ask, letting him change the subject.

Gino nods. "First, I thought you'd like to know that a certain DA's assistant was arrested this morning at the Newcastle Mall. Apparently, Ms. Kluwer was helping her boss."

I laugh this time. "That *is* good news."

"Do you know why she was so interested in you, from the beginning?" Gino asks.

I shake my head.

"Apparently she wanted to use you against Del, to see if she could make him talk to Ray about your dad. Problem was, she never did her homework. Del never knew anything about Mike Esposito."

I stare at him, a hundred questions forming, none of which, I know, he will answer.

"Anyway," he continues, "I think there's a person at the door who would like to speak to you," Gino says, nodding to someone. I twist (a bit painfully—my head is throbbing) toward the door and see Reggie standing there.

"Hey."

"Hey," Reggie replies, as I wave to Gino and wheel toward the door. Reggie and I move into the hall and wait for two nurses to pass us before speaking.

I study my friend carefully. "How did you—?"

"Julia called me on her phone. Vince told her I was your best friend, and she tried the number you used when you borrowed her phone once. Kind of lucky, I guess. You probably wouldn't have called me after the things I said."

I smile. "Of course I would have. You saved us a few nights ago. SWAT came just in time."

Reggie glances toward the room in which Gino is recuperating. "I guess everything worked out."

I nod. "Yeah, it did."

Reggie swallows and looks down the hall. "You're staying with him, aren't you?"

"Yeah, Reggie. I'm going to stay in Newcastle, at least for now."

Reggie says nothing, and we are both silent for a few minutes. "I don't think that's a good decision, Danny," Reggie finally says. "Your godfather is still not a good man."

"I know," I reply, not letting myself get angry. Reggie is right. Frank is a hero. Gino is, well, it's hard to say. I'm already struggling with the fact that Gino may not give up the mob lifestyle. And even if he does, he might be hunted down for being the very rat that he hates so much. He's done terrible things, but now I'm worried about him and his family. I hope my godfather can change, but will he be able to? Will he have a chance? I feel responsible for so much of this.

"I've got to stay for now," I finally say to Reggie. "The Vigliottis are a link to my past—a past I never knew anything about."

225

Reggie nods. "Okay, I understand." He pauses, then smiles. "So, you gonna tell me the juicy details or what?"

I grin and point to a chair. "Sit down. You're gonna love this!"

* * * *

A week later, Reggie and I are gripping the seats in the SUV, both hoping that this ride won't be our last.

"Vince! Slow down!" I order.

"Oh please, don't be such a baby," Vince snaps. "You wanted a trip to Joe's lot—we're going to Joe's lot."

"We want to make it to the lot alive," Reggie retorts. Vince turns from the driver's seat to glare at him, chewing a large mouthful of Snickers, and nearly steers the speeding vehicle onto the shoulder. Reggie reaches out to steady himself as Vince overcorrects the vehicle. "I should have driven you, Danny," Reggie says crossly.

I bite my lip. I love speed, but Vince's driving is downright lethal. "Seriously, Vince. Stop being an idiot. We managed to stay alive last week—let's keep that record going."

Vince doesn't respond, but he does release the gas pedal ever so slightly. He zips off the highway into the car lot in minutes, completing a trip that should have taken at least thirty minutes in just fifteen. He slows the vehicle as it kicks up dust from the lot, coating the army of used cars glittering in the sun. I know we'll probably earn a lecture for Vince's mess.

Vince jerks the vehicle to an awkward stop and unstraps his seatbelt. "Hey, remember when we took on Tommy and his stupid friends?"

I sigh. Vince enjoys bringing up all the times that we have spent together without Reggie. But Reggie doesn't seem to notice—he is captivated by the cars.

"Yeah," I answer. "I heard he'll be taking a few months away from Newcastle High."

"Well, I would too if my dad were behind bars. Ray didn't even get bail."

"I almost feel sorry for the kid," Reggie says, finally joining the conversation.

Vince snorts. "Believe me, you wouldn't if you knew Tommy. He's cut from the same mold as his dad."

"Hey, there's Portia," I say, glad she is here to meet us. We haven't spoken much in the past week; the feelings between us are too mixed up.

I jump out of the SUV and stride over to her, a smile overtaking what I had hoped would be a cool expression. "Hey."

"Hey," she says, returning my smile. She looks adorable in jeans and a sweatshirt with her hair split by two braids. She seems younger, but cute. Always cute.

"You doing okay?" I ask, not really wanting to relive any of the events from last week.

"Yeah." Her eyes sparkle, and I can't move my own eyes from them.

"Hey, lovebirds!" Vince calls, causing both of us to immediately turn bright red. "We gonna talk to Joe or what? You're wasting my time!"

"I gotta talk to your dad," I say to Portia.

"Yeah, I know," she says. "Hey, I wanted to tell you, Tony's really grateful that you helped catch the man responsible for hurting his dad."

"That's great," I say, not really wanting to talk about my rival for her attention. I begin to turn to follow Vince, but she catches my arm.

"It's just that, well, I—"

"What?"

She reaches her hand up around my neck and pulls my head to hers. Then she kisses me. It's quick and shallow, but enough to drive me to the edge of crazy.

"What's going on here?" Joe's gruff voice quickly ends my moment. Portia and I spring back from each other, but she continues to smile.

Joe glares at me. "You coming or what?" he says, and I reluctantly follow him toward the building. Out of the corner of my eye, I see Vince and Reggie making fun of me as they follow, passionately kissing their hands.

"Oh, Danny, I love you so much!" Vince mocks in a very high-pitched imitation of Portia's voice.

"Shut up, Vince. Stop making out with your hand, Reggie. You guys look like idiots," I say, but I can't stop smiling. Nothing can ruin this moment for me, and besides, my two friends have finally found something in common—having fun laughing at me.

Joe makes small talk as we traipse to his small office in the center of the lot. "So, Vince, I hear you may try out for wrestling."

Vince nods. "Yeah, Danny here has practically talked me into it. He and Reggie think they can bring me up to speed."

"Well, you'll probably do okay. I've seen you at work with Tommy Gallo and company. You've got potential."

Vince beams at Joe's praise. "Well, my dad's not convinced—but I'll show him."

We enter the building and Joe motions me toward a chair. Joe sits in the chair behind the desk as Vince scrambles to take the last seat. Reggie rolls his eyes and leans against the wall.

"So, Danny," Joe starts, clearing his throat. "I've heard that you found out a little more about your past."

"Yeah," I answer, my throat tightening. "Apparently I'm not a Higgins at all. I guess I'm really Danny Esposito. Problem is, no one will tell me anything much about my real dad."

Joe spins his chair, which creaks under his weight, so that he can stare out the window. "He was a good man—just got caught up with the wrong people at the wrong time. But he loved your mother, and he loved you."

"But I wasn't even alive yet when my mother left Newcastle. Gino told me she hooked up with Del a week before I was born."

"True," Joe said. "But your father did know about you, that you were going to be a boy. And he made a deal with me. He was already in a lot of trouble by then."

"What happened to him?" I ask, not really expecting an answer.

Joe smiles, but then shrugs. "Like I said, he made a deal with me. And I intend to keep it. I just wanted to wait until the time was right."

Joe heaves himself up and turns to a cabinet, unlocking it and retrieving some papers and a key from inside. He places them on the desk in front of me.

"Danny, I'd like to present you with the title and key to your car."

"My car?" I gasp, excitement and disbelief flooding through me all at once.

"Yeah, your car," Joe affirms. "A nineteen-sixty-eight Mustang. Red. Completely restored and ready to go. Even has a CD player." He points out the window. "Over there."

I'm speechless. I rise from my chair and look out the window at my car, barely able to believe that my dad—*my dad*—had left me such a perfect gift.

"What? That's not fair!" Vince whines. "He can't even drive yet."

"That's awesome," Reggie adds, his envy showing through his words.

"Thank you," I say to Joe, going back to the desk and fingering the key.

"Don't thank me," Joe replies. "I thought about waiting until you had your license, but I think you deserve it now after the crazy stunt you pulled last week. Ray was about to take some of us out, and even though I'm not thrilled that Portia was involved, I also know she won't stay out of a scuffle."

I laugh. "No, she's definitely tougher than she acts."

"Just remember, she's my only child—my little girl. I'll be keeping an eye on you, Danny," Joe warns, his expression turning into that of a protective father. I cringe under his judging eyes, nod awkwardly, and then turn to Reggie.

"Well, I might not be able to drive it, but you can," I say, tossing the key to him. "How about a test drive to the Newcastle Mall?"

"Sure," he replies, smiling as he catches the key.

"Hey, what about me?" Vince demands.

"What about you? You'll wreck it before I ever have a chance to drive it!" I joke.

"Then I call shotgun."

"Shotgun? It's my car!"

"Shotgun!" Vince repeats stubbornly.

"Fine. But then I'm asking Portia to go with us."

"She'll cramp my style," Vince wails.

"Vince, no one could cramp your style."

"You're right," Vince says, grinning. "Last one to the car has to buy Snickers for everyone!"

We rush out the door and into the sun. I laugh as we race to the car, thinking I love my new life that seems to have happened so accidentally. And yet, I only hope Gino will take this chance to go straight, because if not, my happiness will always be in jeopardy.

About The Author

M. M. Cox is a former journalist and public relations specialist who has always been fascinated with stories about the Mafia. She has lived in Los Angeles, Atlanta, Colorado Springs, Boston, and Washington D.C. and enjoys running marathons in different cities. She attended her first writers' conference at the age of 13 and has dreamed of writing books for a teen audience ever since. Cox currently resides in Edmond, Oklahoma, with her husband and children.

Excerpt From Undercover Wiseguy

Chapter 1

This is the end for one of us. The last man standing survives. I can see that he is tiring with each move he tries to take against me, and I can taste victory. He isn't going to make it because I am not giving in.

We circle each other for a few seconds. I blink rapidly to flush the salty sweat out of my eyes. I am so close to finishing him off, I won't give up now. If I can just hold on a little longer, I can take him down. This is not the end for me.

His eyes drop to my feet—just for an instant—and I make my move. I rush him, wrapping my arms around his stomach. We spin and his feet scramble to keep him from falling as I try to trip him. My head is smashed against his chest and my hands are straining to keep their hold on him. He tries to break away, but it's too late. I lift him, and his feet lose contact with the ground. Our bodies slam to the floor.

He's beneath me, but only for a moment. He rolls and is suddenly on top of me, trying to turn me on my back. Yet he's not strong enough to turn me all the way over. I struggle out of his hold and am on my feet in an instant. But he's quick too, and as he grabs me I fall to my knees. Next thing I know he's on my back, his arms wrenching my body, again trying to turn me as I use every ounce of strength I have to fight back.

He's reaching for my ankle, and I know if he gets it I will lose my balance. But as he grabs it, I make my move. I snatch the wrist of the arm he is trying to throw around my head, and I wrap my other arm around his thigh.

We fly backward, and he sails up and over me, his feet flying over our heads before his body crashes back down beside me. In the air, he has managed to twist so that he lands on his stomach, not on his back, but he's momentarily disoriented. My arms grab his body, trapping his arms against him, and I drive him to his back. I'm on his chest, pushing his back to the floor, and after only a few weak attempts to escape, he's finished.

The battle is over. I pinned him.

I strain to my feet as soon as the referee confirms my win. As I stand, adrenaline rushes through me, keeping the exhaustion from overtaking me. High school wrestling matches sap all my strength in a matter of minutes, and my eyes search the area for the one person who will appreciate the struggle I've been through—the one person who has been there for me this past year. He is the reason I am standing here now. I spot him to my right and see that my godfather is grinning at me proudly.

Gino Vigliotti.

I smile back at him because I want him to see that I am happy—happy that I have won, happy that he saw me succeed, and happy with life in general. If I am happy, then surely he will know that taking me in was the right decision.

The referee raises my arm to signal my victory, and I walk—well, limp really—over to Gino.

"Great job, Danny," he says as he smiles again and pats me on the back. I'm taller than Gino now, but I'm still in awe of my godfather. He's lean and wiry, a guy you wouldn't want to take on in a fight, and his keen, dark eyes always make me feel a little unsettled. Right now those eyes are traveling to the other side of the gym, where his son, Vince Vigliotti, is stretching.

"Vince will do great," I say, reassuring myself as much as Gino that his son can handle the next match. I am the reason Vince is competing in this wrestling tournament, and even though he has proven he has a natural talent for the sport, he doesn't have the experience that many other high school wrestlers have. Vince is good enough to win the starting spot in his weight division at Newcastle High, but he is wrestling kids in tournaments who have been competing since elementary school. I've seen Vince's competitor before and think that Vince actually has a pretty good chance of winning this match. Vince is big, like his opponent, but whereas his opponent's size is made up of a lot of fat, Vince, at 18, is solid muscle. He has given up eating Snickers candy bars the past few months, and it has definitely paid off.

"Yeah, I think he'll do all right," Gino says. "But if he wins this, then he'll be wrestling that black kid tomorrow."

I grimace. That "black kid," as Gino has called him, is my best friend, Reggie Allen. Reggie is a talented and experienced wrestler, and I know Vince stands no chance against him. I wasn't too happy to find out that Reggie and Vince have ended up in the same weight class—that means that Reggie has grown a lot this past year. And even though I'm glad that Reggie and I don't share a weight class, it's difficult to have my two friends matched up, especially when they don't care much for each other in the first place. It doesn't help that Gino treats Reggie with suspicion because he is always worried about Reggie's influence on me. Reggie is a straight A student who has won everything from speech contests to science fairs, and Gino is afraid that if I hang out with Reggie too much, I might find my way back to Ridley High.

He doesn't need to worry.

At first I stayed with the Vigliotti family because it was the only place I had to go. I can hardly believe that more than a year has passed since my mom, her husband, and her boyfriend got into a fight, and the result was that I had no home. Gino showed up just in time to save me from foster care, and soon I was part of his family. I don't know if he regrets taking me in because, soon afterward, I destroyed Gino's career – the job that gave him and his family a lifestyle that would make any teenager envious. But destroying that career wasn't a bad thing, really, because Gino was a mobster. And with a little help from my friends, I dismantled the Newcastle Mob by taking down the Mafia underboss, Ray Gallo, who is now in prison for a long time to come.

The best part is that Gino never had any charges brought against him, and in the end, the only person who died was the corrupt district attorney. So, all's well that ends well, right?

This happened about a year and a half ago. I'm now 17 and much more confident and happier than I was back then. Even though all this has taken place, not much has changed for the Vigliottis. There is still plenty of money to go around, and after a month or two of recovering from a gunshot wound, Gino went back to work. He has been just as mysterious as before, and I think the entire family has settled into a routine of not asking him any questions. Does the fact that I don't know if Gino has gone straight bother me? Yeah. But really, I don't have too much time to think about Gino these days.

Dismantling the mob has been just the beginning of so many changes for me. Such as, I now have a new last name because, apparently, my dad was a mobster named Mike Esposito and not my mom's second husband, a fat, cruel man named Del Higgins. But I don't use my real last name because Gino says this would be a bad idea, and although I know my godfather has made mistakes, I don't question him on this point. Seems to me the name Esposito has a lot of baggage attached to it, and I've got enough of that already.

Right now I just want to shower, change, and eat something, but I'm not going to miss the chance to cheer for Vince. After I drain the cold liquid from my water bottle and slip a pair of sweat pants on, Gino and I stand side by side as Vince takes the floor. Reggie is standing across from us. He might be one of my best friends, but here, at a district tournament, we don't spend too much time together. Having already made it to the final match, Reggie is observing this match to prepare himself for his competition, whoever that may be, and I am wondering if he would enjoy wrestling Vince tomorrow. Vince is always finding ways to irritate Reggie, so I can only imagine my friend might savor a win over Vince. And Reggie likes Gino even less, so beating Vince would be a double victory for him.

I glance at Gino, and I can see his jaw is tight. That's the only sign that he's nervous. I know he's learned to control the way he shows his emotions from the years he has spent in the Mafia, but for the record, this is about as tense as I've seen him in a while. He may not have a very affectionate relationship with his son, but Gino desperately wants Vince to win.

I've always wondered if Gino keeps Vince at arm's length to discourage him from being involved in the "family" business. In fact, Gino is friendlier to me than to his own son, which either means Gino doesn't really care if I follow in his footsteps, or he just doesn't know how hard he is on Vince. I don't think those two realize how much they are alike. Gino and Vince are both stubborn, and their dark eyes and black, wavy hair are almost identical. Vince, however, is taller and bigger than his father, and he certainly has a more explosive temper.

I look back at the wrestling mat and try to focus on the matchup, but my eye is caught by a figure at the other end of the gym. He's standing a little behind the bleachers, so I don't have a clear view of him. Vince's match is starting and the spectators around me are yelling, but I can't tear my eyes away from this person for one very distinct reason.

He looks exactly like me.

Well, almost like me. He definitely appears to be just a little older. I try to get a better look at him, but then I tell myself I'm being stupid. With my short brown hair and Italian facial features, I'm sure I resemble many people in New Jersey. I shake my head, and as my eyes dart from the familiar-looking guy back to the match, I quickly see that Vince is struggling. I yell some encouraging words at him, and for a few minutes, my focus is on Vince. In the final minutes of the match, I know that although Vince has done well, he's going to lose.

Immediately I glance back at the person who seems to look so much like me, unable to dismiss him. That's when I see that he has turned and is walking out of the gym. Although I know I should probably referee the exchange between a frustrated Gino and disappointed Vince, my curiosity gets the better of me and I take off around the bleachers. It takes me about a minute to navigate my way through the crowd, but soon I am opening the far door to the gym. The cold January night air stings my face as I scan the area and take in the dark, empty parking lot. Then I roll my eyes. Why am I chasing strangers when I should be encouraging Vince? Just as I'm turning around to go back inside, a pair of slender arms wrap around my body from behind. I smile because there's no need to fight off this attacker.

"Portia," I say, "I'm sweaty."

My girlfriend unwraps her arms as I turn, and she smiles up at me with her big, expressive brown eyes. I've grown taller in the past year and a half, whereas she's still pretty small for a 16-year-old, and I can't say that I mind this at all. Portia always looks cute, especially when she's dressed in jeans and an oversized sweatshirt, like she is right now. At the moment, she's twirling a strand of her long blonde hair with her finger as she reaches out her other hand to touch my skin. "You should put a sweatshirt on—you'll get cold."

I grin and encircle her with my arms. "I think I'll just use you as my human heater."

She grimaces and tries to pull away. "Ew, yuck, Danny. You *are* sweaty."

I release her. "That's what happens when I wrestle."

"Good for you. Now, go take a shower so we can go to the movies," Portia orders.

"Okay. As long as you pick something that doesn't put me to sleep."

Portia pouts. "You don't know me at all, Danny."

I grin again, because I *do* know her. I know she's been eager to see a movie about car racing for weeks. Portia's dad, Joe Saviano, is also a former mobster, and his used-car business barely survived the fall of the Newcastle Mob. The only thing is, unlike the Vigliottis, the Saviano family doesn't nearly have the money they once had, and Portia has suffered some pretty cruel rejection at school. I, of course, having come from extremely poor roots, do not care at all that Portia no longer dresses in designer clothes and accessories. Portia would be beautiful dressed in a garbage bag, and I still can't believe she's mine. But Portia struggles with the way she's treated by the fickle and wealthy crowd at Newcastle High, and it's all I can do not to give her my allowance from Gino. Portia hates being poor, but she won't take charity. So I buy her nice things when I can, and the rest of the time I shoot evil looks in the direction of all those stupid girls who are so mean to her.

Because of my train of thought, I grab my girlfriend's hand and squeeze it as I lead her back toward the wrestling match.

"I hate sitting near the cheerleaders," Portia complains. "And watch out for Lisa. She's been talking about you nonstop like I don't even exist."

"*I* know you exist," I reply, earning a grin from my girlfriend.

"What were you doing over here anyway?" she asks me.

I pause—no need to sound crazy, even though Portia has accepted me as I am, faults and all. But I don't want to lie either. "I thought I saw someone I recognized," I reply. This is true. I thought I saw someone who looks exactly like me.

"You probably did," Portia says. "I'm sure a lot of the students here at Ridley High went to your middle school."

"Sure," is all I say, because I don't want to explain that I actually *do* know almost everyone here, but my status as a student at Newcastle High has scared them away. Or maybe they think I'm cocky now that I go to one of the best (and wealthiest) high schools in New Jersey. Well, they didn't have much time for me when I was the dirt-poor kid in middle school, so as far as I'm concerned, they don't really matter now. The only Ridley guy I still talk to is Reggie, when we're not fighting about whether or not my godfather is working for the Newcastle Mob again. To be honest, I'm a little surprised that the Vigliottis and I still live in Newcastle because I was certain we'd have to run away. The Mafia has a code of silence and loyalty—a code that mandated that at least Gino, and maybe myself, should be killed because of our involvement in the takedown of the Newcastle Mob.

I try to push these heavy thoughts aside as Reggie strides up to me. "So, it looks like I won't be wrestling Snickers tomorrow," Reggie says, sounding almost grumpy about this.

"Vince doesn't eat candy bars anymore," Portia responds defensively, which surprises me, because on any given day, she likes Reggie much more than she likes Vince.

I shrug at Reggie and say, "Better luck next time."

"If Vince doesn't improve, there will never *be* a next time," Reggie states.

"Hey, I'm not that terrible," a voice behind me says, and I wince. Leave it to Vince to show up at exactly the wrong moment.

"I didn't say you were terrible," Reggie states. "You just need a lot of practice. *A lot.*"

"I'm sorry, I wasn't born with my wrestling gear on like you!" Vince snaps.

I groan as Portia rolls her eyes. "Really?" she asks. "Do you guys always have to get into it?"

"Sorry, Portia," Reggie mumbles, and then he turns to Vince. "Next time, win all your matches so I can kick your butt in the finals."

"Fine," Vince growls, even though he probably doesn't think getting shown up by Reggie in the final match would be any better than getting beat on his way to the finals.

Reggie glances over my shoulder and gives me a curt nod. "I'll check in with you later, Danny." He turns and walks away abruptly, and it only takes me a second to figure out why.

Gino is standing behind me, his quick eyes following Reggie as he leaves. "That kid could use some manners," Gino mutters, and I almost laugh because Reggie is actually one of the most polite people I know, just not around the Vigliottis.

"Danny, the wrestling coach wants to talk to you," Gino says, and I quickly turn and follow him and Vince back to the other side of the gym. Gino and Vince head back toward the locker rooms, arguing about Vince's match as they go. Portia and I veer toward the benches. I'm still holding Portia's hand when she stops abruptly and stares ahead with a shocked expression.

"What's wrong?" I ask.

She shakes her head, indicating that she's not going to tell me, and before I know it, the wrestling coach has walked up to us with another teenager in tow. The kid is about my size, but maybe a little more broad-shouldered, although it's hard to tell since he's in a jacket and jeans. He's tanned, which is strange for this time of year, and his straight dark hair is longer than mine and certainly much less sweaty at the moment. But it's the friendly look he gives Portia that puts me on the defensive.

Coach Larson is a gruff, small guy who doesn't realize that this new teenager is making my girlfriend very uncomfortable. I look expectantly at him to explain who this kid is.

"Danny, this is Damian Caletti," Coach Larson says abruptly. "He used to wrestle at Newcastle's middle school before he moved away. His family just returned a few weeks ago. The thing is, Damian's in your weight class. So I guess we'll have to see who gets the starting spot once he joins us."

I try to smile at Damian, but I find this impossible. First of all, I don't want him looking at my girlfriend like he's her new best friend. Second of all, Portia is acting weird, which must mean he's a real jerk. Finally, Damian and I are probably not going to be instant buddies if we're fighting for the same spot on the team.

But Coach Larson is apparently unconcerned with all of this. "Damian, this is Danny Higgins and Portia Saviano."

Damian grins. "Oh, I know Portia. She was my middle school sweetheart."

Somehow the way he says it sounds sweet and sincere, and I hate it. I hold myself in check, reminding myself I'll have my chance at this chump on the wrestling mat, and I'm savoring the image of putting him in a headlock when Damian adds, "Oh, and I know Danny too."

"Really?" Coach Larson and I say in almost perfect unison. I'm suddenly racking my brain for memories of other competitors I faced in middle school. Somehow, I think I would remember someone like Damian. That confident smile would be hard to forget.

"Yeah," Damian continues. "Well, I mean, I know *of* him."

"Oh. Right. Well yeah, Danny's a good wrestler, when he puts the work into it," Coach Larson says.

"I'm sure he is," Damian replies with a nod. "But that's not how I heard of him."

I'm tired of all the hinting. "How did you hear of me?" I demand a bit harshly.

"Damian is Ray Gallo's nephew," Portia whispers, her voice almost inaudible above the cheering of the crowd.

At the name of Gallo, I have to take a deep breath to calm myself. Not only am I responsible for Ray

Gallo being in prison, but I also managed to get his son, Tommy, suspended at Newcastle High. Needless to say, if the Gallos have a sworn enemy, I'm it.

I try to look casual as I eye Damian. "Ray Gallo, huh?"

"Ray's sister is my mom," Damian answers, his easy smile still in place. I think it would have been easier for me if he had been hateful and arrogant. At least then I wouldn't have to guess whether the nice guy act is just that—an act.

However, at the mention of Ray Gallo, Coach Larson has stepped away ever so slightly from Damian. The incarceration of Ray Gallo was big news in Newcastle, and Coach Larson also kicked Tommy off the wrestling team when Tommy was suspended and later expelled for his bad behavior. Coach Larson isn't nearly the enemy of the Gallos that I am, but he's certainly not a favorite of theirs either.

"Well," Coach Larson says curtly, "I'll catch up with you guys later. I've got work to do." With that he stalks off, probably trying to figure out how he can distance himself from Damian Caletti after welcoming him to the team.

Damian watches the coach hurry away with a frustrated look. "Well, there's no way I can keep people from finding out who my uncle is. I guess I'll be the school outcast."

But Damian doesn't look like a kid who has ever suffered from being the school outcast. On the other hand, it's been a bumpy ride for me. I'd say I'm pretty popular now, but that could change at any time. High school is fickle.

"Good to see you again, Portia," Damian says to my girlfriend, and I hate that she actually smiles at him. I mean, I guess that's what Portia does—she's really sweet and not likely to hold anything against Damian if he's nice too. Suddenly, I'm very curious how close these two were in middle school.

"So," I say, not able to hide the edge in my tone. "You guys were a pair, huh?" The words sound stupid even as they leave my mouth, and I suddenly wish I were way more tan.

"Yeah. But Portia was definitely too good for me," Damian says.

"Oh please, you were the guy every girl wanted in middle school," Portia replies, and she giggles. Yes—*giggles*. I know the heat rising to my face is not from wrestling.

"Why'd you break up?" I ask abruptly, trying to bring them back to the important thing—they are no longer together.

Portia's expression becomes serious. "He moved away."

Oh, that's *fantastic*. Damian didn't cheat on her or treat her poorly. Oh no, he just had to leave, something he probably had no control over. This is very bad for me. Very bad indeed.

"Yeah, and Portia doesn't like it when people leave her," Damian replies, and this is the first time I hear an edge of bitterness in his tone. *Good,* I think. *Bitterness is good.*

"Well, I acted pretty immature," Portia offers. "It wasn't your fault."

Okay, if I am going to keep these two from a happy reunion, I have to work fast. "You ready for that movie?" I ask Portia.

She smiles and nods. "Absolutely. I'll just wait here until you shower and change."

I pause, knowing I'm defeated. I'm going to be forced to leave her with Damian for a few minutes. Why can't love be like wrestling matches? I know how to win those. I see the slightest flash in Damian's eyes, and I know that underneath his Mr. Nice Guy act, he still has strong feelings for Portia. But what can I do? Portia can't go back to the locker room with me, and telling her she can't talk to Damian is a one-way ticket to a breakup. She's not too fond of being ordered around.

So I kiss my girlfriend on the lips right in front of Damian, and then I shoot him a glare that I know Portia can't see. I stride off to the locker room trying to look confident even while I'm hurrying so that I can get back to my girl before any permanent damage is done. I angrily stalk to my locker and slam it with my hand. Then I tell myself to calm down; there's no need to lose my head. Damian may have history with Portia, but I'm willing to bet it's nothing compared with what Portia and I have. We came together under crazy circumstances, and we share a common bond because of our mobster ties. Then again, with a last name like Caletti, who knows if Damian has some mobster ties of his own?

CPSIA information can be obtained
at www.ICGtesting.com
Printed in the USA
FFOW04n1320230514
5484FF